THE TINKER & THE WITCH

A COZY FANTASY CHARACTER TALE

G. J. DAILY

CHAPTER 1

A cold wind stirred eddies of deep-purple leaves blanketing the ground. The only light this deep in the forest and this late at night was the faint glow of a single hearth through the wavy glass windows of a cracked and leaning cottage. Standing in the front window, unmoving, was an old woman looking out at the moonlight.

She wore a thick black robe held shut by a frayed rope. Grass and twigs were tightly caught in the hem where it brushed the ground, and her thinning grey hair was pulled up into a crescent moon above her head. A tiny sparrow with a blood-red face, lilac breast, sunset tail, and emerald-green back perked its tiny head out from the old woman's hair, quickly turned, raised its tail, and relieved itself in a streak of liquid down the woman's left shoulder, then nestled itself back into her hair and fell asleep.

The woman did not move nor did she flinch when the wind blew so hard that a branch from the nightshade tree winding around her house crashed across her roof and landed in the yard in front of her. She had not so much as wet her eyes with a single blink in quite a while, because of the moonlight.

It had not spoken to her in a countless age.

But tonight, the raven light carried a powerful message of change.

She began to shake.

"Tha e teachd o thìr eile, air dhìochuimhn', agus gun chuimhne, agus cha'n aithnich iad e," she whispered.

Then, without looking, she pulled a pile of saliva out from the inside of her cheek and smeared a shape of three lines across the pane of glass in front of her as something massive moved across the reflection of her eyes, though the forest before her was dark and empty.

She quickly blinked, took a deep breath, shook her head, and grasped at the sides of her robe to steady herself against what she had just witnessed. But it did not matter. By morning, the old woman forgot the vision. Perhaps the single most important prophecy in centuries finding a woman of no reputation who would not even remember it by daybreak. But so goes history.

A tear streaked down her cheek that she wiped away as she turned and approached rows of jars on the back wall of her cottage.

Small jars. Large jars. Round and square jars. Stone pots with wooden lids and clear crystal vials the size of a thimble, all in some way or another labeled with colors, marks, or little tags tucked under the caps.

She thought for a moment as the sparrow in her hair stretched its legs and shook. A large brown clay vessel on the bottom shelf was marked 'start here,' so she pulled it forward, removed the lid, and smelled the dry, dark leaves crushed into powder. They were aromatic and felt right, so she set the jar down and took a copper pot twice the size of

2

a mug, with a handle and a long copper straw protruding from the lower mid-section, and set it next to the large clay vessel. Then, with that long, crooked finger of hers—its knotty unrelenting knuckles, now nearly useless—she pointed to the jars one by one, trying to remember what each contained, which of them were for drinking, which were for cooking, and which might simply be potpourri. She had at least enough sense to keep everything medicinal and useful somewhere else—she thought she did anyway.

She plucked a small grey jar, a medium grey jar with white freckles, and a tiny, clear glass vial from the shelves and set them next to the brown clay vessel after smelling each. They smelled familiar, but that didn't mean much.

How vicious time can be to those most loyal to it, but she was not concerned with that at the moment. She was still rolling around in her mind some of the fading shapes of what she had seen, and she just wanted a simple cup of tea to help her collect her thoughts.

She looked down into the largest vessel and considered. How much was she supposed to use? A single scoop? Half a scoop? Two scoops? These are the details that make life so effervescent, but she could not quite hold onto them no matter how hard she tried. She poured a single scoop into the copper pot with the handle and straw, then lifted the lid on the grey jar and struggled with the same detail: how much? She decided half a scoop of the brightly aromatic flower petals dried into twisting needle-like threads of vibrant blue. Since the final jar was the smallest in size, from it she drew the smallest portion, only a pinch of what looked like some sort of ground mineral—a dull orange in color. She scooped a ladle of water into the copper tea kettle from a large water collector in the corner of the room and hung the kettle on a hook shaped from stone over her hearth.

While her body still felt in awe of the vision, her mind could no longer find the details. Something beautiful and terrible had just happened, but she couldn't remember what.

She sat down and looked around. She was fine. Everything looked to be in order. *It must not have been that important*, she told herself.

She watched the surface of the liquid, crusted with dried leaves, waiting for it to begin to stir. She knew not to let it properly boil, but she wanted it hot. She didn't remember, but she had let the liquid on several occasions either boil over or boil down to a crust in the pot, completely ruining not just the tea but the pot itself. The only saving grace against the cost of replacing such a unique item was that the coppersmith could reuse the metal, so he had decided not to charge her full price but only the cost of melting and reshaping a new piece, and then at a discount, because she had been midwife to his four children.

As the liquid stirred and the gentle aroma of floral tea began to rise in the room, she carefully plucked the pot from its hook with a darkened cloth lying next to the hearthstone, slowly swirled the liquid trying to not let it splash over the edges, and gently took a drink from the long straw protruding from its side. She winced. It didn't taste right. It never tasted right anymore. She just could not remember the proper mix of spices even though her tongue still remembered, creating a dissonance of how wrong they were.

She rose from her chair, frustrated, and poured the warm tea into the flowerpot next to the water collector, then she squeezed the top of her robe tight and sat back near the hearth as the fire grew in intensity without her touching it.

Though her raven-light vision was quickly fading into an echo of a memory, the streaked shape written in saliva on her window pane remained. It read: Ardimus.

CHAPTER 2

Andrew searched for a few thin slivers of meat on the otherwise empty deer hock hanging by the front door. When he couldn't find much, he took the leg off the hook and tossed it to his best friend, who jumped in the air and caught it in his teeth. Jasper, a mongrel of a dog with black and grey wiry hair, took the bone to his threadbare pillow and laid down to enjoy breakfast. He'd have no trouble picking the bone of its last scraps.

As so many things are, the old cabin was being slowly consumed by the swamp. It had a central living area and two small rooms at the back. Fishing nets and house tools adorned one wall; tinker tools with stamped circles and squares of various thin-rolled metals lined shelves along another. On a shelf, a wooden toy cart Andrew had played with as a child sat next to a child-sized fishing pole. A cast iron pan on a grate over the glowing hearth fizzled and popped, filling the small wood-slat house with the smell of sizzling duck fat.

Andrew—seventeen, slender, and tall with tufts of hair hanging over his slightly oversized ears—knelt in front of

Jasper and pet his head, Jasper's tail wagging but still focused on gnawing the dried meat. "You're starting to look a little lean, boy," he said, Jasper's hips showing through his dirty coat. Then he rose from Jasper's side and leaned towards the fire, rubbing his hands together, trying to warm them before approaching a row of jars on a table by the back wall.

He lifted each of the lids and smelled the contents of each jar. Then he sighed. The fourth had just enough for one more pot of what he considered properly brewed verferra tea.

"Morning," a deep, gruff voice spoke behind him, and he turned. "That smells good," the man said, a blanket pulled over his shoulders and gently stirring the food cooking over the fire. His skin was almost black as ink, with faintly glowing white lines adorning his arms and neck. His eyes and hair were white as snow. Though Andrew was human, the man he called father was Nimic. Andrew knew other humans existed, somewhere, but he had never met one.

Jasper rose and leaned against the older man's leg, who pat the old dog's side.

"That's the last handful of lentils," Andrew replied, pulling a small scale towards him he usually used for measuring minerals but was sensitive enough to also use for tea. Then he carefully measured portions of each dried herb into a beautiful bronze tea kettle with flowers and vines set in relief on the surface. Though Lithuel had hand-crafted the kettle, there was no sign of hammer strikes or solder. Each flower on the kettle surface was tinted white and pink to mimic the swamp lilies floating in clusters around their home.

"Mind if I take this off? It looks ready," Lithuel said,

carefully separating the white flesh of cooked catfish with a fork.

"Go ahead," Andrew replied, leaning down to pinch a small amount from the top of the tiny pile and pouring the contents of his copper measuring bowl into the kettle, then gently tapping the last of the powder residue from his measurements into the pot and returning the clay jars and scale to their proper place at the back of the counter. He lifted a pot of boiling water from the hearth and carefully filled the kettle.

"The rest of our dry supplies are also running low," Andrew told Lithuel. "The deer is done, the lentils are gone, and I used the last of the verferra to brew that," he said, pouring tea into two thick, clay cups with no handles, one of which Lithuel picked up with both hands and smelled.

"Were you still planning on a trip to Jatoba?"

Andrew nodded, scooping a piece of fish and half of the remaining cooked lentils into his bowl.

"I'd rather you didn't. The weather is changing, and I doubt the deer have moved on yet. I saw fresh tracks yesterday. Together we should be able to catch at least two more, which'll last us until the weather breaks."

"The pelts will turn if I wait much longer," Andrew replied.

Lithuel sighed and looked at him. "A few deer pelts aren't worth your life."

"They're worth three weeks' provisions. I'll be fine."

"Then leave the cart. You can make the journey in half the time without it. There might already be snowfall above the foothills."

Andrew looked at Lithuel. Recognizing that look of concern and seriousness that he knew he probably couldn't argue past, he decided not to push it.

"I'll go fishing while you're gone," Lithuel added.

Andrew didn't reply. Instead, he picked up two long, narrow pieces of steel held together with a rivet lying on the table and moved them back and forth. Its movement was rough.

Lithuel watched him. "Maybe you can use a piece of fish bone or leather between the junction to make the motion smoother," Lithuel said. "It's a great piece. You're so much more creative than I was. I would never have thought to build something like that. It was always tools or repairs."

"It probably won't give you all your strength back, but maybe it will help. Besides, this rivet was your idea," Andrew said.

"My idea?" Lithuel asked, taking the item from Andrew and looking closely at the rivet that was both firm and loose enough to allow the metal pieces to move.

"Remember the shears?" Andrew asked.

Lithuel smiled. "You're right. The shears. Those were good sellers. I still have a pair on the shelf by my bed. They're a bit rusted now, but they still work."

"You taught me everything I know," Andrew told him, raising his eyebrow and enjoying his hot drink.

Lithuel moved the device back and forth, considering. "You've moved far beyond anything I might have taught you. You should be off flirting with girls, not worrying about provisions or caring for some old man."

"You're not that old."

"Compared to you, fifty-two feels ancient. Especially with this leg," Lithuel said, handing the device back to Andrew.

"That wasn't your fault," Andrew replied.

Lithuel was quiet for a minute and thoughtlessly

rubbed his left thigh. "I don't want you to worry about me so much; that's all I'm sayin'."

"Jasper was up last night," Andrew said, changing the subject.

"Oh?" Lithuel asked, taking both of their plates to a bucket by the door and using a hanging piece of cloth to wipe away their residue. "Deer?"

"Not likely."

"No," Lithuel agreed. "Not this deep. Any idea what it was?"

"He wasn't growling, only stirring, so nothing for us to worry about. I'll look for sign when I pack Brynlee."

Lithuel nodded and sat back down, rubbing Jasper's head, who leaned hard into his side and looked up at him, basking in the attention.

"Do you need anything before I leave?" Andrew asked.

Lithuel scowled at him. "I'll be fine. I was living in the Dry Places long before I found your skinny ass in the back o' my cart."

Andrew chuckled at that, knowing it was an exaggeration—somewhat of an exaggeration.

"But you really should get going," Lithuel added.

Andrew nodded, took the last drink of his tea, and set the cup by the plates on the back table. Then he put on a thick brown overcoat lined with fine fur and covered with hand-sewn pockets, pulled on a pair of eel skin gloves and a warm hat. He pulled a cloth sack with a sling over one shoulder and lifted a roll of skins bound by twine.

Jasper rose and followed him to the door.

"I'll be back by nightfall," Andrew told Lithuel. But before nightfall, Andrew would question if he would ever see Lithuel again.

Outside, the air was beginning to sharpen with the chill of late autumn.

He pulled the top of his coat shut and tightened his gloves. Thankfully, the short glossy fur inside his coat was iirubee mink, which was dense, waterproof, and warm; both his jacket and gloves were hand-sewn by Lithuel after his accident forced him to give up his lifelong tinker trade.

The house was a wood-slat hut on low stilts standing above what looked like an island of Cyprus trees growing high and thick out of the mud. Surrounding the island for at least two miles in any direction was calm water the color of tea. While some places in the swamp were deep enough for a horse cart to disappear into, never to be seen again, there were also webs of walking paths comprised of shoals and sandbars winding through the dark waters just beneath the surface. While someone with knowledge of Aitecham Tioram, known in the common tongue as the Dry Places, could walk across it with no danger, a single misstep might quickly end a life; unspoken nightmares lived in the low waters if someone didn't know how to avoid them. Thankfully, swamp rats like Andrew, Jasper, Lithuel, and Brynlee knew how to navigate the dark waters well.

Brynlee's breath was a fog in the frosted air, and she shifted as Andrew approached her, happy to see him. She lived in a wood-covered lean-to attached to the house that Lithuel had surrounded with steel fencing, which was time-consuming and expensive to make but far less costly than losing his horse to whatever might be attracted to her from the swamp. Grey and black moss hung from the fence slats and wafted in the slight breeze from branches overhead, and something buzzed faintly in the distance. A medium-sized glowing box was attached to the top of one fence post. Inside it lived a very unusual ant colony Lithuel had traded from another tinker years ago. The ants that came and went were fairly uninteresting; however, the colony's queen produced enough electricity to keep creatures away from Brynlee's fence. The ants were happy to live on this tiny island in the swamp unbothered, and the queen's electricity protected Brynlee—just one example of the careful balance needed to survive and thrive in an environment most wouldn't step foot into.

"Good morning, girl," Andrew said, hugging her neck. While Jasper was Andrew's best friend at home, Brynlee was more like his work wife. She was strong, wise, and full of her own ideas of how to do things. Andrew loved this about her. If a horse could be your mother, this is similar to how Andrew felt about her. She had been traded to Lithuel as a foal because she had been a runt, and the stable master was going to put her down. She had then worked as his cart horse for years after Mayloy could no longer pull the cart and before Lithuel hurt his leg. If it hadn't been for her, Lithuel probably would have lost more than his leg in the swamp that afternoon. The old girl saw it happen and fought like hell to get him home. Since that day, she was no longer just a horse to them but a member of their family.

Andrew poured a cup of oats into a bucket for her and dropped in a few finger roots before pausing to look back at the house. Lithuel told him not to bother with the cart, but Andrew was young and confident he could make it back before nightfall, even with the cart. And why not try earning a little extra while he was there? He hadn't been to Jatoba in months. It wasn't a wealthy town, but it wasn't a poor one either, and they were far enough from the regular trade roads not to be visited often by anyone else.

He chose the driving harness over the riding saddle—brushing her dappled gray hair before carefully tightening the thin leather straps and making sure she was comfortable under the load of his cart.

"There and back again," he said to her, his breath fogging as she turned her head to see him with one eye. Then he climbed onto his carefully organized cart and clicked his tongue twice.

CHAPTER 3

There was a scream.

"What's wrong with her?" the naked woman cried, reaching for her child—blood and sweat streaked across her forehead.

The sparrow living in the old woman's hair startled and fluttered around the room.

The old woman did not speak. Her hands moved with a speed that went deeper than memory. The child was born too soon and was far too young to have much chance, but she would try. She quickly pinched the child's nose, squeezing out any remaining birth fluid, laid the naked child—cord still attached to its mother—on the naked woman's chest and began vigorously rubbing its back.

"Breath deep," she finally said to the crying woman. "Teach your daughter how to breathe with your body."

The naked woman shuddered through sobs and tried to focus. Deep breath. Deep breath. She gently laid her hands on the back and buttocks of her tiny child as the old woman kept rubbing the baby's wrinkled skin.

"Atoorree, atoorree," the old woman began to whisper. "Atoorree, mae-nash tenee. Breathe. Breathe, child."

And suddenly, the tiny child gasped and began to cry.

The mother sighed deeply and began to cry as well, only these were not the tears of fear but of laughter; a cry of happiness.

The old woman did not smile, but her brow did soften.

She opened a small jar of yellow-brown cream made of beeswax, butter, ashwardicus semen, and powdered silver and lathered and softened it in the palms of her hands, mixing the balm with the blood and birth fluid still on her hands from the mother, then wiped the cream all over the child's face, head and body.

"Do not bathe her until nightfall tomorrow," the old woman told the mother. Then she laid her palm on the babe's head and touched the child's forehead to her own. "May the Ruach Ha-Kodesh fill your life and light your way," she told the child. Then she looked at the mother. "Sleep now. Keep her against your breast until she begins to bob. When she does, guide her to your milk. You have done well, mother. Your body has, for a second time, given her life. Now you will feed her when she is ready. Until then, sleep."

The mother rolled her head toward the old woman and looked at her with a smile and heavy eyes. "What is her name?"

The old woman looked toward the child—beyond her to some nameless distant place. "Freowin, for she clung to life."

"Freowin," the mother whispered, looking down at the now-sleeping babe.

The sparrow returned to the old woman's hair as she rinsed her hands in a basin of warm water at the foot of the bed and dried her hands on her robe. Then she gently closed the door behind her and left.

JATOBA WAS a cozy town nestled high in the hills. Most buildings were two or three stories, made of thin, tightly stacked grey stones with green or red wooden roofs and bridges connecting some of the taller buildings. Leather harnesses and straps hung from railings, and images of pack animals and farm equipment were carved into the wooden columns.

As Andrew approached, a valley of short, bright green grass with yellow flowers opened in front of him like a bridal veil leading up to the town, and blue and gold banners blew in the valley breeze. Wooly cows with long red hair hanging down over their eyes grazed in the valley around him.

"Is the tanner in?" Andrew asked a young Minotaur, with the body of a man and the head of a young bull, sitting on a porch on the outer edge of town, who played a long horn that wrapped around him. He opened his eyes from the sound of music Andrew could not hear and pointed up the cobblestone street toward the center of town. Then he continued playing. The music was a special kind of melody only they and their cattle could hear.

Andrew urged Brynlee on.

Wreathes of orange berries and red and purple tinted leaves hung on every door, garlands of the same berries were draped from under eaves and over windows, and people quickly moved back and forth carrying trays of cakes and piled fruits.

Andrew smiled. He hadn't realized when he left home

that it was Eden Vale—a week-long celebration of feasting on candied fruits, cakes, spiced drinks, and merriment leading up to a festival of lights, when a total eclipse of the moon would cause the yellow flowers scattered all throughout the valley to release their iridescent seeds, which would float down through the distant prairies below like a glowing river of light. He hadn't been in a town during Eden Vale since he was a child because he and Lithuel were usually settled in for the season about this time each year. The memory warmed him. It also meant people in town would be in an especially generous mood and looking for unique trinkets to give as gifts, both of which worked well in his favor.

He pulled up to the door where the tanner stood inside a wide room, scraping a large skin with a two-handed blade. The tanner was easily thrice the size of Andrew, with faint blue-grey skin, and though the room was large, the tanner was so massive he looked to Andrew like a grown man sitting inside a child's playhouse. As he approached, Andrew saw that the skin the tanner was working was reptilian. Six large lizard feet hung on the wall above the muscular man, and mounds of grubs crawled in a wooden, flat box in the back corner of the shop. The sharp smell of tanning solution burned Andrew's nose. Several types of pelts, some sewn and some natural, hung from wooden rails along the wall. Andrew could hear the clatter of horse hooves on the stone street outside.

The tanner set down his tool and wiped his hands on his apron. "Welcome. How can I help?"

"I have some pelts to sell," Andrew replied.

"Oh? Of?"

"Deer."

"Kind?"

"Freckled grey tail."

"Have them with you?" the tanner asked.

Andrew nodded and fetched the bundle from his cart.

The tanner untied the bundle and laid the pile of pelts out across a large wooden table coated in sawdust. Andrew watched him gently lift the first. He ran his hand flat across the suede on one side, then turned the pelt over and blew into the brown fir dotted with sand-colored spots, looking closely at the nap. Then he set the first pelt aside and did the same with the other four. He carefully selected two. The tanner's hands were thick and strong yet surprisingly supple, like the skin of a small child. Andrew tried to discern any hint of interest on the Longbeard's face—his nose broad, his eyes grey as hoarfrost.

"These skins have nearly gone off," the tanner said, turning his attention to Andrew. "I'm interested in these two, but the others are already losing their hair." He picked up a pelt and blew against it, showing Andrew how easily the hair fell off onto the table. "I can't use them."

Andrew clenched his teeth. He feared the skins were starting to rot but hoped they hadn't.

"I can see that's not what you wanted to hear," the tanner said. "I might still be able to strip them for cord, but that's about it. I'll give you two silver crowns for the good pelts and trepenny apiece for the others."

This was barely half of what Andrew was hoping to get.

"Can you do three and five?"

The tanner shook his head. "Two and nine is already a deal, with them being potentially unusable. Take them with you if you prefer."

Andrew held up a hand. "No, no. I'll take it."

The tanner nodded and asked, "Is that a tinker's cart?"

Andrew's brow raised. "It is."

"My whetstone was dropped and chipped, and now my pelt scraper is losing its edge. Can you sharpen it?"

"I'd be happy to. It's a penny a hand length, but I can do you one better."

"Oh?" the tanner asked, one of his large, bushy eyebrows raising with curiosity.

"I came across three masterwork sharpening stones in the spring. I've kept one for my own use, but I have one left I might be convinced to part with if you'd like to take a look."

The tanner nodded.

Together they walked out of the warm shop into the sharp air.

Andrew's cart was wooden with a canvas tarp covering a high frame. A lamp hung over Andrew's seat he could light to help him count coin or ply his trade after dark. Drawers lined the cart's bottom, filled with tools, trinkets, and knick-knacks for children. Along the ribs of the cart, underneath the tarp, hung medium-sized tools and a few unique larger items he might sell. Several small cut blanks of metal of different types stood on their edges, carefully tucked away behind a crucible the size of a small lamp, and in a small drawer built into the base of the crucible were various shapes, sizes, and metallic colors of solder.

Andrew pulled back the canvas with a rope and opened several drawers, intentionally leaving them to sit open while he looked for the sharpening stone. He knew that while someone might come for a sharpening or repair, they might also take more than that away with them, so he was always happy to let customers see what he had.

"Here it is," he said, removing a rectangular item from the back of his cart wrapped in grey cloth. Then Andrew unfolded the cloth and handed the stone to the Longbeard, who took it and ran his thumb over its cold surface. While whetstones were usually a medium grey in color, this one was deep black and lighter weight than usual.

"It's not shist," Andrew told him. "It's lechtfelt."

The tanner's eyes widened. "Lechtfelt?"

Andrew knew that would get his attention. Lechtfelt was a strong and lightweight stone mined from the ancestral lands of the Longbeard's people, often used for expensive furniture, jars, and water vessels.

"It's lovely, but will it sharpen a blade? I've never heard of such a thing."

"Try it yourself," Andrew told him.

The two returned to the shop where the tanner had been working the reptilian skin. He reached for his bucket of water, but Andrew stopped him. "You don't need to wet it."

"Not wet the stone?"

Andrew nodded. "And it's very easy to overwork the blade with this. Draw it only twice across the edge—once on either side—and see how sharp it is."

"Twice you say?"

Andrew nodded.

The tanner was more than doubtful the stone would make much of a difference on the folded steel blade of his tool in only two strokes, but he did what the tinker asked. And immediately he could feel a change in the blade. The dirty edge of his tool now glinted in the morning light spilling in through his window, and he lifted it to look at its edge closely. It looked sharp.

He set the stone aside and pulled the tool over the skin. Layers of fat and flesh rolled off the hide beneath his blade like he was drawing a knife over warm cheese rather than dry lizard skin, and he smiled. He pulled the blade over the skin three more times, and piles of dry tissue fell to the floor in ribbons. "The blade wasn't this sharp when I bought it," he exclaimed. Then he reached behind him and removed a slender blade from the back of his belt. "May I?" he asked, holding the knife over the stone.

Andrew considered for a moment whether he should charge for this second sharpening but decided the chance to sell the stone outweighed the penny or two he might get from the sharpening, so he nodded.

The tanner, more slowly this time, pulled the slender fillet knife over the stone at an angle away from himself, only once on either side of the blade, and this time he couldn't help himself—he touched the edge. A single droplet of blue blood rose on the tip of his finger. He smiled large.

"How much?"

Andrew thought for a moment. "As you know, lechtfelt is rare, and I've never seen it as a sharpening stone before the three I acquired." Andrew took a breath, then raised an eye to the tanner. "What is it worth to make your job that much easier?" Andrew asked, knowing that while sharpening knives was valuable, making the tanner's job easier was much more valuable. With a single silver crown worth a standard day's wage and a standard whetstone usually going for two, he was hoping for ten.

The Longbeard ran his hand over his bald head, looking at the stone, which now sat on his wooden table. Then he ran both hands down his long-braided beard hanging down past his knees, lifting it and beginning to absent-mindedly pluck split ends from where it was held tight with a leather cord. Andrew admittedly didn't know any Longbeards personally, but he had never seen this before. Then the tanner dropped his beard and opened his pouch.

He removed three gold sovereigns worth ten silver crowns apiece and laid them, one by one, on the table.

Nothing glitters like gold.

Andrew took a breath.

He would usually barter no matter what the initial offer, but this was already three times what he had hoped to get for the stone, and it had been with him for more than six months, so he knew it wasn't the perfect item for just anyone. This was a craftsman paying for a high-quality tool, not a housemaid for her table knives.

"And for the pelts?" he asked.

The tanner laid two silver crowns and nine pennies next to the gold coins.

"It was a pleasure!" Andrew said, sliding the coins into the palm of his hand and dropping them into his leather pouch. It was turning out to be a worthwhile trip after all.

Andrew pulled his coat collar up over the back of his neck as he stepped out into the cold. Then he closed the drawers of his cart, leaving the tarp open so that any wayward onlookers could see what he had on offer. Andrew was excited about the sale and walked up to Brynlee, who could immediately sense his good mood and kicked her head back in excitement at his arrival. He took a deep breath, trying to contain himself, and pressed his forehead against hers. "We've done some business, girl. Blue skies ahead." Brynlee had heard Andrew say this before and had come to associate it with a heightened level of optimism on his part.

Across the street from the tanner's shop stood a veg stand with blue and green wooden box-crate shelves on either side of a narrow door. The shelves were piled with purple onions, red dragon fruit, pink petiquoa tubers, green and white leeks, and at least three kinds of fingerling potatoes in mounds of loose soil. There were also rows of fresh bread in the window.

Lithuel would enjoy the rare treat of a loaf of fresh bread, Andrew thought to himself, a glow from his sale.

"Happy Eden Vale to you, traveler!" said a Minotaur as Andrew entered the shop. He had powerful muscles, coarse grey hair covering his entire body, and a long braided grey beard. Like the horns of an ox, the shopkeeper's horns were a thick cream-brown, cropped about a hand's length above his bushy grey eyebrows and capped with ornamented brass caps. "From where do you venture?" he asked, wiping soil from his hands onto an apron tied around his waist.

Andrew was hesitant to answer, knowing well that most thought of the Dry Places as cursed and anyone passing through cursed themselves. "South East."

"South East?" The aging Minotaur questioned in a voice so deep Andrew could feel it in his chest. "I know of no villages South East, between here and the ocean."

"My family are fisher people and live in solitude along the coast," Andrew lied.

The Minotaur grunted. That seemed good enough for him. "What are you in for?"

"I saw your bread in the window."

The Minotaur smiled. "My wife's specialty. And we have spiced loaves for Eden Vale! Would you like to taste a slice?" he asked, trimming a narrow slice with a slender blade from a loaf dotted with dried fruit on a cracked but clean cutting board.

Andrew took a bite. The dough was rich and buttery, with chunks of fruit spiced with cinnamon and cardamom and coated in sugar, leaving a soft but satisfying crunch in every bite.

Andrew smiled. "I'll take a loaf. And one of the granary."

The Minotaur smiled back. "Of course you will! Who could say no!" he said, slicing a thicker piece off for himself and tossing the entire piece into his mouth. "It's like a dream, isn't it?" Then he set the two loaves on the counter.

Andrew nodded and began walking around the small but well-stocked shop, enjoying the rest of his slice of spice bread.

Baskets of orange and purple carrots and more fingerling potatoes sat under shelves of black midnight melons, hanging garlic, bright green limes, yellow and sharply aromatic mend-mum bulbs, and blood-red pequoia gourds. Six kinds of eggs lined one shelf, including a small basket of freckled lace the size of his thumbnail and bright blue goose eggs larger than his hand. Jars of different infused oils could be drawn from spouts into either the buyer's vessel or one of the empty clay jars on the shelf next to the taps for tuppenny a jar. At the back of the store were bundles of cut flowers of a dozen different colorful and fragrant varieties. Cloth-lined baskets sat near a scale on the front counter piled with seeds, nuts, and grains of every variety, several of which Andrew didn't recognize.

Andrew filled two burlap sacks with bread, bundles of grain and flour, vegetables and even a few pieces of fruit he had never seen before. He even splurged on a vessel of thick, golden yellow butter. It was cold enough outside that he was confident he could get it home with little worry of it melting. He laid a gold sovereign on the counter, the Minotaur bit into it, and seeing that it was still gold down deep beyond his teeth marks, dropped it into something behind the counter and returned four and six onto the counter in front of Andrew. Maybe he could have dickered for a slight discount, but Andrew was in a great mood and didn't feel like wrestling over trepenny—not this time.

He rested the two full sacks behind his seat in the cart and led Brynlee down the narrowing cobblestone streets to the center of town.

"Tinker, tinker, fix y'er wares! Mend y'er pots, sharpen y'er sheers!" he cried out. It was going to be a great day.

CHAPTER 4

"T inker here! Tinker here!" he called out.

"Tinker, tinker, fix y'er wares! Mend y'er pots, sharpen y'er sheers!" he cried out again as he guided Brynlee through the cobblestone streets. Then he cried out once more when he arrived at a wide circular opening in the buildings near a large fountain of a Minotaur woman pouring an endless vase of water into the basin.

Two shop owners came forward, their knives wrapped in leather, each of which he sharpened and collected their pennies. Several others glanced around the cart, curious what he might have that they had not seen before, but most didn't purchase anything. He didn't mind. His spirits were high.

Jatoba was a mixed village of Minotaur—their face and skin like oxen with long, powerful horns often adorned with etchings and beaded leather jewelry—and Long-beards—a distant descendant of Dwarves, taller than humans by half, strong, and with skin the color of the minerals their ancestors mined millennia ago. Large and fearsome in appearance they were, but friendly.

"Do you mend copper pots?" a Minotaur woman asked, wrapped in a long tunic, her fur a dusty grey.

"I do," Andrew replied. "Trepenny a pot."

She nodded and signaled a much younger Longbeard woman who emerged from one of the homes carrying a stack of three large copper vessels on her hip. The younger woman was bald and so beautiful Andrew had to force his gaze away so as to not be caught gawking at her. Her skin was the same iridescent copper color of the pots she carried, and her eyes a slightly lighter shade. Lines of what looked like copper wire ran across her skin, which varied in color from smoothly polished to tarnished green. She wore a white cloak. She exposed her bare shoulders when she pulled back her hood to speak with Andrew, which was hard for the young man to ignore.

She smiled at him as she approached.

"These need mending?" he asked, his mouth going dry.

Her smile gently grew. "How fine are your skills?" she asked with a voice like music.

He took a breath. "Not one complaint. My father's a master, and I've sat at his knee since before I could walk."

"Good because these are fine vessels, once expensive," she told him.

He looked over the first one. He could tell it was hand-worked but quite smooth. There was almost no sign of hammer on the metal. A hairline crack ran along one side, likely causing it to leak water.

He nodded.

The two smaller vessels were less expensive but still quite smooth and even. Scratching and wear along their bottoms suggested someone had likely pulled them along the hearthstone until they finally split.

"This is a simple mend," he told her, gently touching the hairline fracture in the first one. "But these two need a patch. I'm happy to do the work, but they will cost a bit more than trepenny."

She scowled playfully. "You wouldn't be trying to take advantage of a couple of women, would you?" she asked him.

He began to blush, and Brynlee turned to watch the conversation.

She laughed and touched his arm. "I'm just kidding. We knew it would be more than a simple mend. How much?"

He rubbed his face. He wanted to say eight a piece, four for the mend and four for the copper patch itself, but he hesitated. "How about one and five for all three?"

She glanced at the older woman and back at him, then nodded in agreement.

"Can you leave these with me?" he asked.

The older woman waved him away and took the younger woman's arm, who gently smiled at him. "I'll see you soon."

Andrew blushed again but quickly turned away so she couldn't see the heat rising in his face. His uncontrollable propensity to blush was among the many things he hated about himself. Even the thought of a beautiful woman made his face bloom with bright heat. In the various villages and towns he visited, he often watched men talk to women in a way that caused the women to blush, but he was not one of those men. He longed for that kind of confidence but never found it unless he was talking about his work or his wares.

As the small crowd of onlookers began to quiet, he

climbed onto the back of his cart and hefted the small but heavy iron crucible down onto the largest cobblestone he could find. It looked like an iron tavern mug turned upside down with a small door in the bottom, a hole in the center that would direct heat upwards, and four iron prongs holding a slightly curved iron dish barely the size of Andrew's palm fashioned to hold molten solder.

A crucible like this was unique. Most were large and built of brick or clay—heavy and unmovable in a black-smith's shop—but a tinker had to travel, so someone some-where had once decided to fashion a portable, iron version that could be carried on the back of a cart. However, it required something nearly impossible to come by without traveling to a major city: teefite, a black volcanic rock that burned incredibly hot when met with a magnesium spark. Andrew didn't need much more than a few granules of teefite because of how hot it burned, and once it was lit, it could be difficult to extinguish. Thankfully, the fountain was within reach.

He climbed back onto his cart and collected his copper solder, two metal patches, and his ignition kit: a small pouch of teefite and a magnesium striker. Then he returned to the crucible and knelt before it like he was paying homage to some deity. He opened the pouch and scooped out a tiny spoonful of black powder with a spoon his father had fashioned for the task many years earlier. He gently piled the teefite beneath the iron, tipped the crucible to the side to access the powder, and used the striker to rain blinding white sparks onto the black dust until a loud hiss brought the teefite to life. Then he leaned the dark iron dome back over the heat and dropped three lumps of glob-ulous matte grey solder onto the plate.

He held his hands out on either side of the crucible to

warm them, which felt nice in the growing cold wind. Waves of heat rose from the crucible's vent as the grey solder slowly softened.

"That's her," Andrew heard a Longbeard child say to another, both of whom were sitting on the edge of the fountain. "They say she steals the souls of some of the babies she helps deliver."

"I heard no one knows her family 'cause she killed them all and buried their bodies in her floorboards."

Andrew turned and saw an elderly woman with a dirty grey robe dragging along the ground and hair pulled up in a tall crooked pile above her head.

She was human.

Andrew had heard of entire villages of humans beyond the mountains, but he had never seen any, other than himself.

He rose as she slowly approached him. The whispering children spat in her direction and ran off, and a brightly colored bird cocked its head out of her hair, looked at him, and fluttered off over the shop rooftops. She didn't seem to notice.

Then she took Brynlee's head in her hands.

"She doesn't like..." Andrew reached to stop her, but before he could, she pressed her forehead to the mare's and whispered something to her. Then she approached Andrew's cart, not seeming to notice him at all.

"She *usually* doesn't like anyone touching her face, but she doesn't seem to mind you," he said, slightly bewildered and laying a hand on Brynlee.

Brynlee was calm.

"Can I help?" he asked.

The old woman turned her head towards him but did not meet his gaze. She blinked and moved her head back and forth. She slowly raised a crooked finger towards the cart and then pressed it over her mouth.

"Are you looking for something in particular?" he asked.

The old woman didn't answer.

"Sharpen y'er knives or mend a pot, perhaps? I have other skills as well."

She looked down at the ground like she was trying to remember something, shifting her weight back and forth from her left foot to her right. Then she shook her head, turned, and walked away, having never said a single word to him.

Andrew watched the sparrow flutter back into her hair as she trailed off down the road.

Curious, he thought to himself.

The crucible was warming now, but the solder wouldn't be ready for at least another twenty minutes, so he decided he could use some lunch.

Andrew usually avoided taverns—often too expensive for his purse and too rowdy for his wares—but it was early and he was having a good day. Besides, the pile of handpies stacked on the counter and the alluring fragrance of spiced cider wafting out into the street were calling to him. But first, a shop next to the tavern he had not seen before caught his curiosity.

He drew the tarp loosely over his cart and ran his hand along Brynlee's neck, assuring her he would return soon. She clopped a foot and chewed her bit.

Then he went inside.

CHAPTER 5

The small shop smelled of roses, herbs, and rich soil, a fragrance Andrew knew well from home. Potted plants of various sizes sat on shelves along the walls and the floor. Dried herbs hung from the rafters, and clay pots held powdered medicinals with names like mugwort and xlan.

"Welcome, and peace to you this Eden Vale," a Minotaur woman said, smiling toward him. She sat behind a table towards the back of the shop, embroidering something with pink thread—her robe covered in small, colorful, hand-sewn flowers. "Can I help you find anything special? A gift for a loved one, perhaps?"

The floor behind her table and the entire back wall were glass, looking down into a vast arboretum beneath the shop.

"Thank you, no. I'm only in town for the afternoon and was on my way to the tavern when I saw your store," he replied, stepping towards the glass. "What is this place? I've never seen anything like this?" he asked in awe of the contained rainforest he saw down below.

She glanced up at him from her embroidery and smiled. "Beautiful, isn't it? I collect heirloom cultivars from across the land. Unfortunately, some of what you see there has gone extinct in the wild, though a few of us are trying to bring them back." She pulled her pink thread taut and pierced the needle back into the fabric. "You see those blue ones there, down by the edge of the water?"

There was a spring or some other source of water flowing through the arboretum.

"There?" he asked, pointing.

She nodded. "Um, hmm," she replied, pulling her thread again. "They used to be sought by those in your trade. If you crush the petals and mix them with silver, the metal will glow in moonlight."

"Brynlee phalaenopsis?"

She smiled. "Well done!"

"My mare is named after them. They are my father's favorite flower. The loops in her bridle still glow faintly in moonlight, especially in ..."

"Raven light. Beautiful. I wish I could see that. I know the flower well, but I've never seen any Brynlee silver in raven light. Only a few pieces in dusk."

"It still grows near my home," he told her as something moved on her desk that startled him. A plump little mandrake was sitting in a red clay pot watching him. The plant-like creature, with brown bark skin and branches for hands and roots for feet, smiled when he noticed it.

"Really!?" The Minotaur woman exclaimed, putting down her needlework and leaning toward him. "May I ask where that is?"

He hesitated.

She sensed his hesitation. "I'm sorry. I don't mean to pry. It's just, I thought they were gone from the wild."

Andrew leaned toward the mandrake, who climbed out of her pot and walked towards him. "Hello," she said in the gentle voice of a small child. She was barely eight inches tall with deep green leaves on her head and the back of her hands.

"Hello," he replied.

"What's your name?" she asked.

He had never talked to a plant before. Moving plants were not unusual, especially in the Dry Places, but never a sentient one. Only in stories... "Andrew. What's yours? Or, uh. Do you have a name?"

She giggled and put her hands over her mouth as small light pink flowers bloomed on the backs of her hands. "Of course I do, silly. I'm Fleur de Lis. And I'm happy to make your acquaintance."

Andrew smiled.

"I live in the Dry Places," he finally told the woman.

"I see," she replied, looking away. Then she looked back at him. "There must be interesting flora."

He smiled and nodded, appreciating her willingness to ignore the superstitions. "I saw an Archa Tenech once!"

"Really?" she asked, her eyes growing large. Now he had her attention. "What color were its leaves?"

He thought for a moment. "A silver-grey, I think."

"Then it had reached maturity," she replied.

"I was fishing and heard something big coming out of the trees..."

She stood with surprise, then touched his arm to stop him. "You saw it moving?"

He nodded. "It passed by me, only ten or fifteen feet away, barely a cubit."

"Oh, my goodness." She put her hand over her mouth. "You *are* blessed. I've never even read of anyone witnessing a return before. Did it...did it know you were there? How fast was it moving? What did it feel like? To see it, I mean? I'm sorry, I just can't..."

"It's okay." He sat on a stool fashioned from branches, trying to recall the details of his experience. He hadn't realized the event was significant, but seeing her response gave him goosebumps. "It was an early summer morning, and I was out fishing with Jasper, my dog. He heard it first and stood like he does when he senses something moving through the marsh, but he was calm. When I finally heard it, I could tell it was really big, but none of the trees were cracking or breaking. It was more like the sound of swaying grass. When it came out of the trees, I saw the most amazing thing: huge Cypress and Wellington trees, hundreds of cubits tall, lay before it like grass as it pushed through them, and then they stood up again—solid as wood—after it passed. When something that big comes near, I've learned not to move. So I just sat there. Jasper too. He didn't even woof. He just watched it."

"How big was it?"

Andrew thought about her question and looked around. "Twice the size of this shop, maybe? But the trees growing out of its shell must have been twenty or thirty cubits."

"Incredible."

"And just before it stepped into the water, it sniffed at Jasper, and it turned and looked at me like it was curious. It had no eyes."

"No eyes?"

Andrew shook his head. "I almost reached out to touch it but decided not to. I remember dozens of birds fluttering off from its branches as it disappeared beneath the water, trees and all."

She wiped away a single tear. "Thank you for sharing that with me. May I record your account?"

"Of course. I wish I could remember more."

"Well, if you ever do, come visit me again," she said. "A scholar from the Fryowenn Court had the most beautiful accounting I've ever read. He found one while gathering specimens—its leaves still blue, and its shoots only a few feet tall. He guessed it to be ten or fifteen years old at the time. He returned every year to measure its height and coloring for nearly fifty years, if you can believe that. Until one day, it was gone. From the disrupted soil where it had uprooted itself, he could see that it must have been seventy feet wide, and though he followed its tracks to the sea, there were no broken branches or cracked trees anywhere along its path. The last measurement the scholar took estimated the trees growing from its back to be over 40 cubits high. Can you imagine? Well, I guess you don't need to, do you? No one has ever known how they move through such thick forest without breaking any wood, but I guess it makes sense now. They must have some intuition that protects the trees. They are part of a unique classification of biological plant life called flora animalis. Our little friend here is flora animalis, or animated plant, if you prefer," she said, gesturing to the mandrake, who still grinned at Andrew like he was a new pet.

Andrew remembered his solder and rose from the stool.

"Brynlee Phalaenopsis. An Archa Tenech. I should take a trip to the Dry Places sometime." But as she said it, she unconsciously gripped the top of her robe—a protective measure—and looked away.

"It's not as bad as people think. There is a lot of beauty in the marsh. Maybe I can take you some time? But I think I should check on my solder."

She smiled and nodded. "Thank you for sharing that with me."

"Of course!"

"Come see me again, won't you?" She asked him.

He nodded, then returned to his crucible.

CHAPTER 6

The crucible was now ready, and his solder was properly molten. A single crystal of snow gently landed on his puddle of copper-grey metal, firming a single freckle, then immediately melting.

Andrew looked to the sky.

Grey clouds with thin spots of blue still trying to break through had given way to an entirely forlorn sky with no more sign of the sun.

He was glad for the crucible's heat, but he was hungry. He could still see the pile of hand pies on the counter through the tavern door and smell the spiced drinks, making him wish he had gone into the tavern first instead of the herbalist's shop, even though the conversation was pleasant. But he'd have to wait to eat until after he made his patches—he didn't want his customer to return and find the work unfinished.

Andrew took a small bench from the back of his cart with a wooden arm that rose up between his legs like the neck of a horse. He had three different sizes of round ends he could fit onto the neck, depending on his needs, all burnt from years of use. Then he gathered a small pile of dirt from the street into a pile about the size of his hand, flicked water onto it from the fountain, and worked it into a firm clump of mud.

He fit the smallest of the three heads onto his workbench and draped a thick pad over the head. Then he positioned the cracked water pot onto the wooden head—giving it the calculating look of a master craftsman—and went to work.

Andrew began by painting a dark flux onto the crack with a thin horse-hair brush, then used the mud to build a small dam around the crack into which he carefully poured a thin line of solder that hardened on contact. Once the crack was fully covered, he broke the mud dam away and used one side of a rasp to knock down the rough edges. The other side of the rasp worked the new solder into the old metal until it was so smooth that his knowing fingers couldn't distinguish between the pot's original surface and his repair. He also gave the inside of the copper vessel a quick buff to knock away any prominent barbs, but he was careful not to overwork the inside since this is where the mend found its strength.

Andrew always hummed as he worked—a lullaby, though he didn't know it as such—something from when he was a baby. He didn't know the words—a Human song sung to him before Lithuel.

His hands were getting cold, and the solder was becoming difficult to work with. Music was beginning to pick up inside the tavern, and firelight from the hearth was calling to him.

He buffed the copper pot to a high shine with an oiled rag and set it aside to begin on the other two.

For these, Andrew measured two copper blanks and

laid them over his crucible's edge to warm. Then he painted each of the cracks with flux. Once warm, he shaped the patches over the head of his bench until they perfectly matched the curve of the bowls. Then, some solder, sealing, rasping, and polishing, and he was finished. Good as new.

As the pots began to shine, Andrew watched a Longbeard father return home from somewhere to a wife and two small children who ran out into the street to greet him. Embracing each other, the husband kissed his wife warmly on the cheek, who laughed and pulled him into the house. Scenes like this often pained Andrew down deep; he was happy for them and sad for himself. Lithuel was as much a father to him as his birth father could ever have been, but Andrew often wondered who left him in Lithuel's cart nearly seventeen years earlier.

Were they ashamed of me? he wondered. *Running from something? They cared enough to leave me in someone's cart, but why? Was it a random cart, or had pappa done some work for them? Do I have a brother or sister somewhere?*

He was more than grateful to Lithuel for feeding him, training him, and giving him a home, but it was not his eyes he saw when he looked at Lithuel, not his nose, not his propensity to blush at all the wrong times. Did he have his mother's hair? Perhaps his father's cheekbones? Always the same questions. Never any answers. He sighed and brought his focus back to his work like he always did.

Even though his hands were skilled, having mended pots like these hundreds of times before, it still took him nearly two hours to complete the work, and he had not realized until he was finished that it had begun to snow.

He had lost track of time, and his journey home was at least three hours. Andrew ran a hand through his hair. Maybe he should have gone without the cart after all, but if he had, he wouldn't have sold the sharpening stone. It had been worth it, but he had to get going. However, he had to return the pots first, and neither the Longbeard woman nor the elderly Minotaur had yet returned for them. The crucible also needed at least thirty minutes to cool before he could lift it back into his cart, and thirty minutes was pushing it.

Andrew used the wooden handle of his forceps to carefully push the crucible away from the brightly glowing teefite and poured fountain water onto the embers, which violently hissed and steamed, then a loud crack as the cobblestone split beneath the embers from the sudden temperature change. He was used to this and couldn't do anything about it—another reason why he used as little teefite as possible.

He waved the thick pad from his workbench over the crucible for about a minute, trying to speed the cooling. While a novice might have been tempted to use some fountain water to cool the crucible faster, he knew this would be a critical mistake. If the iron cooled too quickly, it could warp or even crack. He'd have to give it time, time he didn't have.

Andrew rose and entered the tavern.

The sign above the door was a cow's face carved into wood with long red hair hanging down over its eyes and two powerful horns rising up on either side of the words 'The Hiddy Coo.'

A Longbeard woman welcomed him from behind the bar where she carved a dripping hock of some sort of meat that looked delicious—its glaze like a candied mirror. Andrew's stomach grumbled. Her skin was the color of fire agate, and her eyes brown with red flecks. She had powerful hands and muscular arms, with a long, tight braid on her head and a long, tight braid of hair on her face. An apron tied around her waist read: kiss the cook if you dare!

"Happy Eden Vale to you, tinker!" she said swiftly swinging a heavy meat cleaver and snapping the bone in the hock with a bang.

He flinched.

"Thank you. An elderly woman and her stewardess hired me to mend some copper pots, but they haven't returned for them."

"Older? Grey fur? Her arm maiden beautiful, bald, and the color of penny coins?"

"That's them, yes. Do you know them?"

"Aye. That's the lady, Bucktress. She's a regular," the bartender said.

"I need to return her pots to her."

"You can leave them here. I'll see they find her."

"I need to settle with her," he replied.

Bang! The heavy blade cleaved another large piece of bone in twain. "What does she owe you?" she asked, wiping her hands on her apron and approaching him.

"One and five."

"One and five?" she asked in surprise. "I'd have you patch all my pots for that price!"

He grunted and rubbed the back of his neck.

"Or was it a special price for a beautiful woman with copper skin?"

He blushed, and she smiled. That was a yes.

"It's alright. You wouldn't be the first. The lady Bucktress lets her arm maiden negotiate with the men for exactly this reason. She's very good at getting a deal."

His blush washed away to a bit of frustration at that. He didn't like being taken advantage of and liked being made a fool even less. But one and five is what he had agreed to, so he would honor that price and be wiser next time he met a pretty woman.

She reached beneath the bar, counted off one silver piece and five pennies, and laid them on the bar top.

"Chin up, young tinker. She didn't mean anything by it. She was just trying to get the best price, and who knows, maybe she did like you."

He looked to the door. It was snowing harder now, causing steam to rise from his crucible.

"We're an honest people here, and I'd hate for you to leave and not come back, so take a hand pie. On me. Consider it an Eden Vale gift."

While Andrew was not prone to accepting charity, he was hungry and did feel a bit slighted from his foolishness.

"Sit. Enjoy a pie. I insist," she said, her arms as thick as his neck.

The slowly warming tinker swept the back of his long jacket over the stool and sat down.

She nodded and sat a hot, savory pastry in front of him. "Anything to wash it down?"

He slid the coins into his hand and poured them into his pouch. "I smelled something warm and spicy when I came in."

She smiled. "Mulled wine. My own blend. For Eden Vale. It's specially mixed to take all your cares away." She turned to a large cast iron pot bubbling over the hearth and used a wooden ladle to spoon some of the hot wine into a clay mug and sat it before him.

His mouth began to water.

The finger pie was a perfectly flaky pastry, golden-brown and filled with candied fruits and beef in a thin gravy, all of which filled his stomach with comfort. The mulled wine was rich, slightly fruity but not too sweet, mixed with something sharp like ginger and cinnamon, which warmed him from the inside and quickly began to relax him.

Halfway through the mug, he didn't feel drunk as much as incredibly relaxed, like some herb had been added to numb whatever part of him held onto any anger or frustration.

Andrew rubbed his palms on his trouser legs and watched the barmaid continue slicing meat and serving other patrons.

Everything felt like it was slowing.

He ran his hand over the grain in the bar top, its edges worn from years of leaning patrons. A large mirror on the wall behind the bottles had corners etched with images of livestock and scenes of farming. Dry meats hung on the wall behind the bar next to rows of clay mugs and wooden casks of different sizes, all written with a script Andrew couldn't read. A wild fire raged in a hearth the size of the back wall, once built of cream-colored stone that had gone black from years of relentless use and no cleaning. The tavern was as warm and cozy as a mother's hand-knit blanket—a pocket of comfort in the cold storm. The patrons were also jovial and happy to see each other. As they entered, the bartender greeted each of them by name, many of whom had to duck beneath the low rafters when taking their tables. Andrew was an outsider, but no one cared. And apparently, no one cared that he was human, which was nice. Humans were often outcast, ridiculed, and even barred by law from entering some of the larger cities. Andrew wasn't entirely sure why, but he thought it had something to do with some war centuries earlier.

While Andrew sat eating, two men entered the tavern, one a Minotaur and one a Longbeard—both so large

Andrew felt like a grasshopper next to them. But they seemed friendly enough, laughing together as they ate and drank, talking in a language Andrew didn't understand to the bartender and some of the regulars who trickled in. Andrew thought the bartender kept asking him things and filling his mug, but he could never quite remember what she was saying.

Then, after a while, someone began playing a stringed instrument they also blew into, and several patrons started singing. What? Andrew couldn't tell.

He turned to watch the bard play as either the music or the drink in his belly brought the flames in the hearth to life. From the fire came a flickering mother Minotaur and dozens of children holding hands and dancing. Then she brought forth for each of them a small gift that they sat around her and opened. It was a song of Eden Vale.

He wasn't sure if what he saw was real, but he didn't care. The firelight hypnotized him. Fire has its own life, and here in this hearth—and to the bard's music—it had life again.

In his haze, Andrew felt something gently touch his arm, and he slowly turned to find the beautiful bald woman sitting next to him, leaning against his shoulder. She smiled and said something to the bartender, who laughed and poured her a mug of what he was drinking.

He jerked his arm away and stumbled off of his stool.

She was confused.

"I fixed your pots, but I've no more deals to give you," he said to her through a slur.

"What are you talking about?" she asked.

Andrew tried to find his coin purse but couldn't remember where he had put it. "A smile for all the boys, huh?"

"What does that mean?"

His hands dug through his many pockets without luck. "She told me how you get your discounts from all the men."

Suddenly, her hand streaked across his cheek, and he stumbled backward towards the door—his head swimming and pain blooming in his face.

The music stopped and everyone watched.

The bartender and the bald woman yelled something at each other, and the beautiful woman waved a hand in the air before walking toward Andrew and helping him up.

He jerked his arm away again, found his purse, and laid a silver crown on the bar.

"It's not like that. Brutste is my sister, and she loves telling everyone I'm a flirt because I have no husband. She didn't mean anything by it," she said with a look of remorse for striking him.

He tried composing himself as the music began to play, his cheek throbbing.

"How much do I owe you for the repairs?" she asked.

"We're settled," he told her under his breath. Then he turned and left the tavern.

As soon as he stepped outside, a sharp wind nearly knocked him over. It was dark now. His crucible was beneath a growing drift of snow, and Brynlee looked at him like she was wondering where the hells he had been all this time—the cold quickly washing away much of his liquid stupor.

"Stay!" the bald woman yelled over the rasping wind from the open tavern door.

"I have to get home!" he hollered back.

"It's too dangerous! Brutste has rooms!"

He pulled his collar up around his neck, wiped the snow from Brynlee's face, hoisted the now cold cast iron crucible onto the back of his snow-covered cart, and climbed onto his seat, which he had to dust off.

"Don't get yourself killed over some stupid joke. Please!" she cried.

Ignoring her, he lifted Brynlee's reigns and clicked his tongue twice.

Brynlee didn't move.

Andrew clicked again.

Brynlee looked at him like he was being a damn fool.

In frustration, Andrew did something he never did: with a flick of his wrist, he grazed her back with the leather reins.

She snorted and shook her head. Then, under the additional strain of the snow fighting against the cartwheels, Brynlee pressed on.

CHAPTER 7

The cutting snow burned Andrew's eyes as he tried to hide his face from the wind. His hands ached from the cold, even through his gloves—the haze from the mulled wine now frozen out of him.

He started to worry about Brynlee. She was old enough and wise enough to know that they should not have pushed on, but he had insisted in his foolishness.

Andrew pulled her to a stop, no longer able to see the road ahead of them. He turned and looked back, but there was no sign of the road behind them either, other than the quickly fading trail the cart had left in the deepening snow. He decided to retrace his ruts for as long as he could, so he turned Brynlee and the cart and clicked for her to pick up speed, but any sign of even the dimples in the snow from his ruts were gone within minutes. *We must be close to the valley now*, he thought to himself as Brynlee turned her head away from the wind blowing directly in her face. However, the forest was not thinning into a beautiful valley but thickening into denser foliage that began clawing at the sides of the cart.

They had missed a turn.

Andrew looked back again. There was no sign they had just come that way through the snow, beyond a few dozen feet. The cartwheels were becoming too heavy for Brynlee to pull, but there was no sign of shelter anywhere. He could climb under the tarp of the cart if he absolutely had to, but he was worried that Brynlee wouldn't survive this storm without shelter.

He brushed the snow from his hair and looked up through the cutting wind to see the faint outline of a house.

"There!" he cried out to Brynlee. "Shelter!"

Brynlee pushed against the wind, struggling to pull the cart forward until they finally reached a latched wooden fence.

Andrew climbed down from the cart, brushed the piling snow off of Brynlee's neck, unlatched the fence, and high-stepped through the deep snow up the path to the front door, where he saw a flickering light through a front window that filled him with relief.

He knocked on the door and blew into his hands, even though he wore gloves.

There was no answer.

He knocked again and turned back at Brynlee, who looked miserable in the whiteout.

There was no answer.

He leaned toward the window, wondering if anyone was home, and knocked again, this time more of a bang than a courteous knock.

"Hello?" he hollered.

Again, there was no answer; however, he saw something or someone move across the firelight inside the house behind the curtains.

"I'm a simple tinker from Jatoba," he yelled. "My mare

and I have lost our way and need somewhere to shelter for the night. I can pay!"

He tried the handle, but it didn't budge. Under normal circumstances, he would never even consider letting himself into someone else's home for so many reasons, but he was approaching the edge of desperation.

"Please!" he yelled. "We need shelter! We could die out here!"

He kicked the door in frustration, but there was still no answer.

He turned back to Brynlee. His worry had now grown into proper fear, but they couldn't stand in front of this locked house all night. They had no choice. They had to keep going and hope that if this house was here, another might be nearby.

Andrew wiped the snow away again and hugged Brynlee's neck. "I'm so sorry, girl. I got us into a real mess this time," he told her as she leaned into the warmth of his body. Then he made the difficult decision to untie her reigns and leave the cart behind, full of his and Lithuel's entire livelihood—decades of work.

With one hand holding the top of his coat shut and the other holding her reigns, he led Brynlee onward through the snow.

He had no idea where he was or which direction to go. It was dark. There was now not even the faint glow from his lamplight over his cart, and the blowing wind and snow made it nearly impossible to even look up from the ground. He considered curling up next to a tree and hoping for the best.

The snow was nearly up to his knees now.

He could feel Brynlee slowing when the reigns suddenly

jerked out of his hands. He turned to see her lying prone in the thick white. She had tripped.

"Brynlee!" he yelled, dropping into the snow beside her, running his hand along her neck, side, and legs to see if she had hurt herself. There were drops of red in the snow beneath her left hind quarter. *Oh no!* he thought to himself, clenching his teeth. A carthorse's legs are their livelihood; if the injury were bad enough or left unresolved, it might mean her life. If she fell there, she may never rise again.

The back of Andrew's throat began to burn at the thought of losing her there in that dark forest. He laid his head on hers, her light blue eyes crusting with frost. "Help!" he cried out. "Someone! Help!" But the driving wind quickly swept his voice away into the darkness. "I'm so sorry," he told her, his eyes blurring with tears. He did everything he could to at least shield her face from the wind that now felt like needles flying sideways at them as her breathing began to slow. And what of Lithuel? Would he be able to care for himself with his leg nearly useless? What if Lithuel never learned what had happened to them?

He squeezed Brynlee as tightly as he could.

Then silence.

CHAPTER 8

Andrew struggled to open his eyes, crusted shut from snow and frost.

Am I dead, he wondered.

It was quiet.

His body was numb, but he could feel clumps of quickly diminishing snow beneath him as he gently shifted. He figured that if they *had* died, he might at least be warm.

It was dark, but now a faint glow of firelight gently rimmed the edge of Brynlee's ear and the frozen hairs of her mane.

Andrew felt the weight of snow on him but its weight was lessening.

Brynlee was breathing. Her head was lying against his leg and partially underneath his body. Then, through the bitter cold, he sensed the presence of someone standing near him.

He lifted his head.

The old woman with the grey robe from Jatoba knelt next to him, her arm laying along Brynlee's neck with her head on the mare.

Is this an apparition, a dream, or the wine? he wondered.

As she rose, he saw she was barefoot, standing on wet grass with a long, crooked staff in her right hand.

She approached Brynlee's hurt leg and ran her hand down it to the hoof. He wanted to stop her but was still too cold to move. She found blood and rubbed her fingers together, smelling them. Then she tasted them.

Flurries of snow violently whipped around them ten or fifteen feet away, but he felt no wind.

He and Brynlee were now sitting in a circle of wet grass, and steam was rising from his jacket—he also felt warmth on his face from an unknown source, like the warmth of a hearth.

What sort of magic is this? he wondered. *Am I dreaming? Is this woman a witch or something worse? And why is she tasting Brynlee's blood?*

"Stop!" he summoned the strength to call out, but she paid him no mind. Instead, she laid her hand flat on Brynlee's hip and whispered something he couldn't make out. Then she stood and said: "Rise, mother." At that, Brynlee shifted her feet underneath her and stood. However, she did not put any weight on the bleeding leg.

The old woman stepped over Andrew, and Brynlee followed her along a path of melted snow to the door of a leaning cottage with a large tree growing out of its center. Warm firelight spilled out through the open door.

Andrew was surprised to realize they were no more than a few dozen feet from the cottage's front door when they fell in the snow. The blizzard was so thick that only a few cubits was enough for them to have missed it entirely.

Brynlee turned back to Andrew, still sitting on the wet ground. Only then did the old woman seem to notice him, but instead of speaking, she simply motioned him to the house.

CHAPTER 9

"Thank you for helping us," Andrew said, pulling off his wet gloves and kneeling before a roaring hearth. Its heat cut through his layers of wet and frozen clothes, warming him to his core. He wished Brynlee could be next to it with him.

"I thought we were dead for sure out there," he said, not turning his face from the heat, not just yet. "I should have stayed in town, but I didn't think it would come in this fast. How did you find us?"

There was no answer.

He wiped away water dripping down his face from his melting hair and turned.

The old woman stood at a table, her back towards him, working something into a long strip of cloth. The colorful bird he had seen fluttering around her in town watched him carefully from what he could now see was a tidy nest of a hole in her tall grey hair. Then she opened the front door and left the cottage, carrying the poultice with her. Her feet were still bare, and she took no cloak or tunic with her.

Andrew rose from the fireplace and went to the front door.

Brynlee was already feeding at a bucket of something as the old woman whispered to her and gently ran the flat of her hand along Brynlee's side and down her hurt leg. Then she knelt and began gently wrapping the leg in the poultice.

Andrew wanted to ask what she was doing, usually overly protective of the old mare, but it was clear that this woman meant neither of them any harm, so he said nothing.

The storm still raged around the cozy cottage, but he did not feel it. He couldn't even hear it. Beyond the fence line, he could see trees bending in the driving wind, but he felt no cold, no snow, no wind, nor bitter ice from where he stood in the open door. A circle of dry grass on which Brynlee stood surrounded the front of the old cottage. A path through the snow stretched beyond Brynlee out into the storm where he and the mare had been lying.

How is it so calm here and so violent just beyond the fence, he wondered. He had heard of such things, but he had never seen them. *Clearly, she's intuitive. But how could this be?* He had been led to believe that humans were not intuitive, but here she was. Perhaps she wasn't human or not entirely human.

The old woman rose and returned to the cottage.

"Thank you for helping her," Andrew said as she stepped past him.

She didn't reply.

"Can I repay…"

"I heard Mother Mare," she said, cutting him off, her eyes rolling past him to the cabin floor. "She said: '*Take my life instead of his.*'"

Andrew looked back at Brynlee, who was still eating

from the bucket. Light from the hearth spilled out the front window rimming her in a golden glow. He had always thought she cared for him, like Jasper cared for him, maybe more, but he had never heard her speak.

"She spoke to you?" he asked.

The old woman's head swayed in an unusual manner, but she did not reply. The sparrow stretched its wings and nestled deeper into her hair, not taking its eyes off of him.

Andrew closed the front door, now confident Brynlee was safe, and returned to the fire.

A tree grew through the center of the main room that looked like it had once been in a red clay pot that had broken away long ago. The tree's bark was swallowing fragments of the pot, and some lay scattered around it on the floor. The tree's roots had broken through the floorboards, and its branches lifted the ceiling from its rafters. In some places, he couldn't quite tell where the tree ended and the cottage began. Either this tree had been growing here for many decades, or something had accelerated its growth, Andrew wasn't sure which.

The woman sat on the edge of a frayed and broken mattress of feathers lying on the floor near the fireplace. Next to her bed were scattered sheets of parchment covered in scribbles and half drawings of things he didn't recognize, along with a few piled garments, blankets, and her leaning crooked staff that she carried in town and out into the storm.

The area within reach of her bed was a reasonably tidy, lived-in circle of whatever she needed. Everything beyond her reach was dusty and untouched. Old tapestries, unrecognizable from age, hung on the walls, and shelves held utensils and knick-knacks covered in webs. It was like she was camping in the middle of a museum of forgotten memories.

Andrew approached an armchair near the hearth that looked comfortable but broken from age, which released dust as he sat on it. A snake darted out from underneath the chair into darkness, startling him to his feet. Then, something else lurking in the dark corner moved.

He took a breath and pulled the chair closer to the firelight. Under normal circumstances he would not be comfortable staying the night in such a place, but the storm still raged outside, and he knew well not to ignore its ferocity a second time.

He sank into the soft chair, letting the heat of the fire consume and enrich him.

"Thank you for helping us," he said again to her.

The old woman didn't respond. She sat on the edge of her bed, paying him little attention—her eyes looking heavy. The bird in her hair had finally closed its eyes for the night. It must have decided he was no threat.

"If you let Brynlee and I stay the night, we'll leave at first light," he said, but there was no reply.

As the fire began to dim, Andrew thought the least he could do was put some logs on when he realized there were no logs burning in the hearth.

He leaned forward.

Nothing discernible was burning in the hearth. The fire flickered and crackled where logs should be—wrapping and lapping and glowing in the shape of hot coals—but there were no logs, no grass, no fuel—nothing of any sort Andrew could see anyway. But the fire *was* beginning to dim. He could see it, and he could feel it.

"Are you doing that?" he asked, then realized it might be uncouth to question such a thing.

"No."

"No? Then what..."

"No, you don't owe me anything. Tee lea yicktanee loo," she whispered. "I heard the mare's voice. And I came. That is all," she said, looking towards him but not at him, never once meeting his eyes; maybe she couldn't.

"Oh," he replied. "Are you alone here?"

She didn't reply, but the bird half opened its eyes in annoyance, then turned and went back to sleep.

"How long have you been..."

She cut him off again. "Yes."

He paused. "Yes?"

"Wait...," she said.

He waited. "Wait...for?" he asked, leaning forward.

"Wait there for morning light," she replied, pointing towards a back room. Then, before Andrew could ask her anything else, she turned her back to him, tucked her dirty bare feet under her covers, and went to sleep.

Andrew sat there for a few minutes, not wanting to leave the warmth of the fire until its light slowly dimmed and went out. His eyes were now heavy, and he could feel sleep calling to him, so he rose from the soft chair and went to the back room, where he thought he had seen something through the door that might look like a bed.

The room was dark, with a narrow bed on a wooden frame sitting in a corner. The blankets on the bed were thick, and when he pulled the top one back, he smelled the dust in the room stir.

He didn't usually sleep fully dressed, but his coat was now dry, and he wasn't sure of the room, so he kicked off his boots but kept everything else on as he tucked his feet beneath the covers and fell asleep to the thick smell of dust on his pillow.

CHAPTER 10

After some time, he woke to the sight of his breath fogging the air above him. He was cold again. It wasn't bitter, but it was cold enough to wake him.

Andrew tried to pull the blanket up over his face, which helped a bit but not enough for him to fall back asleep. He tossed and turned for a few minutes, then pulled the blanket back and sat up.

Most of the room was dark except for a chest enshrouded in moonlight spilling in through a gaping hole in the roof.

Andrew rose and approached the thin, glistening blanket of newly fallen snow covering the chest and floor around it. It was extraordinary, like something out of an ancient story.

The chest was ornately carved on every side, about the height of his waist and as wide as his arms outstretched. It was the color of cream sandstone with intricate filigree on every edge. The front and sides held the shape of a shield set in deeply etched relief. The lid was a three-dimensional carving of a naked tree with wild roots spreading out and up, encircling a near-perfect likeness of the full summer moon—what many called the raven moon. There were no seams or separation of panels, as though the box had been carved from a single piece of wood. The patina was slightly cracked and reflected the moonlight in such a way that made it look like it was almost glowing, especially the image of the full moon set in the lid.

Andrew had seen fine things in his travels, and Lithuel had taught him to recognize quality in details, material, and craftsmanship, but this was so far beyond anything he had ever seen that he held his breath looking at it.

He then approached a window caked with thick dirt and cleared enough of a hole in the glass to look out. Perfectly glistening snow blanketed the forest beyond the cottage, and the warming light of dawn was breaking beyond the horizon.

He decided he wasn't going back to sleep, so he pulled his boots on and went into the living room.

Though the hearth was not yet lit, the central room was somehow not cold.

The old woman was still asleep, her back turned toward him, and her sparrow sat on the fireplace mantel, nestled into its breast feathers, carefully watching him but not fully waking.

"Good morning," he whispered, taking a few steps toward it but not close enough to startle it. It just looked at him with indifference. Then it lifted its tail and relieved itself in a streak down the wall. Andrew grunted, pretty sure that was on purpose.

As daylight began to raise the curtains on details in the cottage, Andrew saw more of the old woman's story filling tables and shelves.

Things around the home were dirty and clearly falling far into disrepair, but they were tidy; everything had its place. Candlesticks stood in careful attention on either side of a portrait of a young woman with long, blonde hair—the face smudged and scratched out. She was wearing a beautiful lace dress with a green beaded necklace.

Andrew approached the odd portrait and lifted it from the shelf, wiped dust away from its face with his sleeve, and looked at it more closely. The necklace. Where had he seen the necklace?

He set down the portrait and went outside to Brynlee, who was awake and happy to see him.

"Good morning, girl," he told her with a smile and gentle hug. "I'll get you some breakfast shortly." Then he opened a saddle bag and removed a leather book tied shut with a thin strap. He flipped to the back and found the small, hand-painted portrait, the kind sometimes commissioned by a fiancé or spouse to carry in their pocket. It was of a woman with long blonde hair wearing a green beaded necklace.

Andrew didn't know who was in the portrait. Lithuel had found it tucked into his baby blanket. Andrew had always imagined it was his mother. 'For Andrew' was written on the back, which is why Lithuel had given him that name.

He took his pocket portrait back into the cottage and compared it to the one he had found on the old woman's shelf. The necklaces were similar, but since one of the faces was smudged, he couldn't tell if they were the same woman. He turned to the old woman to ask who was in the portrait, but she was still asleep. He would have to wait.

A small painting of an estate hung on a wall, surrounded by trimmed hedges on the far side of a river that almost looked like it was moving until he stepped closer. Little trinkets of fine detail adorned the shelves: A salt dish with a tiny spoon, a fine comb carved from shell, three thin hair ties of different colored fabric laying in perfectly straight lines—all encased in dust.

The old woman was still unmoving beneath her pile of blankets, the sparrow itself having fallen back to sleep on its perch on the mantle.

Andrew's stomach grumbled. He was used to making breakfast and tea for Lithuel, himself, and Jasper before first light every morning, and his stomach was reminding him that he wasn't at home or on his usual schedule. He missed Jasper. He also wanted to give Brynlee some breakfast.

He approached the front window to peek out at her when he saw a word smeared on the glass. Ardimus.

Strange, he thought to himself.

He then wiped away some fog with his sleeve and looked out. Brynlee was standing asleep near the warmth of the house, her breath only gently fogging in the morning air. He also noticed her full weight was on her wrapped leg, a comforting sign.

He gently smiled. This woman had saved their life. There was no question.

Andrew then remembered the children in town whispering about her. "She steals the souls of babies," one of them had said. "And she killed her family and buried the bodies in the floor," said another—the sight of them spitting in her direction like she was an evil spirit. But no evil spirit had pulled him and Brynlee from the snow last night. And why a sparrow? Everyone knows sparrows are creatures of purity, unlike crows or thistle backs.

No, Andrew did not see a witch when he looked at this woman but someone misunderstood and probably wanting nothing more than to be left alone to live her life in peace, as Lithuel had made clear was his wish many times. But what of the intricate trinkets and paintings? And what of the chest in his bedroom? His mind returned to the box with its fine filagree and tree holding a glowing moon in its thick, naked roots. He'd have to ask her about it when she woke. But first, tea.

Andrew approached what he thought was where she prepared food and rubbed his hands together, excited to finally repay her kindness, if only in a small way.

Alright, let's see what our options are, he thought as he began opening pantries, and as he did, a small purple lizard with fine feathers raced out from behind a sack and down the wall, stopping long enough to look at him and flick its tongue before disappearing between the doors of another pantry. Andrew took a breath. Small and medium sacks of what he thought might be mill flours and grain sat on a shelf, one of which began pouring on the floor from a hole in the corner as he picked it up. He juggled the small sack, trying to catch the falling flour and figure out where the hole might be when he felt it move. He quickly set it down on the counter and stepped back as a rock dodger, no bigger than his fist, poked its white furry head, dusted in light brown flour, up out of the grain and looked at him, wondering what had disturbed it. Then it nestled itself back into the sack.

Andrew's eyes were large. He was beginning to wonder if all the food in the house was already spoken for.

He slowly opened another pantry and leaned around, looking past the sacks while not touching any, trying not to disturb anything else that might be hiding in the nooks and crannies. There was no movement this time, so he began poking at the sacks and lifting lids on jars. Still no movement.

After a few minutes of carefully poking around, he found a few handfuls of flower, some oats, raisins, what he thought smelled like cinnamon, and a bit of lard, all of which he rough mixed together in a bowl with some water and pressed flat on the flour-dusted counter into cinnamon-raisin cakes, a simple recipe he learned years earlier—one of Lithuel's favorites. He wished he had an egg to drop into the mix, but he had no luck finding one. He wanted to fry the cakes in some lard on the hearth, but the fire was out, and when he approached it to have a look, there was no sign of ash or log. The sparrow stared at him with a half-crooked glare that asked: *what the hell do you think you're doing?* The thought of it made him smirk, but Andrew found no way to light the fire. *What home keeps no logs, kindling, or strikers?*

That's alright. I'll wait until she's awake, he thought to the sparrow, but didn't say anything for fear of bothering her.

Andrew returned to the food area, set the cast iron pan, stuffed with cinnamon-raisin cakes, aside for the time being, and grinned in satisfaction at the thought of making the woman who saved his life his tea par excellence.

He stood in front of a wall of jars of nearly every shape and size, trying to discern the markings, when he finally gave up and began lifting each one to look at their contents and gently smelling some of the ones he didn't recognize. One was marked 'start here,' which he found amusing. It was black tea, one of the ingredients he was hunting for. Then he picked up a small vial and rolled it around in his fingers, feeling its shape and weight. It was stone alright but also clear as the clearest glass. *This is crystal!* he thought to himself in astonishment. He had never seen this incredible stone used as a vessel before and couldn't imagine its value. He looked towards the old woman who had rolled over in her bed. He could slip the tiny vial into his pocket, leave the cottage, and not have to work again for the rest of the year, maybe longer, maybe *much* longer. It would be missed; surely it would be missed. The sparrow had fallen back to sleep. Maybe it wouldn't be missed. Not at first anyway. But who would he sell it to? Someone in Nevarii, perhaps? He squeezed it. Then he slowly set it back on the shelf, not quite trusting himself to touch it again. It was beautiful.

He thought for a moment about the strange juxtaposition of the cottage. At first glance, it looked like it was about to crumble down around him at any moment, frayed, fading, and slowly being pulled apart by a giant tree, but on further inspection, it was a home. It was warm and cozy, and he felt quite safe. Then there were the fine trinkets, the crystal vial of incalculable value, and the box. Again, that box. It was like it was calling to him to go and have a second look.

Andrew rubbed the nape of his neck and went back to lifting the lids on jars until he finally found what he was looking for. When he did, he set the four vessels on the counter in front of him along with a mortar and pestle. He would only know how much to mix once he knew how much water he was using, so he went to the barrel next to the door and looked for a way to measure it. A wooden ladle was floating on the surface, which helped. *But what can I use to heat the water and steep the leaves?* he wondered. He turned back to the hearth.

The sparrow lifted a single eye to watch him approach, then closed it again.

Andrew found the copper Yerba Mate carafe sitting on

the hearthstone she used for her tea and looked into it. Then he ran his forefinger and thumb over the metal, feeling its thickness—the touch of a master craftsman. The rim was thinning and nearly black from extensive use, but it was quality craftsmanship, no question about it. This would do. This would do just fine. And, it was large enough for them both to have a healthy mug's worth of his special blend.

He slowly ladled two scoops of water into the vessel, carefully estimating its volume, and then returned to the hearth. *No fire.* How could there be no source of fire?! *But there is*, he remembered. She was the source, she was just asleep. He sighed, and the old woman began rousing and rolled over. As she did, a faint flicker of a flame rolled to life in the hearth.

His eyes grew as he watched it start from nothing—nothing he could discern—and he smiled. It wasn't quite as much as he would like, but it might be just enough to get the tea started, so he hung the carafe on the hook and returned to mixing the tea, calculating how much herb and spice he needed for this volume of water.

His skilled fingers carefully scooped, pinched, and measured what he thought was the precise amount of each ingredient into the mortar, relying on his nose to make the final decision. Then, he quietly used the pestle to lightly grind and mix the ingredients just enough to release the aromas and partially revitalize the aging components. Though he considered himself reasonably decent at metals and repairs, he allowed himself the notion that he was actually an expert at this particular blend of tea. And he was right.

With the tea now mixed, he lifted a mug from a hook on the wall and felt it weighed more than he expected when he found a tiny grey mouse curled up in the bottom. At first, he thought it was dead until he saw its tiny sides rise and fall with each diminutive breath. So, he hung that mug back on its hook and fetched another. He was beginning to realize that he would have to get used to various creatures crawling around the nooks and crannies of the old place if he were going to stay for any length of time, an idea just now occurring to him—with the snow as deep as it was outside.

Suddenly, there was a scream.

Andrew turned as the fire roared with so much heat that he had to shield his face, and the sparrow fluttered violently around the room.

"Who?!" the old woman cried. "Who?!"

Andrew squinted past the brightness of the fire, trying to see what was happening as the old woman scrambled over her bed to the back corner of the cottage, reaching for her staff. But before he could say anything to calm her, she stretched her staff towards him and yelled: "Belam mach torem!" as a violent wind tore through the house, ripping the front door open—papers, blankets, and sparrow spinning and flying about. Andrew shielded his face and leaned against the violent gust that was worse than what he had faced in the storm the night before, and before he could catch himself, his feet slid out from underneath him, and he fell, just barely rolling behind the trunk of the tree as the fire from the hearth exploded out toward him. He shrank back from the sustained heat that, within moments, became nearly unbearable, like the heat of a blast furnace.

"It's me!" he cried out, but he could not even hear his voice over the absolutely overwhelming violence being leveled at him. "Please stop! STOP!" He coughed. The air was too hot to breathe.

Then it stopped as suddenly as it began, and Brynlee stood over him, braying and kicking the floorboards.

Andrew scrambled behind her, trying to catch his breath.

The old woman looked at the mare, who tossed and shook her head.

Nothing but the calm flame flickered in the hearth. No papers flew. The sparrow calmly fluttered from its perch on the mantel into its nest in the old woman's hair. Nothing was amiss. But Andrew was still breathing heavily, and Brynlee was responding to something. Something *had* just happened, but what? He wasn't sure. Everything in the cottage looked untouched—not even the dust on the old picture frames had moved. A powerful intuition was at work that made him want to flee, but Brynlee would not move as Andrew rose and tried to pull her reins and lead her to the door.

The old woman approached them both, still holding her staff but now much more calm. She was looking directly at him for the first time since he had met her at his cart, with a mix of confusion and sternness on her face. One eye twitched half closed as she tried to read his face and remember who he was and what he was doing in her home.

"Who?" she asked. "Who!" and she struck the wooden floor with the bottom of her staff, but Brynlee clomped a hoof, and the woman looked at her and leaned away, then asked again, this time more calmly. "Who?"

Andrew looked around, trying to catch his breath. "My name is Andrew. You saved me and my mare last night from the storm, *you crazy witch!*" he wanted to add but didn't.

She squinted and grabbed him by the chin. Brynlee snorted but did not stop her.

Looking closely at his face, she tried to remember if

what he said was true, but she could not. Her first thought was that this was an imposter come to rob her, but Mother Mare told her again to calm down and that this was her boy. She turned to Mother Mare. "Bue lafalem mach a nee noo?" she asked. *What he says is true,* Brynlee replied to her without spoken words. *We mean you no harm. We left the village yesterday, against my wishes, and were caught in the sudden snow. He might be a foolish boy, but his heart is true.*

Still holding Andrew's face firmly, the old woman looked at him again. Then she took a deep breath and let him go.

Jars sat out on her counter, and some sort of cakes filled her pan.

She walked to the mortar and pestle, licked a finger, gently touched the mixed herbs, and tasted them. This tasted familiar. She couldn't remember how, but her tongue remembered. Then she glanced at Andrew and turned to the cakes.

Andrew watched her now from the other side of Brynlee, who—he wasn't sure how—might be able to protect him.

The woman pinched a bit of a raw cake and ate it. Her eyebrows rose. They tasted lovely.

She looked around. *What's happening,* she wondered. *Why does this boy look so scared?* She remembered speaking to Brynlee but not much else. Much of what had happened since she woke was quickly fading.

"What are you doing here," she calmly asked Andrew, carrying the frying pan to the hearth and laying it on a grate fashioned to hold various items above the flame. It was the first time she had spoken to him clearly.

"We were caught out in the storm last night, and you

found us. You wrapped my mare's leg and brought me in," he told her, just beginning to calm. "Don't you remember?"

She looked at the poultice wrapped around Brynlee's leg. *Is it true?* she wondered.

She reached up, and the sparrow hopped onto her finger. The tiny bird chirped and warbled at her for more than a minute then fluttered back into her hair. Only then did the old woman lean her staff against the wall and sit at a small, crooked table.

Andrew could hear the cinnamon-raisin cakes beginning to bubble and squeak, so he slowly approached the pan. The smell of hot fat and cinnamon was punctuating the room, and their edges were starting to brown. He was either going to let them burn, or he needed to flip them. Since she looked calm now and *had* saved their life, he decided to salvage breakfast and hope that food might ease the tension that had not entirely vanished between them.

As the water in the copper kettle began to steam, he found a rag in one of the cupboards and a wooden spatula that he used to turn the cakes. He then poured the Yerba Mate mix from the mortar into the hot water in the kettle and set it on the table to steep.

She leaned towards it and took in its fragrance. It smelled terrific. Her mouth began to water.

Brynlee returned to her place outside after assurances from the woman that she would not harm the boy.

Andrew pulled the pan from the fire with a cloth, never fully taking his attention from the woman, and drew two cakes onto two separate plates. Then he sat down at the table and poured them each a mug of tea.

The woman broke a small crumb off the cake and held it up to the sparrow that quickly grabbed it from her and swallowed it. Then she gently cupped the mug in both of her cracked and crooked hands and smelled it. Andrew watched a smile grow across her face. She cupped a hand over the top and smelled it more deeply, her nose pulling apart the flavor notes, trying to recognize each ingredient. She took a slow sip but did not swallow it, not immediately. Instead, she let the liquid coat her tongue as she felt its texture, its temperature, its darkness—the floral and spice. Then she took another drink. She missed this. She *really* missed this, but why? Where did she know this from? Her entire body tingled. Her fingers felt lighter, her eyes sharper. She could fall into a pool of this hot liquid—sink to its depths, never to be seen again—and she would die a happy woman, but why? Her tongue knew this so well, but her mind did not. After letting her body and senses revel, she tried hard to remember. She dug deep. She fought to grasp for even the slightest hint of what this was and how she knew it so well, but there was nothing—absolutely, infuriatingly, not a single thing. It was as though a loved one were locked behind a door she could not open, no matter how hard she tried. She could *feel* the memory of it so very close, like a word she had used just that morning and now could not remember.

"How is it?" Andrew asked.

"It's perfect," she said quietly.

He smiled.

"How do you know this drink?" she asked him.

"My father. He's made it for breakfast since I was a boy, but his was always too strong and bitter, so I played around with the recipe until I found a mix I like. I really enjoy the contrast of sweetness and spice. I find it warm and comforting."

Warm. And comforting. She liked the sound of that. "Yes. I agree."

She couldn't quite remember why this boy was in her house, but she remembered enough of the conversation with her sparrow and Brynlee to hold onto the important bits. She broke off a piece of the cake for herself this time. It was a little dry but also lovely, and it went well with the tea.

"You don't remember last night, do you?" Andrew asked.

Shame rolled over her like a heavy curtain. "My memory used to be sharp as an adder's tooth, but now..." And she didn't finish her sentence. Instead, her eyes trailed off to somewhere distant. Where? Andrew did not know.

"How long have you lived here?" he asked, recognizing that her memory might be a sensitive subject. "Do you live alone?"

She did not reply. Instead, she took another drink of the tea and another bite of the cake, giving a second crumb to her little feathered friend.

"Well, I'm Andrew. And that's Brynlee," he said, gesturing towards the window.

"Mother Mare," she whispered. "Mother Mare. Lorna. Mother Mare," her lip twitching to one side as she spoke.

"Lorna? Is that your name?"

She took another drink of tea with no reply.

He wanted to ask where she was from, who the woman was in the frame, or if she knew any other humans, but such questions felt futile.

As they ate, the little grey church mouse that had been sleeping in the mug on the wall clambered up onto the table, yawned, and took a large crumb of cake in its front little paws, sat back on its haunches and began to eat, not bothered in the slightest by the presence of the two humans. And while Andrew paused, eyes wide watching the peculiar scene, the old woman didn't seem to notice at all.

"You seem to have a lot of..." he hesitated, not wanting to offend. "Friends."

Her eyes met his. "No friends," she replied.

He felt a pang of sadness for her.

"Not alone. But no friends."

He pushed his cake around on his plate, now not quite interested in finishing it.

Somehow, the food and fragrance of the tea held her memory in place long enough to allow them something of a conversation.

Her head swayed to the left and the right. He studied the odd movement, her hands, her hair, her smile as she took another long drink of tea.

"How are you able to talk to Brynlee?" he asked her.

The woman's head swayed his direction, but she did not meet his gaze as much as look at his chest. But again, she did not reply.

He wasn't sure at this point if she was intentionally ignoring some of his questions or was somehow unable to answer—perhaps unable to even understand them.

"Now things seem to simply slip away," she replied to his previous question. "No friends. Not alone. No friends, never alone," she whispered into her tea and took another long draft, her head swaying more and more, like a boat on choppy waters.

"Well, thank you. For having us," Andrew said slowly. "You saved our lives last night. And you might not remember that, but I will never forget it." He turned to the window, where he could see Brynlee pulling up long green grass in mouthfuls. "I was so stupid." He looked away, now feeling the pangs of his own guilt and shame.

"I don't know what I would have done if I had lost her last night."

"I don't know exactly. Intuition. Since I was a girl. Intuition. Yes," she said, looking up towards Brynlee. It was as if it took her several minutes to answer his questions.

Intuition. That word captured Andrew's attention.

"Perhaps. Perhaps she saved you: Mother Mare," the old woman said.

Andrew nodded. "Twice, I think," he said, remembering the terrible flames and wind. "Why do you call her that: Mother Mare?"

"She is a mother. Once a mother, never not a mother. Never a mother, I, but mother, she. Clear as firelight in darkness," she told him.

Andrew shook his head. "I've known her since she was a filly. She has never born a foal."

Now her eyes rose to him, crystal clear, and she calmly said: "Don't you see, child? You are her foal."

Oh, great spirit! he thought to himself and swallowed. That was heavy. He looked towards Brynlee again, but now he saw her in a new light. Of course, he was her foal. Why had he never thought of himself that way? Moments sprang to life in his memory: moments of her keeping him and protecting him, watching over him while he slept at night on the roads, laying close to him to keep him warm in autumn, trying to stop him from leaving Jatoba, stepping into the raging fire to protect him just that morning.

There was quiet between him and the woman for the rest of her cinnamon cake as his thoughts crawled across the scattered artifacts of a life once lived, now hanging on the walls and sitting on the shelves. Then, the box came back to mind.

"May I ask you about something?" he asked.

Her eyes rose, and she looked in his direction but did not meet his gaze.

He'd take that as a yes. "That's a beautiful chest you have in the back room. I've never seen anything like it."

She scowled and looked away.

Now, he was hesitant to go any further with it.

"Is there any more?" she asked, reaching her mug towards him.

He smiled and poured what remained of the tea into her cup. She also smiled and cherished the dark liquid again, her eyebrows raising with contentment.

"I can tell you how to make it." Then he stopped. *Foolish*, he thought to himself and shook his head. *She won't remember.* Then he snapped. He had an idea.

"Damn stubborn fool!" she blurted out.

He froze. Was she talking to him or...

"He doesn't talk to me anymore. I apologized, but he won't give me my secrets back!"

Andrew took a breath. "Who won't give you your secrets back?"

She didn't respond.

Again, they sat quietly for some long, awkward moments before his mind returned to how he might help her remember how to make the tea. Then he rose to the jars still sitting on the table. He was a tinker, after all; he could solve this.

He fetched the small salt spoon he had seen on a shelf earlier, dropped it into the first jar, and with a piece of chalk he found on a shelf, he wrote on the jar. It already said: 'Start here,' so he scribbled: 'three scoops.' On the second jar, he wrote: 'second—two scoops.' On the third jar, he wrote: 'third—two scoops.' And on the fourth, smallest jar, he wrote: 'fourth—three pinches.' Then, underneath those words, he drew a line, and beneath the line he wrote: 'add to half kettle of water.' He lined the four jars up next to each other on the back of the table where she could easily see them.

"Now you can make yourself a proper cuppa, even after I'm gone," he said, proud of himself.

"Gone?" she asked.

He looked out the window. The sun was glistening brightly off the snow, but the snow was deep—too deep to venture out into.

He nodded. "Last night, I promised you that Brynlee and I would leave at first light, but I'm not sure we can with how deep it is out there."

"Stay," she said. "Or leave. Leave or stay."

Lithuel came to mind. He was probably worried about whether Andrew had made it through the storm or if he had stayed in Jatoba overnight. Andrew also needed to find a way back to his cart—if the storm hadn't ruined it.

"I'm not sure I have much choice," he told her.

She rose and reached for her staff.

This made him a bit nervous with what happened the last time she wielded the long dark staff, with its spiraling web of branches at its top, but he held his nerve and stepped out of her way as she approached the front door and went outside. He followed her.

It somehow did not feel cold outside, even though at least a foot of heavy snow covered the entire forest everywhere except the cottage. Andrew was beginning to think that either the woman, the house, or something in it was resonating heat, and with the fire flickering out after she fell asleep and sparking to life after she rose, he was willing to lay a silver crown on the barrel head that the source of the heat was the woman.

Andrew watched her approach the fence line, still bare-foot, and Brynlee stepped towards him.

She drew the interlaced ovoid of branches at the top of her staff towards her mouth, cupped a hand, and blew into them. As she did, they began to glow like the embers of a fire. Then she stretched out her staff as a path of snow melted away as though being met with a steady flow of hot water. After thirty or forty cubits of snow had melted down to the steaming grass beneath, she turned to him. His eyes were large. This was extraordinary. How could a human do such a thing? Perhaps she was *not* human. She looked human.

She pulled each of his hands towards her so that they lay open and flat. Then she spat into them, rubbed the spittle across his palms, and motioned him to rub them together, which he did with disgust. Then she leaned the staff down so that its end was between her and Andrew.

Andrew watched a small, single branch grow out from the end about the length of a finger, and she smiled like a mother holding her infant child for the first time. She carefully broke it off and handed it to him.

He wasn't sure what to do with it until she took him by the wrist and led him to the edge of the cold, wet ground. She held the small branch up to his mouth and motioned him to blow into it. He hesitated. But she nodded again. Then he blew onto the branch as she had, and its natural end began to glow like a tinder.

She smiled. Then she pulled Andrew's wrist and stretched his hand and the branch out over some of the pristine, glistening snow undisrupted by her staff. It melted for him just as it had for her. It did not rush away at the speed or volume it had before her staff, but this tender branch clearly held some small portion of the power that was either hers or her staff's—he was still unsure which. But, wherever the power came from, he could feel it, and he was touching it.

She let go of his wrist.

Andrew slowly waved the branch back and forth, and as he did, snow melted away for nearly half a cubit from the glowing end.

He shook his head. "This is amazing!" he exclaimed. He looked at his hands, which were not burned, though he could feel the warmth of the twig on his face.

Then she held up a single crooked finger and looked at him sternly. "Haya hachama!" she told him. "Be wise." Then she grabbed his wrist again and blew long and hard on the branch as it began to glow so brightly he had to turn his face away. She flicked his wrist, and a large bush not ten cubits from him burst into such flames that he dropped the stick and stumbled backward.

Andrew watched as she calmly picked up the violently glowing branch and cupped it in both hands. Its light quickly dimmed and flickered out. Then she calmly handed it back to him like she was passing him the salt. He, however, wasn't sure that he wanted to take it. But she gave him a look of assurance and motioned him to do so.

He slowly rose and took the branch from her. It now looked like any simple twig he might find in the forest, and he felt no heat from it.

She returned to the house.

He looked at Brynlee, who had startled at the explosion but looked calm enough now.

Remembering what the woman had said about his mare, he rubbed her neck and hugged her face. She closed her eyes and leaned into him, welcoming his embrace.

CHAPTER 11

After exchanging well wishes with Lorna, Andrew returned to find his cart buried in heavy snow, which he slowly melted away with the small rod she had given him. It was difficult for him to accept that the woman who saved his and Brynlee's lives would probably not remember them by the afternoon, but at least she could wake every morning to a proper cup of his special blend. The taste of his tea would have to be enough.

Andrew pulled up to the squat swamp cabin he called home. His whole body ached. Fear can exhaust you, and he hadn't slept well. He was glad to be home.

He stowed his cart, fetched Brynlee some fresh hay, and went inside. The house was empty and quiet. No sign of either Lithuel or Jasper. Even though it was sometime between supper and dinner, the hearth was cool—unusual, but nothing that worried him. He welcomed the solitude. As comfortable as he tried to be talking to strangers, it was always peace and quiet that renewed his spirit.

He knelt, lifted a scratched floorboard in the corner of his bedroom, and looked down into the soft swamp soil below the cabin, where a mud crawler the size of his hand skittered away from the light. Andrew reached beneath the flooring. Finding a long, taunt rope attached to a hook, he began to pull. It was dry at first, but as he carefully lifted it through the floor, the rope became damp and thick with mud. At its end was a mud-caked sack protecting a small but heavy box. He left the rope and sack hanging from the hook and carried the box to the kitchen table, where he had said his goodbyes to Lithuel the morning before. The metal box was about the size of a loaf of bread, tin-grey in color and nearly smooth on every side. It was a puzzle box with no apparent locks, latches, hinges, or doors—another of Lithuel's ingenious contraptions.

Andrew slid a panel on the right side of the box up with his thumb, releasing a panel on the opposite end, which he slid back. He then slid a front panel down that unlocked the lid.

Andrew often thought Lithuel should have worked at one of the academies or a lord's court, but he was content with the tinker's life. "Safe and fed. That's enough," Lithuel had always said.

Rows of silver crowns and gold sovereigns filled the box so tightly that extra coins were squeezed between the rows. There was even a platinum raicham worth 100 gold sovereigns or 1000 silver crowns, a value far too high for most to trade outside the cities. With a single silver crown being a skilled worker's standard day's wage, the box held more than ten years' wages, more than enough for Lithuel to retire on, which is what he was doing. And they both knew that if anything ever happened to him, the cabin and all its contents were Andrew's, which meant—by extension—that this box also held Andrew's future.

He dropped all but a silver coin and the copper pennies

from his purse into the box, returned the panels to their locked position, and lowered the mud bag with its precious contents back into the wet soil beneath the house, which swallowed it again.

Andrew rubbed the back of his neck, wondering what Lithuel might be doing. He and Jasper had probably gone off fishing.

Even though his stomach was calling to him, he could barely move, so he kicked off his boots and fell onto his bed.

A WET TONGUE on his cheek startled Andrew awake. Even though Andrew felt like he had just fallen asleep, the cabin was dark now save for the flickering glow of the hearth from the main room. Jasper's head was resting on Andrew's feather mattress, and his tail was wagging with anticipation. Andrew could smell the soothing fragrance of logs on the fire and Lithuel's rich wine broth with heavy cream, making his mouth water. The cabin was warm.

With a heavy hand, Andrew pulled Jasper up onto the bed in a tight hug as Jasper rolled back onto his feet and shook with excitement now that Andrew had awoken entirely on his own and with absolutely no help from Jasper's wet tongue that had gently tickled his cheek.

"Hey, boy!" Andrew laughed as the scraggly dog rolled around on him and licked his face vigorously.

Hearing Andrew's voice, Lithuel poked his head into the bedroom. They tried to give each other some modicum of privacy, though the house had no doors to close except for the front.

"Hey! There he is. Hungry?" Lithuel asked, a long dish towel tied around his waist.

"I could eat the ass off a horse," Andrew groaned, trying to pull away from Jasper's rambunctious kisses.

Lithuel winced. "Wow. Now I've got that image in my head. Thanks for that," and he dipped back into the kitchen. "I might not have a horse's ass, but I do have some cockles, freshly harvested," Lithuel hollered from the kitchen. "And I saw you found some fresh bread. And butter! Come eat!"

Andrew rose and leaned against his bedroom door frame.

"You look a bit dazed. How was the trip? It looks like you've stocked us up with food for at least a few weeks," Lithuel said.

Andrew nodded. "Jatoba was great. I sold the sharpening stone."

"Really? Well done!"

"Yeah, but I also got caught in the storm."

Lithuel paused and looked at Andrew with concern as he set two bowls of cockles on the table where a knob of bread and corner of butter were already waiting. Then he poured two mugs of wine, everything within reach of the table so that he didn't have to move his leg much, and sat down.

"Are you alright? I saw Brynlee's leg is wrapped. And you took the cart."

Andrew nodded again, feeling a bit embarrassed about the cart, and sat down to the bowl piled with circular shells about the size of a large coin in a thick pink broth covered in red and green diced herbs. This was one of Andrew's favorite meals, and though cockles were abundant in the mud flats about thirty minutes to the west of their home, they could only be harvested at low tide. Lithuel often saved them for special occasions, like a homecoming or birthday, since his legs weren't strong enough to stand in the ankle-high mud for long anymore.

"You were right. The snow came in much faster than I expected," Andrew said.

"Why didn't you stay in town?"

Andrew didn't immediately respond to that, now feeling both embarrassed and a bit foolish. "It's a long story."

Lithuel looked up at him from his bowl, nodding. "Well, I don't have to go jogging for at least an hour, so..."

Andrew smirked.

"I sold the skins and lechtfelt stone and got us stocked up before heading into town center when an old woman asked if I could mend some of her copper pots..."

"Which you can..." Lithuel added, tossing a corner of bread to Jasper.

Andrew nodded, not yet having touched his food, which didn't go unnoticed. "And she had an assistant with her."

"An assistant?"

"A beautiful assistant."

Lithuel's eyes rose, and he nodded. Now Andrew was getting somewhere. He plunged a chunk of his bread into his broth and took a bite.

"We negotiated a price, and they left their pots with me. While I let the solder heat, I shopped around for a bit."

"Okay?"

"Then I took their pots into the tavern to leave with the barmaid, when she told me that the pretty girl often dickers with the men in town for unfairly low prices."

Lithuel set his spoon down. "What does that have to do with you?"

"I might have only charged her one and five for the mends," he mumbled under his breath.

"One and five?" Lithuel asked, leaning back on his chair. "She must have been something for that price."

Andrew pushed one of the small shells around in his bowl. Then he shrugged. "I had done well with the stone and was in a good mood, so I went to the tavern for a drink and to warm myself a bit."

"Uh, huh," Lithuel said, and Andrew glanced at him. He had a grin like the cat that caught the mouse. "Or three."

"Or three."

"And?"

"When I heard she had swindled other artisans, I might have taken it personally."

"Did she swindle you? Because flirting and swindlin' ain't the same."

"Well. No."

Lithuel's arms were now crossed across his chest. "I'm waiting to hear how this caused you to get caught in the storm."

"After a bit, I'm not sure how long, she came in. So I left."

"Was it already snowing by then?"

"Yeah."

Lithuel sighed. "How did Bryn hurt her leg?"

Andrew sighed. "The snow came in quick. I tried turning us back, but the path was already covered, and I got lost. Then she tripped."

"Tripped? That ol' mare could walk through this bog blindfolded. What do you mean she tripped?" Lithuel asked, pushing his bowl away from him. His convivial mood was melting away.

"The snow was coming in hard and fast. And before I knew it, she was lying in the snow with a hurt leg. I thought that was it, we were done, when this old woman shows up, in the snow, barefoot!"

Lithuel was listening carefully and leaned forward, his elbows resting on the table, his bowl only half eaten.

"She was human."

"Human, you say?"

Andrew nodded. "And intuitive! She used this long, gray staff to melt away the snow and bring us into her home.

Then she wrapped Bryn's leg and put me up for the night. Only, the next morning, she didn't remember I was there, and when she woke, she used this incredible intuition to nearly blow me out of the house."

Lithuel rubbed his chin. "What kind of intuition?"

Andrew shook his head. "I don't know, but she used it to create this...this hurricane that knocked me over before the fire from her hearth blew at me hotter than an oven. I barely hid behind this huge tree growing up through her house, or I would have ended in a bad way."

"A tree? In her house?" Lithuel was trying to track what Andrew was saying but was getting a little lost.

Andrew nodded again, finally taking a bite of his now lukewarm cockles, and describing some of the peculiarities of her house to Lithuel.

"I have no doubt that we would have died in that storm if it wasn't for her, then the next morning, she nearly kills me herself," Andrew reiterated.

Lithuel looked out at Brynlee through the front window, trying to process everything Andrew had told him. "Maybe she didn't trip."

"What do you mean?" Andrew asked.

"You said the old woman—what was her name —Layla?"

"Lorna."

"Lorna. You said she could talk to Brynlee and even hear her through the storm?"

Andrew nodded.

"Maybe Brynlee somehow knew the woman was there and stopped."

Andrew hadn't considered this. "But she hurt her leg. I saw the blood myself."

"Maybe she hurt her leg on purpose. Maybe that's what it took to get you to stop."

Andrew's stomach sank. *Well, shit.*

Lithuel could see that this idea saddened Andrew, so he reached across the table, took Andrew's hand, and squeezed it.

"The woman called her Mother Mare. She said she was a mother because I was her foal," Andrew said.

Lithuel took a deep breath and rubbed the back of his neck, continuing to process.

"How much did you get for the stone?" Lithuel finally asked.

"Really?" Andrew said, looking up at him.

Lithuel flicked some broth at him, startling Jasper, and Andrew laughed.

"Three sovereigns and then some for the pelts."

Lithuel nodded. "That's a good price," he replied, tossing a few spoonfuls of broth into his bowl, dropping in a large knob of bread, and handing the bowl to Jasper, who took to it in a second.

Andrew pushed his wine around the table for a few minutes while Lithuel finished cleaning up and went to the hearth to enjoy his evening pipe.

"She also had this chest or box of some kind."

"Who? Leyla?" Lithuel asked, looking for his strikers. His pipe was full, but he needed something to light it with.

"Lorna," Andrew corrected. "I woke that night and found this chest, but it wasn't like anything I've ever seen."

"Uh, huh," Lithuel mumbled, patting his pockets. "Have you seen my strikers?"

Andrew shook his head, half ignoring the question.

"It was a little smaller than this table and had the most beautiful carvings, only they looked more like bones than filagree."

"Bones, you say? Where are my damn strikers!"

Jasper rose and left Lithuel's side for Andrew. He didn't like it when Lithuel raised his voice for *any* reason.

Andrew finally realized Lithuel was getting frustrated, so he rose and went to Lithuel's jacket. But he didn't find anything. There were no strikers around the dining room or in either of their rooms. Then Andrew had an idea.

"Did I mention that she gave me something?"

In frustration, Lithuel slammed his pipe on his arm table, eyeing the hearth fire to see if he could fetch a small tinder to light his pipe.

Andrew stepped out of his bedroom with a small twig in his hand.

"What am I supposed to do with that? Pick my nose?"

Andrew smiled, very gently blew into it, and flicked the end at the hearth, which surged with heat.

Lithuel nearly fell backward off of his chair, and Andrew laughed. "What in the nine hells is that?"

Andrew carried the twig, shielding its end like a match, even though no natural wind could blow it out, and motioned Lithuel to take up his pipe again. With hesitation, Lithuel did so. Andrew then used the glowing end to light the pipe. "It was a gift from Lorna. She grew it out of her staff." Andrew handed it to Lithuel, who gingerly held it by its far end and felt its heat with his hand. "It's a striker that doesn't burn out."

"Even if it gets wet."

"You're serious?"

Andrew nodded. "I accidentally dropped it in a puddle, melting the snow off the cart this morning."

Lithuel motioned to Andrew if he could dunk it in his wine. Andrew shrugged. So, Lithuel gently plunged the glowing end into the red liquid, and after a few seconds, the wine began to bubble and steam. Lithuel pulled it out and looked over it again. The room now smelled of hot wine.

"When does it go out?" he asked.

"It doesn't," Andrew replied.

"Okay?"

"I have to put it out." Andrew cupped it in his hands as the glow dimmed between his fingers. Once it was extinguished, he touched the end. "And now it's cold."

Lithuel pinched the end. Andrew was right. It was cool to the touch.

"Can you do that to something else? Another stick?"

Andrew shook his head. "It's not me. It was her. She somehow put something into this."

Lithuel handed it back to Andrew. "Don't tell anyone about this. Some would kill you for less than this."

Andrew looked at it, glad it looked innocuous when extinguished.

"Tell me about this box," Lithuel said. Andrew now had his *full* attention.

CHAPTER 12

Andrew stayed home for the next few days, resting and helping Lithuel with some fishing.

It was night now, an incredibly dangerous time to be out in Aitecham Tioram, but Andrew was hunting something he couldn't easily see in daylight, and his thoughts were once again with Lorna. How alone she was. How the children in town had mocked her. Did others mock her? Who was she? Was she really human? If so, how was she intuitive? And what about those expensive bobbles scattered around her house? She had saved his life, and he was becoming increasingly antsy to find a way to help her. "If she's as alone as you've made out, she's lucky to have met you," Lithuel had told him, though Andrew felt like the lucky one.

And what about Brynlee? Had Brynlee really spoken to her? Did Brynlee falter in the snow on purpose? Brynlee had a steady stride, he knew that much, but would she really hurt her leg to get him out of a storm?

And what of that box? It was beginning to inhabit his dreams. Was it a chest? A table? Why did the raven moon carved into its lid capture and cast back the light the way it did? Was it carved of some special wood? Shell? Some sort of formica? Was it intuitive like Lorna? So many questions; so few answers. In his mind, the chest had grown from simple curiosity to this strange and vibrant thing, drawing him back to it like a hungry man to food. And what had Lorna meant when she said someone was keeping secrets from her? Had someone somehow locked the box and hidden its key? He found no seam or joinery when he inspected it. No lock. No keyhole. Perhaps she was talking about something else. The way he had found it in the moonlight and the circle of snow now felt unnatural, but he wasn't sure why.

Andrew had several times dreamed about the chest. When he did, the tree on the cover would grow out of the ground and become a forest so large he could not see the canopy, with falls of water pouring from the clouds high above. But there had been no waterfall on the box—not one he could remember. Why was he dreaming about a forest? Lithuel had said that he thought the box was probably a chest or table, and someone must have built it, which stirred Andrew's curiosity even more.

Jasper huddled low in the boat as Andrew quietly pushed them across a small lake he and Lithuel called the Oubliette, or Place of Forgetting, saying if anyone ever fell in, no one would even remember they had existed. They did not fish on the Oubliette for at least two reasons: the first was that they regularly heard dire noises from the distant island in the center, and the second was that they never found any sign of fauna along its muddy banks, which suggested even the local wildlife would not come near this place.

There was no moon this evening, making the night

swallow the boat in vivid darkness, precisely what Andrew wanted. If he could not see, perhaps whatever else was out there might not be able to either, at least not as well as in daylight. Instead of piloting the boat by sight, he paid careful attention to the feeling of his long setting pole against the bottom of the lake as he quietly pushed the flat-bottom vessel across the water.

It was so quiet Andrew could hear the gentle motion of the dark water breaking away from the front of his punt until tiny lights skittered across the water and vanished.

As Andrew felt the bottom of the lake sinking beyond the reach of his pole, he gave one last strong push and pulled the pole up into his boat, hoping to quietly glide the rest of the way across the water.

Suddenly, another flicker of golden light flittered across the water and disappeared. Then another.

He heard the gentle hiss of his boat pushing through reeds and bullrushes as tiny golden lights rose from the marsh grasses and fluttered about, lighting the surface of the island in front of him. He smiled and held out a hand as a small lantern fly alighted on his palm. Then, gripping the reeds, he slowly pulled his boat up onto the grassy shore and climbed out, motioning to Jasper to stay, who moaned a bit but did as he was told.

A faint blue light glowed through the small trees that grew thick on the island. Andrew hoped that meant he was close.

Lithuel had taught him to travel the Dry Places with a walking stick, saying that most of what you have to worry about—and can survive an encounter with—can simply be pushed out of the way with a long stick, which worked as well for marsh cats as it did for mud vipers. He knew well, however, that no sword or shield could protect from some of what lurked in the dark waters, which is why he would get what he came for and get out, leaving nothing the wiser —hopefully.

He used his staff to push through the slender trees, trying to find the source of the blue glow, until he came upon three slender flowers growing out of the side of a fallen wooden stump. The flower had round white petals and looked up to the dark sky, each petal glowing a very faint blue.

"Brynlee phalaenopsis," Andrew whispered, using a slender pocket knife to pry the plant up by its roots and wrapping the ball of soil in a small square of cloth. Perhaps the herbalist woman with the cute little mandrake back in Jatoba might know something about the chest, especially if he came with a gift.

Just then, there was movement behind him, and he froze.

The movement was close enough that the hairs rose on the back of his neck. Whatever it was, he could sense in the blackness that it was large—large enough that Andrew could hear the tender trees snapping above him.

He slowly and as quietly as he could, reached into his back pocket for the wand Lorna had given him when suddenly every lantern fly on the island took to the air and began circling the small plot of land, casting the semi-moist ground in a haze of golden luminescence. And that's when Andrew saw the creature's silhouette through the darkness.

It slowly moved opposite the tree from where Andrew had harvested the blue flowers, not seeing him for the tree. It was half the size of Andrew's entire cabin and walked on all fours like a giant gorilla; however, it had thick green scales intermixed with the long black hair covering its body. As it pulled up a fist of the trees and began chewing, Andrew saw powerful fangs coated in a thick drool that nearly liquified the fibrous branches it was eating. It seemed to him a terrifying cross between an enormous gorilla and a dragon.

Even though it had not yet seen him, the beast was now between him and Jasper in the boat. *Jasper!* Andrew thought. *If he barks!* He had to do something, and he might only have a few seconds.

Then the beast stopped chewing and turned its head towards him, sniffing the air.

In a moment, it rose on its legs and charged with a violent show of aggression—first beating its chest, then spraying a mouthful of the acidic saliva—towards whatever was hiding in the grass; however, the beast must not have known what it was looking for because it ran past Andrew and tore at the grasses at the edge of the water. At that, Jasper sprang from the boat and started barking. Startled by the sudden noise, the Ape-Dragon pulled back for a moment, looking at the dog barely the size of its forepaw, when it lowered a predatory hiss at Jasper—a mouth full of viper teeth lengthening towards him and a frill of jagged skin raising on its neck. Before Jasper could be eaten, Andrew blew onto the wand as hard as he could, causing the ember on the end to flame brightly enough to draw the immediate attention of the beast, and Andrew flicked his wrist towards it. The night erupted in light as the Ape-Dragon exploded in violent flames, writhing and falling back into the dark water with a screaming so deafening that Andrew dropped the wand and covered his ears. As the scream stopped and Andrew regained his composure, the beast slowly rose from the water, its flames now extinguished. Andrew picked the wand up from a small plume of fire growing in the grasses where it landed and raised it again, his hands shaking uncontrollably.

The beast was now a mass of violent anger, rising up on its hind legs, stretching its arms wide, with its throat expanding and not one but two sets of eyes glaring down at Andrew with clear intent. It then opened its mouth—a green light growing from somewhere deep inside—when something long, reptilian, and many times the size of the Ape-Dragon lunged out of the dark water, grabbed the beast by its head, and pulled it under with a quick jerk back and forth.

And suddenly, the night was quiet. Only the sound of Jasper's energetic barks could be heard.

The lantern flies continued their calm flutter in a unified circle above the island.

"Shhhh," Andrew finally pulled himself together enough to command Jasper, not wanting to attract any more attention than they already had. He couldn't believe what he had just witnessed. This place was dangerous—there was no question in his mind—but Andrew could never have imagined what he had just seen. He quickly cupped the stick in his hands, darkening it, and scooped up the bundle of flowers lying at his feet.

"There is always a bigger predator," Lithuel had once told him.

Andrew slowly climbed back into the boat, his hands violently shaking. He was terrified. He had never been so scared. Whatever creature had come out of the water was still alive and well *in* the water and just below the boat. But he had to cross the water to get home. No wonder he and Lithuel had never seen any animal tracks along the shore. Apparently, everything but the stupid bipeds sensed the presence of an apex predator.

Quiet be damned, he thought as he dropped his ores into the water and rowed until his arms hurt.

CHAPTER 13

The next day, Andrew knocked on the wooden doorframe of the herbalist's shop, and the woman Minotaur looked up, smiling large and beckoning him in from the cold. She wore a green shawl with fur trim, and thin strips of leather adorned with beads hung from her horns.

"Happy Eden Vale! From where do you travel today, tinker?" She asked, rising to greet him at the door. The mandrake giggled and waved at him from her pot on the counter. Bright blue flowers sprang to life all over her fibrous body in excitement.

"I've come from home, and I brought you a gift," Andrew said, holding out a small cloth sack.

"A gift?" the woman asked, with a look of curiosity. Then she gingerly took the tied bundle from him and opened it at the counter. As she did, a faint blue light lit across her face, and her eyes grew large. "Brynlee Phalaenopsis," she whispered. Fleur de Lis put her small hands over her mouth in awe. "You found one?" the woman asked, looking up at him.

"I did. It grew on an island in the middle of a large lake near my home." He stopped there, not wanting to worry her with his account of how he was almost eaten trying to gather it. "But this isn't the only reason I've come."

"Oh?" she asked. "Come with me." And she went to the front door, flipped a sign written in a script Andrew couldn't read, and clicked a simple metal lock on the door. Then she returned to the counter, lifted a small stone hanging around her neck, and kissed it. As she did, a panel in the clear glass floor opened, and she motioned him to follow her.

The arboretum beneath the shop was much larger than Andrew could see from the window. A spring flowing through the garden fed countless varieties of fragrant herbs, glowing mushrooms, towering trees, and tiny toad-stools. The air was rich, moist, and filled with the fragrance of something akin to lilacs and orange peel. There were more than a dozen varieties of fruit trees, bushes bubbling with iridescent nectar, and hanging vines that Andrew thought were watching him, which gently moved as he passed by. Then there were the walking sticks—literal walking sticks—crawling across beds of moss and grass.

In the center of this part of the garden was a pond with dozens of brightly colored, long, slender fish swimming beneath the surface. Small piquets no larger than his thumb leapt like jewel drops from aquatic lilies into the water and swam away.

A yellow bulbous creature that looked like a gourd with eyes turned to watch the woman approach it. She carefully stepped out onto a row of stones that rose from the water to meet her. When she reached the small island in the middle of the pond, she smiled and pet the yellow bulb that resonated deeply at her touch. Then she removed a small tool from under her cloak, knelt next to two clusters of the glowing blue flower, and planted the gift Andrew had brought her. With satisfaction, she stood and turned to Andrew with a smile, returning the tool under her cloak.

"This is a special gift indeed. Thank you for thinking of me," she said, motioning him to return to the shop with her. As he did, large purple flowers bloomed around them, the stones in the pond sank again, and the bulbous creature began singing a faint but beautiful tune. Something across the landscape sang back.

Before climbing back up the ladder to the shop, Andrew stopped for a moment and looked around. He wondered how far it went; he had never seen such a place. The very walls were alive with countless types of crawling grass and fluttering birds and butterflies.

Once they were back in the shop, she turned to him. "I did not ask your name the last time you visited my store. I am..." she let out a melodious sound like a cow singing. "But you can call me Daphnie."

He smiled. "My name is Andrew."

Daphnie gently bowed to him, then asked: "How can I help you?"

"There is an older woman who lives not far from here. I saw her first in town when I was here last time. She came to my cart, and I thought she wanted to buy something, but before she said anything, she just walked away. She's human, with a long grey robe and..."

"A small bird in her hair?"

Andrew nodded.

Daphnie smiled and returned his nod. "Lorna. Yes. I know her well." Fleur de Lis listened intently but said nothing.

"You do!"

"In a way, yes. She has been a part of our community for as long as I can remember. She helped my mother calve me. Her eyes were sharp, and her mind was clear then. But her memory has since deteriorated such that she no longer recognizes me. It's such a sadness to see. She used to be so lovely, with her long, golden hair."

Andrew remembered the portrait of a young woman with long, blonde hair in the lace dress—the face smudged and scratched out.

"My mare and I were caught in the storm that night, and she brought us in and gave us a safe place to stay."

Daphnie smiled. "I'm not surprised. She has always been so kind. She has a mother's heart but no calves of her own—none that I know of."

"I was wondering if you could tell me more about her."

Daphnie looked away. "You will forgive me, young tinker. I can sense that your heart is true, but I am reticent to share too many details of someone else's story. Her story is hers to tell."

Andrew was disappointed. "I understand. She saved my life, and I'd like to repay her kindness. But I don't mean to pry."

Daphnie looked on at him for a moment, considering his countenance and what she might be able to offer Andrew that would not intrude on Lorna's privacy while still empowering him to help her. Fleur de Lis had climbed out of her small pot and snuggled up to Andrew's hand resting on the countertop. She was now asleep.

"Before I leave, can I ask about one other thing? If it's too personal, I'll be on my way?"

Daphnie motioned him to proceed.

"That night, I was a guest in her home and couldn't

sleep. When I rose, I came across some sort of wood crate. I'm not sure what it was exactly, but it was beautiful. It had intricate carvings on all sides and a tree of incredible detail on the top. Well, I've been dreaming about it, if you can believe that. And I'm just curious to know if you've ever seen or heard of such a thing. When I asked Lorna about it the next morning, she mumbled something about someone keeping secrets from her. Perhaps I'm just foolish," he said, rubbing the back of his neck and looking away.

Daphnie listened carefully with her head turned slightly to one side. "A tree, you say?"

Andrew nodded.

"What sort of tree?"

He pointed to a slip of parchment on the countertop and a stick of charcoal. "May I?"

She slid them to him. Then he drew, as best as he could, the shape of the long roots that rose up like a circle surrounding the naked branches and the full raven moon.

"And that moon. I swear, it was glowing like the brynlee phalaenopsis do," he said, pointing to the crude circle in the middle of his sketch.

Daphnie lifted the page and studied it carefully. She tapped her chin with a forefinger, then rose from her chair and approached a row of manuscripts of various sizes with bindings of different colors and thicknesses. She ran her finger along the row of books on the first row and then the second, stopping at a slender volume, which she brought to the counter and laid open in front of her. Andrew saw no words or images on its pages until she laid her hand on the first page and whispered a simple prayer: "Great Ruach. Grant us wisdom." And as she spoke, lines of script wisped across the page, like smoke fading in reverse. Then she pinched a pair of spectacles to the bridge of her nose and leaned forward, gently turning each page and scanning the script with a finger. After a minute of searching, she smiled and turned the book towards Andrew. "Was the tree you saw something like this?" she asked, pointing. In the middle of the page was a near-perfect sketch of the tree on the top of the box—its naked roots rising above its crown to hold the full raven moon.

His eyes grew. "That's it!"

She read the page.

"It says here that this is an image of..." She paused. She looked up at him over the top of her spectacles. Then she returned to the page and kept reading for another moment, in silence, before removing her glasses, setting them aside, and closing the book.

Andrew didn't like the look of that. "What? What is it? It's an image of..." and he leaned towards her.

"It is the sigil of the Shimar Etsell, known in the common tongue as Night Watchmen or The Shimmering."

"Shimar Etsell?" Andrew repeated.

"Very little is known of them."

"Then why do you look nervous?" Andrew asked.

"Because, the tree is an image of something I *do* know something about. It is what is known as a Grace Giver. A creature of myth."

"A creature?"

She nodded. "As a young calf, I would sit by the firelight listening to my gran tell stories of our people. She would then play her lute until the firelight itself came to life and danced to her tunes."

That must have been what Andrew saw at the tavern.

"And one of the stories was a calves' tale, a fay story if you will, of a creature that would appear where no one expected and in a different form every time. To one, it might appear as a fish in a lake. To another, it might be the boulder on a mountain face or perhaps a great world tree holding the very light of the raven moon," she said, touching the sketch Andrew had made. "It is said that whoever finds a Grace Giver will be granted a single Grace, but with such a gift comes a dire warning. This is why I hesitate to share this ancient of my people's stories, and only because I do believe you want to help the old woman."

"What is the warning?"

She looked at him with an intensity he had not previously known from her—more beast than human.

"It gives as much as it takes."

Andrew swallowed. "What...does that mean?" he mumbled.

"The tale teaches that whoever finds a Grace Giver should only ever ask as little as they possibly can. Else, nothing at all. For if they ask for treasure, their land may be left baren, and they may starve to death; if they ask for eternal life, it may cost them the lives of their children."

Andrew stared at the sketch.

"But these are just stories. As I said, a creature of myth," and she slid the sketch to Andrew, who picked it up. Fleur de Lis was snoring a faint snore, like the sound of a tiny snail chewing.

"And what of the..Night Watchmen? The Shimar Etsell?"

She hesitated.

"Did the book say anything else about them?" he asked, trying not to push, but he had come too far to leave without something a bit more substantial than a child's story of an imaginary creature that granted wishes.

"Because you have been kind," she said. Then she wrote

a single word on the corner of the sketch and wished Andrew a pleasant Eden Vale. As he stepped out into the cold, he unfolded his sketch to find a name written on the corner: Ki Lo Kan.

CHAPTER 14

Brutste smiled as Andrew entered the tavern. It was the early afternoon, and only an elderly couple sat in a back corner enjoying a cheese plate with apples and bread for lunch. Pieces of a dismantled tool lay before her on the bar, and she was trying to fit a wooden handle back onto a blade.

"Happy Eden Vale, tiny tinker!"

Andrew scowled at that moniker. He didn't usually think of himself as tiny, but he supposed he probably had to be one of the smallest men in this town, no matter the age.

"It looks like my sister didn't run you off after all," she said, pushing on the tool so hard her biceps strained. She wore a cream-colored tunic and simple brown breeches with a row of carving knives tucked into the front of her apron band. Her long beard was braided into three medium-thickness braids woven with the same yellow flowers that would release their iridescent seeds in just a few days. A large vat of dark purple wine sat on the hearth, slowly simmering, with a layer of fruits and spices floating on its surface, releasing alluring fragrances into the air in bubbling fits and spurts. "You looked a bit worse for wear last time you tumbled out of here," she said.

No thanks to you, he thought but didn't say. He just sat at the counter and watched her wrestle with what he could now tell was probably some sort of circular meat-cutting device.

"What can I get you?" she asked, with a clearly feigned smile, slamming the wooden handle down on the bar top so hard it startled Andrew.

"Have any tea on?" he asked, blowing into his hands. The roads had all been plowed, and the sun had now been shining for a few days, but it was still crisp and cold outside. He was glad for the warmth of the hearth, he just needed to give his bones a chance to thaw.

"Aye. Always," she replied. "Anything to eat?"

He pointed to the currently smallish stack of Eden Vale pies sitting on a tray behind the counter.

She nodded, wiped her hands on her apron, and set to fetching him a proper cuppa and a finger cake that she let warm on a thin stone on the hearth.

While the cake warmed, Andrew slid down the bar to where the pieces of tool were splayed across the counter. He looked at them for a moment, trying to imagine what the puzzle was supposed to look like, then picked up the handle and blade that Brutste had been fighting with, carefully turned the blade into the handle, and felt it click into place. Piece by piece, he put her entire tool back together before she even had the chance to set his finger pie on a wooden platter in front of him. And after she did, she rested a fist on one hip and watched him.

"No trouble for your tiny fingers, aye?"

He was starting to understand that she probably didn't

mean anything by her slight jabs. "I've been building stuff like this since before I could walk."

She picked up the meat cutter. "Hmm," she said. "Well, food's on me then."

He shook his head. "It's not necessary. I'm not here on business. My fingers just needed something to fiddle with."

"Dust thou refuse an offer from a Longbeard woman!" she said, slowly reaching for a knife in her belt.

His eyes grew and she started laughing. "You need to calm down, tiny tinker," she said, reaching across the bar and squeezing his shoulder with a startling amount of force. Then she did pull a blade from her band and leveled it at him. "You've made friends here," and she used the knife to slice his pie in half for him, stowed the blade, and turned to fetch his tea.

Andrew picked up the pie and took a bite. The perfectly flaky crust tasted of salted butter, while its filling was both rich and spicy, a bit like the bread he had bought from the vegetable stand a few days earlier. Apparently, spiced fruits were a popular flavor during Eden Vale.

Brutste set a well-worn clay cup in front of Andrew and began to pour from a tin pot when a hand covered the mug. Brutste glanced up, cast a smirk, and simply turned and walked away.

The beautiful bald woman with skin the color of newly minted copper pennies stepped behind the bar and hung a long white cloak on a hook near the shelves.

Andrew rolled his eyes. "You work here now?" he asked.

"Actually, I own the place."

Andrew shot her a questioning glance.

"My sister and I own it together—passed to us from our father."

She was much more beautiful than he had remembered.

Her eyes glistened perfectly brilliant copper, now so deep they were nearly rose-colored. *Weren't they lighter earlier?* he wondered quietly to himself. Now in daylight, he could see more clearly the intricate web of metallic texture covering her neck and most of the naked skin on her head, cheeks, and chin.

She reached below the bar and laid before him a fine grey cloth.

"What's this?" Andrew asked, unsure how to interpret her body language. Her countenance was serious, but not angry.

"I'm not what you think I am," she replied, shooting a dagger of a look across the bar at her sister, who grinned and shook her head from the other end, where she finished polishing the blade of her tool and began cutting thin slices of meat. "Consider this an apology."

Incredulous, he watched as she set a round, stone platter on the grey cloth. On the platter, she sat six smooth grey river stones, an intricate brass bowl, a small set of tongs, a small brass spoon, an oddly shaped brass bowl barely two fingers wide, and a pair of beautiful clear cups with brass handles and brass rims. She carefully moved everything around the stone platter just so, then disappeared into a back room. Andrew wasn't sure what was happening, but the dishes on the tray were beautiful. Intricate. She returned carrying two boxes. One was a medium-sized box with a diamond-shaped lid and a small brass clasp. The other was barely the size of his palm and the color of cream eggshell. She set the boxes on the counter, opened the diamond-shaped one, and carefully removed a jar the size of a teapot with no spout. Instead, it had handles on either side of its textured brown and grey surface. A crescent window in its belly held a brown translucent stone that looked like a large jewel. Brass fili-gree adorned the pot and its small teardrop-shaped lid.

She set the pot on the tray and opened the smaller of the two boxes, removing something that looked like a blue enameled egg dotted with white and pink flowers, and she carefully set the enameled egg on the two-finger-width brass dish, nose up. The enameled egg had a tiny brass pull top.

"You didn't have to run off," she said to him.

"You slapped me."

"You deserved it," she replied with a bit of attitude, opening another small box that she had fetched from beneath the counter, and used the brass tongs to pluck what looked like small round balls of bullion, then leaned forward and carefully stacked them into a small pile the shape of a pyramid on the brash dish.

Maybe he had deserved it. He couldn't quite remember what he had said or did that night. "You tried to take advantage of me!" he retorted more sharply than he intended. When he did, he saw Brutste glance at him and then continue to slice her meat. It was hard to have a conversation like this with family listening.

The bald woman straightened. "I *negotiated* with you. You could have said no."

Fair point, he thought, not wanting to say what he truly felt, which was that he didn't really care about the few pennies lost; he was hurt because he thought she was flirting with him.

After filling the pot with hot water, she went around to the other side of the bar, pulled up a stool next to him, and adjusted the cloth and platter so that it lay out on the bar in front of them both.

She was close enough now that he could tell she

smelled of something intoxicating, both herbal and creamy. Whatever it was, it forced him to swallow and have to consciously regain his composure. He licked his lips and felt himself beginning to blush.

He turned away from her. *Not now!* he scolded himself and bit the inside of his cheek.

She gently ran her hand along his forearm and took his hand.

He had to quickly decide whether to let his guard down and show her he was embarrassed or walk away. A part of him wanted to run, but the ceremony felt special. The pot, the dishes, the cups. They weren't standard bar fare. So he sighed and looked back at her. As he did, her gaze softened ever so slightly at the sight of the heat in his face, but she did not comment nor take advantage. Instead, she softly said, "This is the ceremony of Lassára Tye." She turned his palms up and, with the brass tongues, set one of the brown balls in each palm, then closed her eyes. He closed his eyes as well.

"Great Ruach. Grant us grace. Thank You for Your gifts, for we know that every good and perfect gift is from You alone. And help us show others the compassion You have shown us."

When she released his hands, he opened his eyes.

Her hands are so soft, he thought to himself.

She removed the lid from the pot as a plume of steam rose from the hot water inside. "One for you," she said, using the brass pinchers to take one of the small balls from his palm and drop it into the water. "And one for me," and she dropped the second into the pot, set the pinchers aside, and closed the lid.

Andrew watched as water behind the large brown jewel

in the belly of the pot flared to life with what looked like wisps of swirling gold.

"Look, I..." he began to say, but she stopped him and gently shook her head. So, he sat quietly.

Once the swirls faded into a calm glow from behind the jewel, she held the top of the pot with one hand and pulled on the teardrop lid with the other, drawing tea into a long tube built into the underside of the lid. Then she held the tube over Andrew's cup and gently released the tea. She repeated the process for hers. Returning the lid to the jar, she rolled her wrist, exposing what looked like a thin line of polished copper wire running from her palm to her elbow. She lifted the enameled egg with two fingers, gently added a few drops of cream to Andrew's cup, then hers, and returned the enameled egg to its base. Andrew sat quietly watching her slender fingers move like a carefully choreographed dance. Her face was calm. Finally, she used the brass spoon to stir each cup precisely three times, set it aside, and lifted Andrew's cup to him with both hands, bowing her head until it nearly touched the top of the bar.

He gently took the cup from her, mirroring her movement, unsure if he was also supposed to bow, but it didn't look like she was expecting him to do so, so he just waited. The tea in his cup was a rich translucent copper color closely resembling her skin; only, the tea glistened with sparkling flecks of light.

She lifted her cup and saluted him. He returned the gesture, and together they drank. When she did, her eyes were closed, and she took in the fragrance of the tea deeply and with a smile.

He took a sip and felt the warm liquid coat his tongue before evaporating. He could taste it, but there was nothing to swallow.

Then she opened her eyes and calmly looked at him like a sly cat with a full belly. "I'm sorry," she said.

"Wow. Why do I feel like you really mean it?" he asked sarcastically.

She smiled gently and took another sip of her tea. Andrew did the same, enjoying the wonderful flavor but missing the warmth in his belly a common cuppa builder's brew gave him on a cold day like today.

"Where's your cart?" she asked, slowly opening her eyes and resting her cup on the bar.

"I left it behind."

"Oh. Why?"

"I'm on something of a journey," he replied, taking another long drink of his evaporating tea.

"To where?"

"Ki Lo Kan," he replied.

He watched her face go through at least three different shades of emotion as she tried to process what she had just heard. "Why? What is there for you in the Ki Lo Kan Forest?"

"I don't know exactly," he said, setting his cup on the stone platter. "I'm trying to help someone, and I think someone or something in the forest might be able to help me do that." Then he raised his eyes and looked at her. He had an idea. "Do you know the old human woman who walks around town? Grey robe. Bird..."

"In her hair?" she nodded and smiled. "Yeah. I know her well. I think everyone does. She spends most days just wandering around the village like she's looking for someone, not really talking to anyone. Some think she's a little crazy. Who knows, maybe she is, but I don't mind that personally. She doesn't bother anybody. My sister and I keep a tab open for her, but she rarely comes in, and when she does, she just orders some vegetable soup and leaves."

"How long has she wandered the village?"

She shook her head, considering his question. "I don't know. Since I was a girl? I think my mother knew her."

Andrew perked up.

"Can I speak with her?"

Her face became downcast, but only for a moment. "She passed on. More than ten years ago."

"Oh. I'm sorry..."

She held up a hand. "It's alright. My father raised us until I was nearly eighteen. Then he took ill. It's been just me and Brutste ever since. Until she went and got married, that is!" she hollered in Brutste's direction. Brutste chuckled and shook her head.

"Aye! It's not my fault no man will have ya! You've got too much skin. You need to grow a beard!" Brutste hollered back.

The woman with the copper skin smiled and shook her head.

Andrew watched her take her last swallow of tea and set her cup on the tray next to his. He thought about the elderly Longbeard couple he had seen in the tavern earlier, both of whom had, well...long beards—the man's growing wild and loose while the woman's was woven with the same yellow flowers as Brutste's.

"May I ask?"

"You may," she replied, "But I may not answer."

He thought about how to frame his question to avoid being rude. "Clearly, your sister...and other women in town...can grow..." and he stopped there, gently rubbing his chin.

Her eyes raised. "You'll have to buy me dinner for that one," she said, a whisper of a flirting smile curling the outer crest of her lips.

Dinner. He liked the sound of that.

CHAPTER 15

Andrew and the beautiful bald woman spent the next couple of hours laughing and chatting, having moved to a booth towards the back of the bar.

Even though the tavern slowly filled and the revelries increased in volume as the night went on, Andrew was careful to avoid Brutste's mulled wine this time. He was enjoying their conversation and didn't want to repeat his foolish behavior from a few nights before.

Andrew did most of the talking, telling her about living in the Dry Places, how it wasn't nearly as bad as everyone made it out to be, as long as you know where to walk and what to avoid, and how Lithuel had raised him and taught him everything he knew about being a tinker.

"It sounds like you love him," she said, a flickering candle reflecting off her metallic skin.

He thought about that for a moment. "I do. I really do. He's all I've ever known, and he's given up a lot for me."

"You're lucky," she replied. "I would pay my weight in

solid platinum Raichams to have just one more meal with my da',” she said thoughtfully.

He wanted to ask what had happened to him, but he was worried it might steer the night into a different mood, and things seemed to be going well.

He told her how he too had lost his family, never having known them. Then he reached into one of his coat pockets, removed the small painted portrait of the woman, and handed it to her.

“Who is this?” she asked, looking at the fading image on canvas.

He sighed. "I don't know. Maybe my mother?"

She turned it over. ‘To Andrew’ was written on the back. She looked at him and could see the pain on his face.

"It's the only thing I had on me when Lithuel found me."

“Found you?”

Andrew nodded. “He was leaving Nevarii when he heard me cry out from the back of his cart. He went back to town and spent two days trying to find whoever left me, but no one knew anything about a human child."

She squeezed his hand.

The weight of the conversation was beginning to tire him, and she could see it on his face.

“I should probably get going,” she told him, gently touching the back of his hand. “Thanks for the conversation.”

He could feel himself beginning to blush again, and she saw that too but didn't say anything about it. She just smiled.

"You know..." he rubbed the back of his neck. "I plan on getting a room upstairs if you want to join me."

She smiled a coy smile, looked away, then back at him. Then she leaned towards him and kissed him on the cheek.

"Good night, tinker," she said and began to rise.

"You never told me your name," he said, reaching for her.

"Something to look forward to," she replied with a grin. Then she collected her cloak from where she had hung it earlier, kissed her sister on the cheek, who smiled and waved her off, and left.

Andrew hated to see her go.

THE FOLLOWING DAY, Andrew stopped by the veg stand to purchase a small sack of each ingredient for his special tea blend, some fruit, veg and a loaf of spiced bread. He and Brynlee then went to Lorna's cottage.

When he arrived, the house was quiet. Snow still piled much of the forest beyond the plowed trails except for the dry circle surrounding Lorna's peculiar home.

He laid Brynlee's reins loosely over a nearby branch, took the sack of food in one hand, and quietly approached her front door. He had not previously noticed a leaning fence surrounding her property with a broken gate covered in thick weeds.

Andrew set the bag on her doorstep and leaned to look in her front window, hoping not to startle her after she had nearly killed him last time, but everything was quiet.

He looked around the back of the house and saw no sign of her, so he looked in through the front window again, trying to see if her hearth was lit. The hearth was dark, but the sparrow slept on the mantle.

Andrew smiled. He had become fond of that little bird.

If it was there, Lorna was too. He left the sack of food on her porch and turned to go, then paused. He thought about the wand now resting inside his jacket pocket. He did not intend to keep it, but something urged him to hold onto it for a bit longer. It had come in handy back in the swamp, and he *was* on his way to an unmapped forest with no roads.

I will give it back to her upon my return, he decided.

As he returned to Brynlee, he lifted the leaning fence, trying to determine how broken it was. One side was still entirely usable, having only slipped its post. The other was cracked where the hinges were meant to hold the gate. Then he tore the weeds away from the undamaged gate.

He fetched some tools and wire from his saddle bag, mended the cracked post, set the left side, and re-hung the gate. Then he checked how it swung and latched it. Good as new. Well, not good as new, but perfectly functional until he could properly replace the cracked post, which he made a mental note to bring with him the next time he came.

While he worked, Brynlee enjoyed mouthfuls of the exposed grass near the house. As he mounted her, he looked back at the leaning cottage that once resembled a witch's shack, but he now saw as the cozy cottage of someone he cared about, someone he hoped to see again upon his return—hopefully with some answers.

CHAPTER 16

The Ki Lo Kan was a forest Andrew knew little about other than it was large, untraveled, and across the Ridge Back Mountains from his home, which meant he would be traveling roads he had never traveled before. He had packed several days' provisions and let Lithuel know exactly where he planned on leaving the road to venture into the woods. His father had offered to go with him, but they both knew it would be too much for him. The going was slow at first due to the thickness of the snow this high in the mountains, but by fortune or by grace, he still had what he was now thinking of as the warming rod from Lorna, which helped him remove snow as he went, even if it did get a bit arduous after the first hour. He was also traveling without his cart. He had decided that even if he could find business along the way, such a journey across unknown landscape might be too much for Brynlee—too far a distance with the cart in tow. Her leg was strong again, thanks to Lorna's compress, but that had not changed her age.

As the snow began to thin and mountain stones gave

way to tundra and prairie, he thought about how he had never been this far away from home before. It reminded him of the first time he traveled with the tinker cart and without Lithuel. Lithuel had hurt his leg only a few weeks earlier and they were running out of supplies, so he went to town and did what he had seen Lithuel do. It was scary, but he was successful. When he returned home the next day, Lithuel greeted him at the door with Jasper. "I have nothing left to teach you," Lithuel had told him. "Today, you are a man."

He also remembered the strange days in Jatoba and the friends he had made along the way: Daphnie and Fleur de Lis. Brutste. The beautiful woman who hadn't given him her name. Lorna and the little sparrow. He had once thought of himself as a loner, traveling from town to town, plying his trade, but he didn't feel quite so alone anymore. "You made friends here," Brutste had told him. He imagined what it might be like to live in such a town. Perhaps he could open a tinker shop rather than hauling his cart back and forth. Could there be enough business in a single town for a tinker? Knives didn't need sharpening every day. Perhaps he could charge four pennies instead of three, but that seemed ludicrous. Lithuel had charged trepenny and that's what he charged. No. He doubted anyone would ever pay four. But maybe he could also sell pots and tools and utensils? Even some of his machines? He did enjoy meeting new people. They might not always be accepting of a human in the cities, but that didn't seem to matter as much anymore as long as he avoided the wealthier districts where security was paid to thumb their nose at anyone even remotely different.

The day was beginning to warm as the road led through an open valley as it had on the southern slope, once again dotted with the blooming yellow flowers that were the hallmark of Eden Vale, and now there were so many of them he could smell their sweet honey fragrance in the air. *Is this the sweet flavor everyone keeps trying to capture in the food?* he wondered.

He stopped for a moment by a creek that had formed along the road, let Brynlee graze and have a drink for a few minutes, relieved his bladder behind a tree, and fetched from the saddle bags the small pocketbook of bound parchments that he had made for his wandering thoughts. He had even wrapped a thin piece of charcoal with cloth to use as a writing tool without getting his fingers black. *Perhaps I could sell these*, he wondered, looking at it and watching Brynlee in the late morning light. The warming day felt nice after being so cold up in Jatoba for the last day and a half, and as he flipped to a circular sketch in the center of his book, he caught movement out of the corner of his eye. An iirubee mink—its body long and narrow—came out of a bush, dove into the water, then returned to the rocks with a glistening golden trout in its sharp teeth. The squirming fish was twice its size, which didn't seem to bother it for a moment. The small creature—slick brown fur dripping wet —casually watched Andrew as it stopped to tear off a few quick bites. Then it grasped the fish in its mouth again and disappeared back into the bush.

Andrew smiled, flipped to a new page, and quickly sketched out the shape of the mink's face—with fish in mouth—before he forgot its details. Then he climbed back on Brynlee and clicked twice for her to continue on.

Sometime after a short stop for lunch, he and Brynlee came to a narrow bend in the road that doubled back and curved east again. The road was still beneath them, but it had become faint and overgrown by this point, looking to his eye as though no cart or horse had passed over it in at least several months. He now had a choice: did he continue along the road, probably never making it to the Ki Lo Kan Forest, or did he leave the road and follow the slowly widening chalk stream north through the thickening trees?

He thought again about Lorna and the box, about Daphne's warnings, and about Lithuel.

"What do you think, girl? We've come this far? Shall we continue?" he asked Brynlee, who turned to look at him.

She nodded and looked forward.

He smiled. Her confidence renewed his strength.

"There and back again," he told her. "We'll just go and return."

Then he clicked twice, and she stepped away from the road and into the forest.

CHAPTER 17

The backcountry was beautiful. No woodsman had felled any of the old-growth trees, allowing thick varieties of flora to flourish, including yellow moss that clung to tree trunks and webs of trumpet vines lacing between the high branches. Little clusters of mushrooms poked their heads through the loam and danced with patterns of changing colors as he passed by. Small woodland animals, birds, and varieties of rainbow-colored spiders with wings raced away from the sound of Brynlee walking through the undergrowth. This place felt very alive, like the trees, fungus, and everything in between were all somehow connected.

Daphnie would love these, he thought to himself, stopping by the creek to fill his water skin and let Brynlee have a drink, finding patches of flowers with black stems and almost completely transparent petals. As he reached to pluck one, all of the patches of the flowers up and down the creek vanished into the ground in a moment.

Brynlee lifted her head at the sight, then went back to drinking.

When he rose, he turned to see a canine of an unknown variety watching him closely two or three cubits from where he stood—head lowered, lapping up water. It was purple and blue and barely the size of his water skin. It looked neither afraid of Andrew nor aggressive, so Andrew simply watched as it had its fill of the cool, crystal-clear water and casually trailed off into the forest.

As he and Brynlee continued on, the chalk stream widened into a river that he had to cross for the steepening bank on his side. The water was also picking up speed, and the trees were becoming so tall he had trouble seeing their canopy high above him.

He stopped for a moment and realized he had seen this place before, not in the waking world, but in the sleeping, and somehow, he knew beyond knowing that there was a waterfall ahead, and beyond the falls a forest of trees so tall you could not see their crown from their roots.

As they rode, he removed the small pocketbook from his saddle bag again and flipped to the circular drawing in the center of his book. It was a crazy idea he had for a device that would tell you the time, even if it was night or a stormy day. The circle in his book had marks and numbers around its face. Beneath the dial were different mechanisms he was exploring that would allow the tiny needles on the face to move at a constant and steady motion. If he could get the device to move at a reasonably precise rate, he should be able to set the dial, start the movement, and track time, if only for a few hours per winding. It would be groundbreaking. He knew the applications of a way to track time without the sun had been explored by several scribes using water, candles, threads, and sand. But none of them were precise, and most of them involved consumables, like candles carefully marked. They also each had their draw-

THE TINKER & THE WITCH

backs: water around machines, sand was heavy, candles imprecise. He dreamed of something better. But how to keep the hands running at a smoothly controlled pace? Then he saw it in a shop about three months earlier: a Bantam artificer had built a child's toy with a winding spring that unwound slowly that made it look like it was playing an instrument. And it dawned on him that he could use something like that for his time device. What he now wrestled with in his pocketbook was how to build it into a box small enough to fit on a table. If he could do this, it might be useful for work. He had already begun testing different mixtures, lengths, and thicknesses of metal for the winding spring, but he was not yet happy with the results.

When he looked up from his charcoal scribblings, he heard the sound of rushing water and knew, clear as a chiming bell, what it was. It was also getting later in the day, and he would need to start looking for a campsite soon. The river was moving quickly now, and the bank had become rocky. The trees around him were nearly as wide as his cabin back home, and the sound of the rushing water was quickly growing in intensity.

I hope Lithuel is well, he thought, climbing down from Brynlee to give her old back a rest and craning his head to see if he could fathom the height of the trees he stood between. They were growing quite far apart now, and smaller bushes and vines still crept across the ground, but not many other varieties of wood. He could also see the river cresting maybe ten to fifteen cubits ahead of them, near a large outcropping of rocks.

As he came to the outcropping where the river disappeared over a fall into clouds of thick mist, he looked beyond into the forest.

"Are these the shadow falls?" he wondered aloud to

Brynlee, who couldn't hear him over the sound of the rushing water. Beyond the plumes of rising mist created by the falls rose the most incredible trees Andrew had ever seen anywhere outside of his dreams. They were real. Even though he knew they must be growing from the forest floor hundreds of cubits below, he could not see that floor. Instead, the silver-blue trees rose in front of him so high they completely vanished into the clouds above, giving the appearance that they grew down from the clouds more than up from the ground.

After taking in their grandeur for several minutes, he began looking around the edge of the falls, trying to see if there was any way to descend. But he found none.

Brynlee left him and circled a spot under a tree.

He wasn't quite sure how late it was, unable to see the blue sky through the canopy above, but the light was dimming, and the air was cooling, so he set up camp for the night.

The tree Brynlee had approached was hollow on the side facing away from the mist of the falls, which Andrew decided to use for camp. He also preferred building a fire somewhere that could disperse the smoke rather than letting it rise into the clear sky and pointing a brown arrow down onto his exact location for anyone or anything that might get curious.

Brynlee was happy to graze at the mouth of the hollow even though it was plenty large enough for her and her five cousins to come in for the night. Andrew unrolled his bed, set out a circle of stones he pulled from the river, and gathered some logs for fire. Then he filled a small pot with water from the creek and poured in a third of the diced vegetables and herbs he had brought from home. He set the pot on the unlit logs and took a small box out of his bag the size and length of his thumb. Inside was a fat, fuzzy little green grub with red stripes that he carefully removed and pet for a moment. It looked up at him.

Under normal circumstances, he would coax the grub to light the logs with a fire breath that came naturally to it and then feed it some fresh leaves before returning it to its box until he needed it next. But he no longer needed it and didn't like the idea of keeping a creature unnecessarily cooped up. He also had a good idea it would not pupate into whatever it was to become so long as it was in captivity. It had been collected from a forest much like this one, once upon a time, and it was time to let it go—a sentimentality to small creatures most people did not bother with, but he didn't care. Why kill a spider if he could carry it outside? So, he stepped out of his campsite and held the grub up to the thickly split bark of the tree until its tiny grasping feet took hold on the loam.

Returning to his unlit fire, he removed the warming rod from his coat pocket, gently blew on it until it was glowing red, then slipped the hot end underneath the stacked logs. Within minutes, the fire was burning strong. Once it was, he dimmed the warming rod and put it away.

It was all but dark now, and it began to rain.

The sound and smell of the rain contrasted against the warm crackling of the fire was cozy and comforting. The sight of Brynlee standing just inside the opening to take part in the warmth also made him smile. He knew she would stand careful watch over him all night and until the end of time if she had to.

He rose and hugged her neck and fed her one of the apples he had hidden in his bag for her as a treat at the end of each day. She leaned into him, letting him know she indeed loved him. Then he returned to his bedroll.

His stew was rich and filling, and after sneaking out into the drizzling rain long enough to rinse the pot in the river and refill it with water for tea, he settled into bed for the night. He had also packed and lit a small wooden pipe with savory smelling herb, a rare but loved treat for cold nights that Lithuel also enjoyed. Its aroma took him back home to his place by the hearth, where Lithuel and Jasper were sure to be settling in for the evening with a cup of warm wine and a tightly packed pipe.

Cupping his tea in both hands and letting the smell of his pipe fill the tree hollow, he sat watching the firelight until his eyes grew heavy.

CHAPTER 18

Andrew woke to find someone sitting near him, tending to the fire. Startled, he scrambled away.

The figure calmly watched him, their features in some ways masculine, but their hair was long and as smooth as strands of silk with beads and feathers woven in, which made their gender hard to determine. Perhaps they had no gender. The figure had large, emerald-green eyes with two pupils and a narrow mouth with what looked like a whisper of a mustache made of skin. They wore long, loose robes of natural green and brown fibers tied at the elbows and knees with leather straps, and they were kneeling barefoot opposite the fire from Andrew.

Narrowing their gaze at Andrew, they slowly blinked solid black, translucent eyelids, then asked: "Why have you entered my forest?" with a calm and confident voice, almost animal in nature. As they moved, a length of metal glinted in the firelight beneath a long dark-green outer cloak obscuring most of their form.

Andrew sat up. "Are you Shimar Etsell?"

They did not respond.

"I've come looking for the Shimar Etsell."

They glared at him.

"I was told the Shimar Etsell might have carved a box... or chest, and I needed to know more about it."

They rose and approached Brynlee, holding their hand out to her to let her nuzzle their palm with her nose. Andrew could now see that the figure was quite tall.

"Your mare asked me not to kill you. Leave. Before I change my mind," and they began to leave the hollow of the tree when Andrew spoke up.

"The box had a carving of a tree on the lid, and I need to know what it is," he said, scrambling through his saddle bag for the image he had sketched for Daphnie.

The being stopped and looked over its shoulder at him.

Andrew unrolled the parchment and held up the sketch. It was harder to see the being for the dark forest behind them, their robes and colors blending perfectly into the texture of the night forest.

They took the parchment from him, studied it closely, then calmly dropped it into the fire.

Andrew somehow knew not to reach for it. It didn't matter anyway since he had sketched it, and unless his dreams began to fade, he would not be forgetting the tree anytime soon. Then the robed visitor turned to leave.

"It's a Grace Giver, isn't it?" Andrew asked. "The tree. On the cover."

The Night Watchman turned to him with a look of fierceness and resolute control, only slightly curling their upper lip in disgust. Then, a glint of bright metal flashed before Andrew faster than he could process what had happened. And returning the blade to its saya beneath its robes, the being disappeared into the rain.

Andrew's lip began to sting, and he touched it. A hairline of red rose on his upper lip the length of the tip of his finger. Seeing the blood, Andrew knew that the being could have separated his head from his shoulders and that no one but Brynlee would ever have been the wiser.

Through the entrance, the Night Watchman looked on at Andrew as it mounted bareback a green steed twice the size of Brynlee with legs that articulated the opposite direction of hers and a fleshy prehensile tale like a large monkey with no hair. Then the green horse slowly stood on its hind quarters, moving more like a sloth than a horse, and reached up above the entrance to Andrew's campfire hollow and climbed the tree, gripping at the crevices of the bark with hooves split in twain like those of a mountain goat, only with a third fleshy hoof-piece that grasped narrow edges like a thumb.

As it climbed, Andrew leaned into the drizzling night and watched the green tree horse disappear up the length of the tree with the Night Watchman holding onto its waist by the strength of his legs and his fingers entwined in the horse's mane.

Andrew touched his lip again. Though his lip still stung, the bleeding had already stopped, which meant the cut had been shallow and clean as a razor. Never had he seen such precision. They had moved faster than the flit of a dragonfly's wing and had left a mark without doing any real damage.

Brynlee stood just inside the hollow, out of the rain.

"Thanks for the heads up," he told her. She only looked at him.

CHAPTER 19

Andrew decided that while he would not venture any farther into the forest, there was no need to leave before daybreak, so he and Brynlee stayed the rest of the night in the dry hollow. And again, he dreamt of the tree.

This time, he was in Lorna's forest. It was dark, and she was there with him, but she didn't know he was there, no matter how hard he tried yelling to her. The tree itself was her home, its roots and branches wild and reaching, and somehow it clutched the bright raven moon in its canopy. Lorna was blindfolded and stumbled through the forest looking for the front door, but she could not find it—a warm light glowing between the edges of the doorframe. He tried to tell her where the door was—how to open the door—but she could not hear him.

When he woke the next morning, breakfast was already cooking on his fire, and whatever it was smelled delicious.

"I heard you met Aefook Aenoosho," a voice cracked near the fire.

Andrew rubbed the sleep from his eyes and sat up on an

elbow to find a Night Watchman of the kind who had visited him the night before, poking at a pan on the fire, only this one had hair twice as long and ashen grey, pulled up and tied in buns on top of his head save for a few strands that hung down on either side of his face. This one's robes were also green but more ornamental and would not blend into the forest as easily.

Andrew played with the strange sound of that name in his mind: Aefook Aenoosho, unsure he could make those sounds, the 'k' sounding more like a click with the tongue than the velar sound a human might make at the back of their throat.

"He almost killed me," Andrew said.

"If he had wanted to kill you, we would not be speaking. Besides, you offended him."

"How so?"

The old man did not immediately reply but shot Andrew a knowing grin. "He said that you spoke of our diety. By grace, you did not know its true name; else he might have killed you twice."

Killed me twice? Andrew wasn't sure what that meant, but he didn't like the sound of it.

"So, the tree on the box is a...," and Andrew stopped himself out of respect for his visitor and whatever a Grace Giver might be—assuming they were real.

The elder Night Watchmen cast a handful of something into the pot on the fire and stirred it with a long wooden spoon. "Tell me about this box," he said, scooping a portion of the cooked food, which Andrew could now see was some kind of porridge with fruit and nuts, into a small wooden bowl and handing it to him. A broken piece of thin brown bread stood in its center.

Andrew held the bowl in his hands and could tell

through its wood that the porridge was hot, but he had no utensil. Then he smiled, realizing that that was exactly what the corner of bread was for, and used it to scoop some of the delicious and enriching porridge into his mouth. As his eyes grew, the old man smiled.

"Good? It is my wife's recipe." Then, the old man rose and approached Brynlee, holding something wrapped in a large leaf. "May I?" he asked, holding the bundle up to her.

Andrew assumed he meant he wanted to feed it to her. Andrew nodded.

The old man smiled large and gently pet her back, whispering something to her that sounded more like music than words. She was happy to take the bundle and enjoyed it. Then, the old man returned to the fire.

"You don't sound like the other one," Andrew said, taking another bite. "And you're nice."

The old man gave him the gentle smile of a wise grandfather. "It is in Aefook's nature to be wary of...outsiders. I see where his blade kissed your lip. That was both a warning and a courtesy. Besides, I have lived among your kind. In another life," he said, looking for a moment out past the entrance of the tree hollow.

Andrew didn't respond to that but kept eating.

"Tell me about this box," the old man said, kneeling near Andrew.

Andrew set his empty bowl aside. "So, it is a box?"

"I have no idea. You have yet to tell me about it."

Andrew situated himself. "Several days ago, I was caught in a storm, and the woman who gave me and my mare shelter, was sick in her mind. She wanders the village talking to herself, and the children in town are afraid of her. But she's *not* dangerous! At least not much," he added, remembering how she *had* almost killed him. "It's just that it's like her memory is broken. You can tell her one thing, and she'll forget you said it, then start talking about something completely different. And before the end of the conversation, she may not even remember that she had been speaking to you at all."

The old man stroked his long, thin beard as Andrew spoke, careful not to interrupt him.

"That night, she let me sleep in a back room, but I could not. New place and all..." he trailed off, then brought himself back. "There was this box, or chest, or whatever, unlike anything I've ever seen, and my father taught me how to recognize fine craftsmanship. But this was something other than craftsmanship. It was more like it had *grown* there somehow; it was so perfect," he said, gesturing with his hands as though he were about to reach out and touch it.

"Describe it to me," the old man said.

Andrew held out his arms. "About this wide and this tall," he said, holding his hand above the ground waist high. "The surface was covered in fine carvings on every side, and the top..." Andrew paused and thought for a moment. Then he found a stick and began scratching at the soil, and the old man leaned forward.

"There was this beautiful tree on the top, but it wasn't carved *into* the box. It was carved like a statue so that it stood off the box, with its roots stretching out and reaching up above it. And in its branches rested the raven moon," he said, trying to trace the shapes he spoke about in the crude soil. "And I might be falling into a madness, but I'm pretty sure the raven moon it held was glowing." Then he looked at the elder.

He could not read the old man or tell what he was thinking. His expression was thoughtful but emotionless.

He sat on his knees and bare feet in a kind of kneeling position that Andrew thought must have hurt, but he hadn't so much as shifted his legs the entire time Andrew spoke.

"And one other thing," Andrew was hesitant to add, but he decided he had come far enough to find the Shimar Etsell, and here was one speaking with him. He may not have another opportunity. "I've been seeing it in my dreams."

"Your night visions, you say?" the old man asked, taking a deep breath. Andrew tentatively nodded.

The old man thought for several minutes quietly, then said: "How do I know you did not read about this or learn of it from someone other than yourself?"

An odd question, Andrew thought to himself, unsure how to answer. "I don't know. Why does that matter?"

The old man ignored the question and asked another of his own: "What material was the box?"

"Wood."

"And what color was the wood?"

Andrew decided to be precise and looked around. Then he rose and approached Brynlee. She had always had a cream patch on her hind quarter. "Only very slightly darker than this," Andrew said, pointing at the patch. Brynlee shifted.

The elder nodded. "And what was the shape of the leaves," the old man asked, narrowing his eyes at Andrew.

Andrew's brow raised. This one was easy, though it was a bit unusual, now that he thought about it. "It had no leaves," he confidently replied, crossing his arms.

The old man clenched his jaw. "You could not have seen an Igbaya," he mumbled, half to himself and looking away.

"Why not? What's an Igbaya?"

The elder returned his gaze to Andrew. "Only seven

were made—all gifts. I thought they had all been lost," his voice trailing. "You said an old woman has it? Where is this woman?"

And for the first time, Andrew realized that Lorna might be in danger if the chest was valuable and the wrong person wanted it. So, he didn't answer.

The old man saw his hesitation and took it for honor more than guile. The boy did not know who he was or where his people tarried. He *had* been forthright about the Igbaya until asked about the woman's location. *He's protecting her,* the old man thought to himself, carefully reading Andrew's body language.

"How do you know there were only seven?" Andrew asked.

The elder sat back, his appearance fading into that of a proud father. "Because I made them."

"So, you can tell me how to open it!" Andrew exclaimed —hands wide in excitement.

The elder shook his head.

Andrew's arms dropped. "Why not?"

The old man approached the fire and scooped out a bit of the porridge with a triangle of the brown bread and ate it using no bowl—considering. Brynlee had already spoken to him about Andrew and the storm and meeting the woman; he knew these things before the boy had even awoken. He only asked to see if the boy would tell him the truth. She said they were looking for someone in a distant forest and asked if he could help them. "Please be kind to him," she had asked—an unusual request. Kindness was a gift of grace. Something rarely seen in the lands where the belly's hunger drove nearly every decision. It was difficult to explain, but the elder—nearing four centuries young— could discern beyond words or logic that this boy was blessed by grace, possibly even anointed; he could feel it deep within. *And dreams?* Perhaps a Grace Giver was calling to him. If so, who was he, Petook Aenoosho Pellotuloma Pembrook, to stand in the way of a Grace Giver?

Andrew watched quietly as the old man took another bite of porridge, considering. Then the old man finally spoke, "You cannot open it because it is not yours. Only its master can open it. With a word, phrase, or song, something personal to them—chosen at its giving."

"But if you made it, wouldn't you know what that is?"

Petook shook his head. "That's precisely the point, don't you see? The Igbaya were made to protect items of great value. *No one* can open them but their master. The master decides the passphrase upon sealing it the first time."

"There has to be a way. What if someone forgets? Can it be somehow reset?"

Petook rose. "It is not possible."

Andrew stood with him. "Is there a safety word or some way..."

Petook shook his head, dismissing the idea outright.

"What about forcing it?"

The old man shot him a glance as though he had just been offended. "If you try to force it open, it will swallow whatever it holds, causing those items to be forever lost. If what you say is true, whatever it holds may be gone for good." Then Petook gently ran his hand along Brynlee's neck one more time as he left the hollow, and Andrew followed him out.

"What do you mean, its master?" Andrew asked.

The elder gathered his robes and mounted a beautiful green-grey tree horse much like the one the Night Watchman rode the night before, only this one was much more graceful in appearance, with large, colorful flowers woven into its mane.

"My people believe you can never truly own a living thing."

"A...*living* thing?"

The old man nodded. "They were alive. And not just alive. Igbaya are peetekum," then he paused, trying to find the word in the common tongue. "Sentient. The *chest* is sentient. And if my memory serves me correctly, this was a particularly moody chest," he replied, then began to lean forward.

"There must be something I can do to help her open it! Something. Anything."

Petook looked on at him for a moment, considering the gravity of one remote but possible solution, then decided against it. "I am sorry. I can see you care for her, but it cannot be opened. Not by you. If you want to help her, help her find her memory." Then he whistled what sounded like a bird warble, and the horse leapt vertically onto the tree and began climbing.

Andrew's gaze followed the horse and its rider until they were out of sight, considering what he had just learned. *It cannot be opened by me? What exactly does that mean?* He had not for a moment thought this...Igbaya... could be alive. He *had* considered it might have grown out of the ground, but it was also clearly square—not a shape found in nature.

CHAPTER 20

The ride back to Jatoba felt long. Andrew was disheartened with the news that the chest could not be opened—a whisp of white cresting the high and distant peaks of the Ridge Back Mountains, reminding him that snow would soon return to the valley.

Keeping my secrets from me, he remembered Lorna saying. *She must have been referring to the chest.* Maybe he could help jog her memory somehow—help her remember how to open it. However, she had indicated that she had already tried.

As he and Brynlee slowly climbed in elevation, he could feel the day cooling again, even though it was not yet midday.

When they stopped for water, Andrew found in his saddlebag three small bundles like the one the old man had fed her, each wrapped in a large leaf and twine. When Andrew unwrapped one of them, he found what looked like a large oat cake mixed with nuts and something thick and sticky like dates. He broke off a corner and smelled it before tasting it. It smelled sweet and tasted even sweeter. Both he and Brynlee could eat this, and probably half of one each due to their size, which meant that he had enough food for him and Brynlee for at least three meals. It also looked like it would probably keep just fine wrapped in the large leaves for at least several days, if not much longer.

After only a few bites, he felt very full, as though he had just eaten a large meal, but not heavy as if that meal were rich and full of gravy. He did not know that, to the Shimar Etsell, this cake was considered a perfect food.

Every detail of the last twelve hours played over and over again in his mind as he passed the small black flowers, the place along the river where he had watched the mink catch a trout twice its size, and eventually, the shallowing of the water enough to cross back over. He thought about sketching once or twice but just wasn't interested. His motivation had left him.

JATOBA WAS EVEN MORE RICHLY ADORNED for Eden Vale, now only two nights away. Orange and white banners—long and embroidered with gold and blue threads—flitted about in the wind. The afternoon breeze was steady and cold, cutting through his jacket and reminding him of the storm that had started his futile journey. He was ready to be home, ready to be warm, ready to curl up underneath some thick blankets with Jasper and smoke a stout finger-full of savory herb. He had made enough money during his last visit to last him until spring. And that was just fine by him. He was tired, frustrated, and disappointed. The idea that he could do nothing for Lorna felt like he was pushing against an immovable rock. Under normal circumstances, the aroma of cakes and bread baking in what smelled like every home would have made him ravenous, but he just didn't care.

Andrew quietly rode past the tavern, glancing in through the door, hoping to see a certain copper-skinned beauty, but he did not. He wasn't sure what he'd say even if he had.

A sign hung on the door of Daphnie's shop in the red script he couldn't read. He tried the handle, but it was locked—yet another disappointment. Turning to leave, he saw movement and leaned to look in the window. Daphnie sat barefoot with legs crossed in the center of the shop, holding her hands out to her sides with palms up like she was praying or meditating. Small storm clouds crackled and broke above her head between the old wood rafters, dropping a gentle rain onto all of the plants in the store. The ring on her left hand was glowing blue and flickered with white light whenever lightning crackled above her. Fleur de Lis slept on her shoulder—little vines from her arms and legs hooking into Daphnie's garment.

It was a marvel to see. She was using intuition to water her plants. What other jewels or beads were possibly intuitive of the dozens she wore? Something about this changed how he thought of her. She wasn't just a simple shopkeep in his mind any longer, she was powerful. Were all of the women in this town extraordinary in some way?

He considered leaving without bothering her, but he thought she deserved an update—even if he *had* failed—and wasn't sure when he would be back through town, possibly not for some time. So, he gently tapped on the glass.

She first shot a frustrated glance through a single open eye until she realized who was standing at the door. When she realized it was Andrew, she smiled, wrapped a shawl over her bare arms, and came to the door. As she did, the clouds fled, and the rain stopped.

"Welcome, friend! Happy Eden Vale to you," she said, gesturing him into the shop. She was not at all wet from the rain.

A fine layer of droplets lay on everything in the store like a blanket of tiny crystals, enriching the colors and herbal fragrances, making it feel like her gardens below. No wonder she could keep such a variety of flora.

"I wasn't sure you'd be in. Let me feed and water my mare quickly," Andrew replied.

Daphne rolled her fingers through the air towards Brynlee as a tender shoot pushed its way through the paving stones in the street and quickly grew into a bush of leafy green vegetation before the dappled horse. Brynlee stepped away from it at first, then tentatively leaned forward to have a smell and began nibbling the tender shoots. Daphnie carefully ran her hand down Fleur de Lis' back and whispered to her, "Come, come, little one. Help our friends." At that, Fleur yawned and stretched. She rolled off Daphnie's shoulder and into her open palm. Daphnie gently set the little mandrake on the ground, and Andrew watched as she stumbled her way out of the shop and up to a small water spout in the street. She scratched her head with one branch as she grew a second branch up to pull the handle on the waterspout. As it trickled out into a basin beneath it, Fleur grew some of her roots and started soaking up some of the water herself—a contented look on her face, her eyes still closed from her not-yet-complete nap. Once Brynlee had a few mouthfuls of vegetation, she approached the water basin, took a good drink, and returned to the bush, which looked not to have lost any of its leaves, though Brynlee pulled them off in steady mouthfuls.

"Now, tell me of your travels. Have you learned anything new about this mystery of yours?" Daphnie asked, sitting on one of the stools on the front side of her counter. "I have been considering it while you were away."

Andrew nodded, dropping his shoulders.

Daphnie could now see he was downtrodden. "What's happened?" she asked, her large head cocked to the side in concern.

"I found them, the Shimar Etsell."

Daphnie's eyes grew. "They are real? Extraordinary! How did you find them?"

"It's more like they found me. I followed the road north until it split away from the creek and decided to continue along the waterway into the forest."

"In case you got lost...wise."

He nodded.

"I rode all day. Near nightfall, I came to the edge of a waterfall. The trees there were..." His thoughts trailed off, trying to find the words to describe their incredible beauty. "Unlike anything I have ever seen. They were as wide as this shop. Wider. Above the falls, the trees were so tall I could barely see their branches above. But below the falls, the trees grew from the forest floor all the way up into the clouds. They were like gigantic floating columns as far as I could see."

Daphnie's eyes were huge, trying to follow everything he was describing.

"And there you came across a village or ..."

He shook his head. "Nothing like that. There was no sign of anything. Bryn and I took shelter inside one of the trees as it was getting dark. I was planning on looking for a way down the falls the next morning, but I never had the chance. That night, when I woke, someone was sitting at my campfire."

"And, it was..."

He nodded. "I wasn't sure at first, but he asked me why I was in his forest. I told him I was looking for the Shimar Etsell because I needed someone to help me with the chest."

"You determined it is a chest?"

Andrew nodded. "I'll get to that."

She gripped the edge of her cloak in anticipation but tried to remain quiet as Fleur de Lis climbed up onto the counter, hefting a tea cup and platter with some difficulty. Still dreary-eyed, she walked away and returned with a second cup and platter. Daphnie did not take her eyes from Andrew, though he watched Fleur as he spoke.

"He threatened to kill me if I didn't leave."

Daphnie leaned forward, touched his forearm with concern, and covered her mouth.

"But he said that my mare had spoken to him and that he would let me live if I left *his* forest immediately. I told him that I had come looking for someone to help me open a box, which he didn't seem to care about until I mentioned the tree carved on the cover. So I showed him the drawing. The one that I had made for you?"

Daphne nodded in understanding.

"Which he looked at then threw on the fire."

Fleur planted her feet, growing roots a bit wider than usual and reaching her branches down behind the counter. Then she pivoted back and winced as she hoisted a steaming teapot up from somewhere, making Andrew wonder where the hot tea had come from—Daphnie still unphased by Fleur's acrobatics. She didn't even reach to take the pot from the little sproutling.

"Then I made the mistake of asking if it was..." and he instinctively hesitated.

Daphnie's face questioned the pause.

He looked around. "A GG," he said in a low whisper.

It took a moment, but then she realized what that meant.

Fleur slowly lifted the teapot above her head, filled each cup halfway, gently set the pot back on the counter, yawned, and climbed back into the red clay pot to finish her nap.

Daphnie collected a cup, handed it to Andrew, and began sipping from the second.

"But I didn't call it a GG to him. I called it a...you know what," he said, tenderly touching the still red line on his lip. "When I did, he drew a blade and swung it so close it grazed my lip."

Daphnie gently moved his chin to get a good look at the red line, and when she did, Andrew saw her clench her jaw, and her left eye twitched. The gesture was protective and welcome, and her touch was comforting after such difficulty.

"Then he left."

"Just left?" she asked.

Andrew took a breath. "When he left the hollow where I camped, it was like he almost disappeared into the dark forest. And then he mounted this..." Andrew thought about how to describe it. "This horse. But unlike any I've ever seen or heard of in fay tales. It was twice the size of Bryn and green."

Daphne sat back. "Green, you say?"

Andrew nodded enthusiastically. "Dark green, but that

wasn't the most incredible part. As I stood there watching, the horse climbed straight up the side of the tree, with the rider on its back, like a lizard or monkey."

Her eyes were large, and her head leaned forward, thinking. Then she held up a finger for him to pause. She rose and went to her shelf of books. Returning to him, she set a thin volume on the counter between them labeled *Snowing Butterflies*, and she leafed through its thin stack of transparent pages covered in lines of delicate wisping script written in light blue ink.

"What is this?" Andrew asked, gently touching a page. He could see the words both across the page and down through the book, which looked to almost shift as he slightly leaned towards it. "I've never seen such a book?"

Daphnie glanced at him with a grin. "No, not many have. This is Scritt writing, and they don't easily part with their texts."

"How do you have it?"

"A very good friend made it for me," she replied.

"And you can read it?"

She took a breath. "Not as well as I'd like. This is not writing like we know. When I look at these pages, I see words. When a Scritt looks at these pages, they hear music. They don't just *read* the book, they look *through* the book. You see these?" she asked, pointing to small dots and dashes around the outer margins of some lines of text.

Andrew nodded.

"These record inflection, tone of voice, body language." Then she found what she was looking for. "Did it look something like this?" she asked, tapping a sketch of the head of a tree horse in the top corner of the page. The drawing was rough ink quickly brushed with varying shades of now fading green watercolors. But it was a tree horse alright.

"Yes, that looks about right."

She turned the book and read:

Three days into the deep wood, I had been following the tracks of a viperwhirl when I came upon a clearing between fantastic hornbeams. Tired from the chase, I rested my mount when I saw it: a green steed, dark as vine leaves, on the knee of a large tree root, grazing as easy as a fawn in a spring pasture. Only, it stood at such a height on the curving branch that I first thought this could be no natural Equine and I must be seeing visions, or perhaps I had fallen asleep waiting for my mount to rest. But, either by day vision or by night, I could not let such a sight pass by without a closer look, so I rose and gently approached it. And though I know how to creep quietly enough to touch a deer nibbling lavender without spooking it, this creature knew me at my first movement. Then I knew I was not having a vision because the magnificent creature startled, causing it to rise and dart in a moment but not across the clearing. Rather, straight up into the trees! It moved its legs like a marmoset, grasping at the tree's limbs with hooves more finger than hoof and a long hairless tail that swung to balance. And so is the witness of Teatay, Hunter of Nerivay, this fourteenth year of Queen Plema, may she live forever.

"Other than this one account, I've never heard of any such thing," Daphnie said, carefully studying the small sketch. "When I read it here, I assumed he had seen something of a strange small mammal. Like a tiny dear that had climbed for safety or some such thing."

"It was no small animal," Andrew said. "It was probably twice the size of Bryn."

"And the Shimar Etsell was riding one? Incredible."

"They both were," he replied.

Daphnie set the book aside and darted her gaze back to Andrew.

"Both?"

He sighed. "Because it was raining and late, I decided it would not hurt to hold over by the fire and leave at first light. When I woke the next morning, another Night Watchman was in my camp. This one was older and didn't seem quite as...militant."

"Militant?"

Andrew nodded. "The first was serious, unwilling to answer my questions, and definitely had a blade. The other was...nice."

"What do you mean nice?"

"He seemed like a happy grandpa. He actually made me some breakfast, fed Brynlee, and was more than a little curious about the chest. I asked if he knew of a way to open it, but he said it was not possible. I asked how he was certain, and he said he was certain because he had built it —seven actually. Apparently, they were gifts. He did indicate that it was a...GG on the cover."

"He built it? Then, it *must* have been something exceptional. I've been doing some research of my own, and the Shimar Etsell craftsmanship is legendary amongst some of the oldest families, but because of their incredible value, these items are never seen by the common people. One story, for instance, spoke of a small boat crafted for the first son of the Burreem. It is said that it was stronger than lechtfelt, cut the water like an oiled arrow tip, and had an intuitive underbelly that could carry the fishing catch of three imperial schooners, though it only took four men to pilot the craft."

Andrew's eyes were large, trying to imagine such a vessel.

She continued, "It is said that they spend *centuries* perfecting the use of a single material, then imbuing the item with intuition. And when one of their craftsmen has created what they consider a perfect specimen, they break the tools they used to make it so that it can never be built the same way again."

The thought of destroying his tools was literally unfathomable to Andrew. Most were hand-crafted by either Lithuel or himself, and a few, like his crucible, were worth just about as much as Brynlee or his cabin. His tools were an extension of his hand. They were like family to him. Simply unfathomable.

"Well. There's more," Andrew said.

Daphnie shifted in her seat and poured them both another cuppa.

"He said the chest is sentient."

Daphnie stood and looked around, trying to process what she had just heard. Then she turned back to him. "Sentient?"

Andrew slowly nodded.

"Oh, that changes everything. I think it's time you meet my friend."

CHAPTER 21

A race nearly as rare as Humans, Andrew had never seen a Scritt before. What little he had heard of them was that they were a highly intuitive race who worshiped writing. If Daphnie was correct, they saw writing in three-dimensional terms, recording body language, movement, mannerism, tone, dialect, inflection, intonation, accent, and so much more in how they annotated their texts. Surely, this Elrift would have some answers.

It took Andrew half a day to find the nearly overgrown stone path Daphnie had told him about that wound up and around a part of the Ridge Back known as Table Mountain.

"Just past the leaning man," she had said, which didn't mean much until he came to an ancient stone statue nearly a hundred feet high of a wise old minotaur leaning out of the cliff face, looking over the valley below. Trumpet vines grew down from his head like long strands of hair. He had a shepherd's staff in one hand and a sword in the other.

"This must be it," he told Brynlee.

Little yellow warblers with grey wings chirped at him

and Brynlee from the long, reaching branches of horn-beams as they made their way up a slender slope of loose slate to a stone door covered in vines. The door was round and painted in the circular script Andrew recognized from Daphnie's book.

He reached for the door, but before he could touch it, it gently rolled open, and standing in the entrance was an Inkling. The Inkling stood barely half as tall as Andrew with a white beard that came to a point and tufts of white hair sticking out of his double-lobed and pointed ears. His eyes were large, looking up at Andrew through a pair of bi-focal lenses that clung to the end of his button nose, and tufts of blue hair intermixed with bright blue hedgehog-like quills stood up and were tied back through a blue-felt dome of a cap lined with brass buttons. He wore fingerless gloves and brown leather boots with scuffed brass toecaps. His finger-tips were stained with yellow and blue ink.

"Yes?" he asked in a high and nasally voice.

"Elrift?"

The Inkling scowled at Andrew. "I am not he. What do you want?"

"I don't mean to bother you, uh, sir, but is Elrift available? Daphnie sent me," Andrew replied, holding up the flowers Daphnie sent as a gift.

The Inkling narrowed his gaze and sized up Andrew and Andrew's horse. Since they did not appear to be much of a threat, he stepped aside, indicating that Andrew could enter the long stone hallway behind him.

"You will need these," the Inkling said, holding a pair of darkly tinted goggles up to Andrew and turning a nob to tint his own glasses.

Andrew put the goggles on, which blocked out almost all light once the front door closed.

Then, trying not to trip on any of the stacks of leather, thread, and binding material lining the hall walls, Andrew followed the clicking sound of the Inkling's metal boots.

They passed several doors covered in the same circular script until they came to a large set of double doors that moved weightlessly at the Inkling's softest touch. The script on this door was etched in deep relief like the doors of a church.

As the door began to open, light poured out into the hall so bright Andrew had to shield his face even with his heavily dimmed goggles.

"Master, we have company," the diminutive fellow said, a shadow stretching out behind him across the floor as he stepped through the door.

Andrew strained to see who the little man was talking to through the brilliantly glowing light. There was movement. Then Andrew's goggles further auto-tinted against the phosphorescent brightness, allowing him to begin to see.

They were standing in a cathedral-like room with floor-to-ceiling windows in the far wall, looking out to the vast horizon and over the valley below. Countless shelves of books rose to the high and distant ceiling. Andrew didn't know this many books existed in the entire world, much less in one place. The sheer volume was dizzying.

Elrift slowly turned towards his visitor and very slowly smiled. He sat on a platform in the center of the room on what looked like a throne of pillows facing the tall windows. Four bright lamps beamed down on him. He had a small, bald head, tiny eyes, three long spindly arms, and three long spindly fingers on each hand, lying open on books sitting on a high, tilted table before him. His skin was translucent. Andrew stood amazed at the sight of Elrift's nervous system, pulsing purple heart, light purple veins, and skeletal structure, exposed like a living anatomy lesson. He wore nothing but a thin fabric wrapped around his waist.

Elrift was so exposed, Andrew wondered if he should turn his face away until he raised a hand to Andrew in welcome, every movement barely one-third what someone might consider normal speed.

The Inkling turned a rather large knob for his tiny hands near Elrift's chair as the lamps dimmed and clicked off.

Andrew undimmed his goggles and blinked, trying to adjust his eyes to the now moderate level of light in the room. As he did, Elrift's translucent skin became an opaque goldenrod.

The Inkling snatched the bundle of flowers from Andrew and climbed a small staircase next to Elrift's chair, clearly built for him, and handed them to his master, who scowled.

"Be...kind...Pectree," he told his companion, who grunted. Pectree looked at Andrew, sighed, nodded in agreement, then stepped away.

Elrift's scowl returned to a warm smile at the speed of pouring molasses. "Beauti...ful," he said, smelling the flowers, then plucked the head of one and ate it. "Daph knows... just how...to...butter...me up," he said with a warm and content grin. "How...is...my old...friend?" he asked. He spoke so slowly Andrew had to pay attention.

"She's good. She looks healthy and happy. The town is getting ready to celebrate Eden Vale."

"Eden...Vale?" Elrift asked. Small mounds of flesh where eyebrows should be raised on his forehead, though there was no sign of hair anywhere on his body.

Pectree climbed the steps again, this time carrying a long shawl he tossed up over Elrift's shoulders.

"Has...it been...so long?" Elrift asked.

"What do you want?" Pectree asked, his quick movements around Elrift reminding Andrew of a busy bee buzzing around a flower lazily blowing in a light breeze.

Elrift slowly scowled again, which Pectree saw and sighed again.

"I mean, how can we help?" Pectree asked, punctuating his last word with something of an annoyed grunt.

"Daphne said that you might be able to..."

"Excuse...my...friend," Elrift interrupted. "He...forgets... his...manners..."

"No problem," Andrew replied. "Daphnie just thought..."

"It's...been...so long...since...we've...had guests."

Andrew smiled. "No problem. Daphnie just thought..."

"How...can...we...help?" Elrift finally concluded, plucking another flower and very slowly eating it.

Andrew paused, trying not to interrupt him again.

Pectree stood, tapping the metal toe of his boot halfway up the small wooden staircase like he just didn't have time for this nonsense.

After a moment, Andrew replied: "Daphnie thought you might be able to help me with a bit of a mystery I'm trying to solve."

"A...mystery?"

"Yes," Andrew replied. "You see..."

"I...love...a good...mystery."

Andrew waited. Then, after another pause, he told Elrift and Pectree about Lorna, the chest, his journey into the Ki Lo Kan Forest, how he met the Shimar Etsell, and his dead-end.

About halfway through the story, Pectree rolled his eyes and vanished off to somewhere Andrew didn't know where. Elrift just sat quietly listening, almost completely motionless.

Elrift slowly touched the spot where a chin should be, considering. Then he held up a finger.

"A...closed...door...is still...a door," he said. "What one... must find...is...the key." Then he rose from his seat and stretched his surprisingly short legs. With one arm, he lifted what looked like an umbrella, which he opened to a beam of light that shone out from underneath it, and he sighed a contented sigh. He descended his platform and walked to a back corner of the large room. Andrew followed him, fascinated by his appearance and having to adjust to his speed.

"Excuse...me. I...slow...down...without...light," Elrift told him.

Slow down more than this? Andrew thought to himself but said nothing, out of courtesy.

As Elrift approached the stack he was looking for, the wide stone tiles in the floor rose up before them into a stair-case by some unseen force. He and Andrew climbed them to a fourth row of shelves, probably three cubits from the ground, as a wooden walkway telescoped out from the stack to create something of a long and narrow platform for them to walk along. Elrift then gave a kind of humming whistle, causing the shelves to open like rolling doors. Behind the shelves were more shelves, layers and layers of shelves, that opened into a long hallway of shelves of books.

"I apologize...for the...cramped space. It...can be...diffi-cult...to find...room...for my...collection," Elrift told Andrew. Andrew's eyes were wide. There was no natural way for so many books to be held in such a space. They slowly walked down the hall and turned a corner. Elrift then made another humming whistle as a row of books rolled out from the stacks like a wave until the wave stopped at a set with spines projecting blue script, like floating holograms of writing.

"Ah...here...we...are," Elrift said, still holding his umbrella-lamp in one hand and reaching for one of the books with another. Andrew watched with fascination as every part of Elrift that remained under the umbrella-lamp was translucent while every part that reached beyond the lamp's light became opaque and goldenrod. As he pulled the book into his lamp light, the book became an almost invisible block of floating blue text, like he was holding a three-dimensional cube of floating letters. Instead of turning pages, he moved the book around, examining it from different angles. As he did, the letters shifted in direction. Then Elrift gave out a loud warble chirp, chirp, and a small door in the far wall swung open as Pectree came skittering across the room. Andrew turned and realized they were standing on the platform overlooking the large room, not in a hall or behind the first row of shelves, which made him a bit dizzy trying to process the fluid dimensions of the bookshelves.

"Tea," Elrift said, and Pectree nodded and skittered away.

"Reclusive...people...the Shimar...Etsell," Elrift said as Pectree returned with tea and biscuits for both Andrew and Elrift, laying the spread out on a small table on the main floor. Then Elrift slowly motioned Andrew to join him for tea and biscuits.

Over the next hour or so, Elrift described to Andrew how the Shimar Etsell, known as Night Watchmen to some but more formally known as the Shimmering, were a tribal people living closely with nature. Elrift knew of no record of their history, mythology, or societal structure; only that they were a proud and extremely xenophobic race, though some oral tales suggested they had not always been so. It seemed to Elrift that they had once been open to trade with outside cultures, often working for noble families, until they inexplicably disappeared many centuries ago. They had been highly regarded for their knowledge of medicinal herbs, plant culture, animal husbandry, and skill with their crafts, particularly musical instruments. "A...highly...intuitive...race," was how Elrift described them.

"Why are they known as the Shimmering?" Andrew asked, but after consulting and considering his texts, Elrift found no answer.

"Interesting," Elrift said, studying a cluster of text deep inside the cloud of writing.

"What?"

"Twins," Elrift replied. "Every...one."

"What does that mean?"

Elrift either ignored or didn't hear the question.

"What about Grace Givers?" Andrew asked casually, dipping a biscuit in his tea.

Elrift looked up from his text. He heard that.

Another chirp-click called Pectree, who swept the book away, scooped up a small stool near the large staircase, returned the book to its exact place, and quickly put the stool away as the staircase became flat floor tiles again.

"Now this...is...a different...thing...entirely," Elrift replied.

Andrew then remembered his mistake with the first Night Watchman and was unsure how Elrift would respond.

"What...is true? What...is tale? Hard...to know. Even...for me. In...the beginning...was...the Word. The...Word... became Grace. And...from...that Grace...came life. All...life." Then Elrift slowly explained how it is said that the Great Ruach created many worlds, all connected, and that in each, beings existed to maintain balance, and these beings were known in this world as Grace Givers. It is thought that a Grace Giver had given the Scritt their language and the Minotaur their strength. The Scritt thought of them as the pure word, capable of both truth and illusion, while others thought of them as fire, both purifying and dangerous.

Andrew was beginning to find the constant duality of the Grace Giver stories both fascinating and unnerving.

"Prophecy foretells...of...an age...of grace...that will... return...again...to...our land. May...it...come...quickly," he finished. Then Elrift rose from his chair and clicked twice.

Pectree quickly came to his side.

"And now...forgive me. My light...grows...dim," he said, looking noticeably exhausted from the conversation. Then, with a click and a whistle, he returned to where Andrew had found him.

Pectree held out a hand for Andrew to follow him out, which he did.

As the front door rolled open to a gust of cool evening air, Pectree finally spoke again: "Consider yourself fortunate, boy. Master has not spoken so much in..." and he thought for a moment, "Eighteen seasons."

That's oddly specific, Andrew thought.

"Please send Madam Daphnie our regards."

And as Andrew held up a hand to thank Pectree for his time and hospitality, the door was already rolling closed.

CHAPTER 22

Andrew knocked on Lorna's door. He had been considering for some time how he might safely approach her. It seemed like her memory held together better when they were eating, so he had some more tea and a couple of Brutste's finger cakes, hoping not to scare her.

At first, he was going to loop Brynlee's reins over a branch but decided to let her into the front yard, hoping Brynlee's presence might remind Lorna who he was.

The fence was still standing, though the gate hung open, and things seemed quiet. Then he knocked.

There was no answer. Then he saw Lorna's sparrow flit across the front window.

He waited patiently until the door finally opened and Lorna peered out with a look of frustration and hesitation.

Andrew smiled. "Hello! I don't mean to bother you, but I thought I would stop by. I'm on my way home and wanted to see how you were doing. I've been..." he paused, unsure how much to tell her. "...on a journey."

She didn't answer.

"I brought you something," he said, holding out the cakes wrapped in paper.

Her eyes darted away from his, and she started fidgeting nervously, slightly shaking her head and blinking quickly several times.

This isn't working, he immediately thought to himself.

When Lorna saw Brynlee, her demeanor softened to a curious look like she had just seen an old friend, and without a word, she pushed past Andrew and approached the old mare, gently caressing her neck, mane, and forehead. Then, after a minute, she whispered: "Hello, mother."

Andrew smiled.

"Oo nee nachtanay oo," she spoke gently. "Felesh oom crestley noomanay oo?"

Brynlee shook her head.

Lorna looked at Andrew.

"Oo nee peleshtem?"

Brynlee nodded.

"Crestfell elah felcorum?" she asked.

Brynlee shifted and shook her mane.

Andrew had learned not to question these things. They must be speaking to each other. How? It was beyond his knowing. But he wanted his turn with Lorna, so he decided to try something else.

Reaching into his coat pocket, he slowly removed the warming rod and held it out to her, curious to see if she would recognize it.

She slowly stepped towards him and gently took it, pulling it close and holding it tight as though she had found a precious heirloom, thought to have been lost to the ages. After a moment, she said,

"This is yours." And she slowly handed it back to him.

"So, you remember me?" he asked with excitement.

She did not reply. Instead, she walked back to her cottage, leaving the front door standing open.

Returning the warming rod to his jacket pocket, he stepped inside the musty, dusty cottage that was starting to feel more like home.

"I thought you might like some cakes," Andrew told her, looking around. "It's almost Eden Vale. Will you be celebrating?"

She fiddled with her robe and moved some things around on the counter, not really tidying but more moving things for the sake of movement. Her sparrow alighted from wherever it had been back into her hair.

"Jatoba looks beautiful. It's been so long since I celebrated Eden Vale. The cakes are delicious," he said, setting them on the kitchen table. He saw that some of the tea jars were open, and a half-brewed cup of tea sat on the counter, which made him smile. He touched the liquid with a finger and tasted it. It wasn't perfect, and it was cold, but it was pretty close. He was glad that she had been able to follow his instructions. Part of the loaf of the spiced bread he had left for her sat partially eaten on the counter.

"I've been traveling the past couple of days, looking for someone who can answer some questions for me," he said, turning back to her. "Do you remember telling me how someone was keeping secrets from you?"

She didn't respond.

He sat in the dusty, but comfortable, armchair near the fire and considered how to frame things in a way that wouldn't be aggressive or unnerving to her, but he wasn't exactly sure how to do that.

"I think it's your chest that's keeping things from you,"

he said, closely watching for any sign of upset or recognition.

"Do you remember when you got it? Was it a gift?"

"No celebrating," she finally said, responding to his earlier question about Eden Vale. She didn't understand what this boy wanted. He was speaking so fast.

Andrew watched her carefully as she stood with her right shoulder towards him, shifting back and forth from one foot to the other. She wasn't engaging with him, but she didn't look scared either, so he decided to continue. He told her about his journey into the Ki Lo Kan, encountering the Night Watchmen, and speaking with Elrift, hoping she might remember something.

While he spoke, she wandered around the outer edges of the room, reaching for—but never touching—items on her shelves.

"I met the man who made the chest, but he said there was no way to open it unless you might remember something about it. He said only you could open it, with a word or song or phrase." He saw no sign of recognition in her body language. "Does any of this sound familiar?"

Lorna didn't respond.

What chest? she wondered. *What is he talking about?* The presence of this stranger in her home was starting to make her anxious, though Mother Mare told her they knew these woods and had passed by only days earlier. Just then, her sparrow fluttered from her hair and landed on the boy's shoulder, which made Lorna look towards them with confusion. *Does Vetta know this boy? How?*

Andrew could tell she didn't remember receiving the chest. Of course not. If she didn't recognize him, how would she remember something from a long time ago?

Perhaps it had been a gift to a family member or distant relative. Maybe she had never known anything about it.

He sighed. Perhaps this was all futile.

"I stopped by two nights ago on my way through town. I brought you some provisions and fixed your gate. I thought about knocking but didn't want to bother you."

What is he talking about? When did he leave provisions? Lorna wandered, looking around, her discomfort growing.

Andrew wished she could remember him, even for a few minutes. He had so many questions about who she was and where she came from. She was like him. Her hands were like his hands; her skin like his skin. He stood, but she pulled away. He took the small portrait from his pocket and held it up to her. "Do you know this woman?"

She glanced at it.

"Is it you?"

She did not respond.

Andrew sighed. There was nothing more to do. He desperately wanted to know more about the woman in the portrait, whether she could be his mother and why Lorna had an image that looked so much like his own, but instead of answers, all he kept finding were dead ends.

It was nearly dark now and starting to snow, which he wasn't about to underestimate again.

"I should probably be going," he said through the weight of his sorrow and disappointment, returning the portrait to his pocket. "I will try to stop in again next time I'm in town, but I'm not sure when that will be."

As he turned for the door, she grabbed his arm. "Thank you," she said, not quite looking directly at him.

His eyebrows raised in gentle hope. "For what?"

She did not reply. Instead, she said, "That is yours," pointing towards the warming rod in his coat.

Lorna might not remember who he was, but she could see the fragment of her staff resonating with the name of its new owner. Then she released his arm, sat back on her cot by the hearth, and started rocking back and forth as the sparrow returned to its nest in her hair.

Just before he left, Andrew heard Lorna quietly say, "You may return."

CHAPTER 23

The night was now cold and dark, but Brutste's tavern was warm and welcoming. A steady snow fell across the southern sky blanketing Jatoba in a crisp quietness only snow can bring.

As Andrew approached the tavern, he could hear the sound of Brynlee's breath, her hooves clipping-clopping on the paver stones, and laughter spilling out through the tavern's open door up ahead. Warm light filled the street, melting a semi-circle of snow away from its narrow entrance.

Andrew led Brynlee up between a ferlorn, standing twice as tall as her with its six legs, and a hairy ox with long red hair hanging over its eyes strapped with a riding harness and reins, which was quite unusual; perhaps a child's pet.

"Be good," he told her, petting her forehead and unfolding a blanket from his bag to drape over her back for the cold night ahead. He also broke off a large piece of the cake the Night Watchman had left for them and fed it to her. Then he went inside.

The first thing he did was scan the bustling tables for a certain copper-toned someone. No luck.

Brutste smiled from the distant side of the bar as he walked in. She was wearing a mustard-yellow dress with ruffled sleeves that was quite fetching. Her hair was braided up into spiraling buns on either side of her head, and her beard was tight curls dotted with small yellow flowers.

"Happy Eden Vale to you, tiny tinker!" she said, wiping out a mug and setting it in front of him.

The tables were full of laughter and merriment. The same musician he had previously heard was tuning his stringed, wind instrument and flirting with a young Minotaur woman with narrow horns, barely a hand's length, and wearing a diadem of woven white and yellow flowers on her head, periodically punctuating their flirtation with a snort of laughter that startled Andrew the first time he heard it.

"From where do you travel on this *dark and snowy night?*" Brutste asked, her eyes large and with a smile from ear to ear.

"From the Ki Lo Kan Forest," he replied, squeezing between a powerhouse of a Minotaur and an even larger Longbeard woman with frosted grey beard hanging loose and wild down to the floor, each talking to their own parties and laughing in the local language.

"Now, that's a name I haven't heard in more than five seasons. What were you doing *there*?" Brutste asked.

"Looking for answers."

"Any luck?"

He sighed, shook his head, and dusted some snow off his jacket.

She could tell from his body language he wasn't in a jesting mode tonight, and she was busy, so she quickly wiped the bar before him. "I'm sorry to hear that. What can I getcha'?"

He thought for a moment, then asked, "Do you have any rooms?"

She gave him a comforting half smile. "I keep one for friends and family or spill-over on especially busy nights. You can have that," she replied, turning to a box on the wall behind the bar, fetching a bulky brass key with the number one on the wooden tag, and laying it before him on the bar.

"Very kind," he replied and thought for a moment about what he might want to eat. *Oh, sod it!* he thought to himself since he was home for the night. "I'll take a fist of your Mulled Wine."

Her eyes grew large as she wiped out another mug. "Remember what happened last time?"

"I'm a big boy," he replied.

She shot him a to-each-his-own shrug of her shoulders, scooped a tankard full of wine from the barrel behind the bar, and set it before him with a slosh of dark red onto the wood, which she quickly wiped up.

"Vittles?" she asked.

"In a bit," he replied and took a long drink.

She had seen this before and knew that what she sold was comfort for the soul more than fullness for the belly and left him to his drink.

Especially mixed to take all your cares away, he remembered her telling him the first time he had ordered a tankard of the sinfully deep-red elixir. Warm. Sharp yet soothing. Fruity but not too sweet. Rich and aromatic. Tannic to the sides and back of his tongue but not too dry. He took another drink. He held the mouthful for a moment to really let the cinnamon tickle the insides of his cheeks. Then he slowly swallowed. Damn, it was just so good.

The edges of his reason were softening, and he soon forgot any frustrations from his journey as the musician began playing his Aeolian harp—its ethereal, melodic sound rising above the laughter in the room. Andrew turned to watch him play as the musician darted a look and a grin at the young woman leaning towards him. She spun one of her many necklaces around her finger. Licks of fire from the hearth rose and took the shape of a man and his bride dancing to the sound of the notes, periodically embracing for an extended kiss.

Then Andrew saw an older couple rise from a back booth and leave, probably deciding that the start of the music was the end of their night before the real revelries might begin.

Andrew held a finger up to Brutste, who excused herself from the woman she was talking to at the other end of the bar and came over.

"Any...special? Tonight?" he asked, taking longer than he realized.

She grinned and said something that he couldn't quite catch.

"I'll just be..." He pointed to the now empty booth at the back where he could sit quietly watching the party from a safe distance and get properly tossed before stumbling his way to bed. "And keep these coming," he nodded and pointed at his now half-full mug.

She nodded and slipped into the back room.

Andrew used the large, solid shoulder of the man sitting next to him to rise from his barstool. The Minotaur glanced at Andrew, then quickly ignored him, seeing Andrew's size and the drink he carried. *No hurt nor harm*, the farmer decided. Then Andrew carefully maneuvered through the cluster of tables and people to the empty booth.

Once he arrived, he sank into the padded seat and waited for his food. How long? He wasn't sure, but by intuition—either real or imagined—his mug never went dry. And, after some further blurring of the edges of his reality, Brutste approached his table and sat before him a knob of bread and a bowl of something that smelled delicious— some sort of stew with thick, chunky vegetables and pieces of meat he didn't recognize on first glance. A fish head glared up at him from the center of the bowl with a long nose and wildly uneven, sharp teeth.

She smiled, but it was no joke; this was the night's special.

"What is thhhhis?" he slurred.

"Sand shark," she replied. "The monger had a crate arrive this afternoon, and I scooped 'em up. It looks a little scary, but I think you'll like it. The cheeks are especially delicious!" she told him. Then she returned to the bar. As she did, Andrew watched her react with a flourish to a well-built man barely half her size walking in from the snowy, cold night and dusting a handful of white powder off his shoulders. He was completely bald from the shoulders up.

Andrew watched with curiosity as Brutste picked the man up with both arms, as he put his hands on either side of her face, and the two kissed passionately.

Could this be...her husband? he wondered. *Her* bald *husband?* The irony of how much grief Brutste had given her sister for being bald made Andrew chuckle.

He took another long drink and thought about how to approach the stew. It smelled quite lovely, but he wasn't accustomed to eating food that looked back at him. Perhaps he could nudge the face aside? He gave it a poke. Then he decided to try the bread first, tore off a corner, and soaked it in broth. It was quite good—a stream of hot liquid running down his chin. He took the scratched and nearly flat spoon and fished out a piece of a purple root vegetable. This was also soft and delicious.

Alright. I can do this, he thought, taking a larger bite, this time with a piece of the beige fish meat.

He glanced up to where Brutste had been, and that's when he had a vision—a copper-toned vision.

CHAPTER 24

S he entered the bar laughing and talking to patrons like they were members of her family.

Her skin looked darker in the mottled tavern light than it had during the day, but now it shimmered. He tried not to stare as she took off a warm-looking brown cloak—once again revealing her slender shoulders—and hung it on a hook behind the bar. Then she kissed Brutste's cheek, who said something to her, and they both glanced at him. This made him suddenly self-conscious, and he felt himself beginning to blush, so he quickly looked down and away, fishing for another bite of bread and a long drink of wine.

Brutste took her husband by the hand and whisked him off into the night as her sister tied an apron around her waist and began pouring drinks and laughing with the patrons at the bar.

Andrew tried to keep his eyes off of her and on the musician, but it was like trying to ignore a lighthouse in a dark storm. And more than once, he thought he caught her tossing glances in his direction.

After some time, she approached his booth.

"Evenin'," she said.

Andrew sat up straight and smoothed the front of his shirt. "Eve-ning."

She could immediately tell where he was on the four-sheets-to-the-wind scale.

"Enjoy the stew?" she asked through a slender whisper of a half smile.

To Andrew's surprise, his bowl was empty, and the shark's head was torn to bony bits. He wasn't sure who had eaten it, but he wasn't hungry anymore—the only sign of the nob of bread was scattered crumbs and a melted butter stain in his lap. He raised his eyebrows and gingerly shifted the spoon around on the table before setting it in the bowl and pushing it towards her.

"Can I get you anything else?" she asked, her look razor sharp; her eyes polished new pennies.

He nervously rubbed his knees and licked his lips.

She noticed, and her ears pulled back; her look glistened with knowing. Andrew was naive and helpless in this tavern of giants—friends and family of hers—nearly all of whom would leave hearth and home to defend her honor, but she did not wield this with a heavy hand. Instead, she simply looked at him with calm compassion. Something about this tinker was both foreign and fetching to her. The more he tried to hide his rosy cheeks and nervous behavior, the more he telegraphed how much he liked her. But he wasn't forceful or brash like the other heavy hands that often tried to take her home. She saw from a distance when he thought no one was watching how meticulous and capable he was with his tools, how gently he touched his mare, how he laughed in Daphnie's shop when talking to Fleur de Lis. He was like a song or bit of poetry on a farm—something fascinatingly different in a place of working hands and harsh tools. She *saw* him. She couldn't help but see him. Like a lighthouse in a storm.

He tried to talk to her through heavy eyes. "Would you... How have you been? Would you like to loin me? Uh, join me?" he asked.

She smiled. Clearly, he had no idea what he was doing; however, this naivety was somehow enduring. "I can't. I have to tend the bar," she softly replied.

Another strike against him. It seemed the day would not relent. "Ah, I see," he replied.

Her calm and compassionate look broke in a brief moment of confusion, then returned. "How about I bring you another drink?" she asked, taking his nearly empty mug and bowl.

"Sure," he slurred, his head slightly bobbing.

He wouldn't remember in the morning, but the mug of wine she brought him this time was a watered-down version Brutste kept for when someone wanted to buy her a drink or started getting rowdy.

As she delivered his drink to his table, he stood and started fishing for some coin. "You said you'd tell me your name," he mumbled.

"My name?"

"Next time...I came. Your name. But, maybe you're too busy for that too."

Perhaps he wasn't *quite* so fetching when he was drunk.

"Your money is no good here," she told him, gently touching his arm as he found his purse and tried digging out a silver crown for the food and room.

He pulled away. "Then consmidder it a...tip. I can pay for myself. Thank you very much."

As he began to walk away, she grabbed his wrist. "Feyloren."

"Feyloren?" he asked.

"My name. Feyloren."

Andrew turned and stumbled away.

Someone has laid crooked stairs, he thought to himself as he tried to maneuver the narrow flight. He could still hear the music from downstairs as he tried his key in a door three times with no success before realizing he had the wrong door. *Does one come before or after two?* he wondered, trying to do the math, but then he got lucky and found it.

SOMETIME LATER—IN the darkness of the night—Andrew slowly roused to the motion of someone in his room.

He wasn't alone.

He felt a tug. Someone was pulling off his boots, then his trousers, and finally his coat. The warming rod clattered on the floor as it fell from his jacket pocket.

With heaviness, he lifted his head.

A copper shape—gently outlined in moonlight spilling in from the window—moved through the darkness. Only, this time, there was much more skin than just a pair of bare shoulders.

The covers pulled back.

A warm breath. That smell. That damn intoxicating aroma caused him to stir. She was warm and soft and close now.

He could hear her breathing.

A hand touched his bare chest, the covers pulled up, and a firm but light head rested on his shoulder.

Then he was gone.

CHAPTER 25

The next morning, Andrew slowly woke to find Feyloren still lying next to him, he'd be damned if her breathing didn't sound just like purring. He glanced below the covers. Her arm was draped over his chest. They were both in thin undergarments. He could now, for the first time, see the exquisite texture of her long bare legs, one intertwined with his and the shape of her ankles and feet.

Did we? He couldn't remember. He had hoped, feigned to imagine...but now he couldn't remember? What a fool he was.

He continued to look at her, not wanting to move for fear of waking her and by some chance she might fade to wherever dreams come from. Perhaps this wasn't real. Perhaps this was a result of Brutste's mulled elixir. Perhaps the wine held some hallucinogenic compound and he was still cold and alone in bed. But she was so soft and warm and smooth. And that smell again. He had never had a night vision that smelled so wonderful.

He closed his eyes and—moving as slowly as he

possibly could, trying not to wake her—took in the fragrance of her naked head.

Damn it! What have I possibly done to get her into bed? he tried to remember.

He didn't want to leave.

After a while of lying there together, Feyloren began to stir and gently groaned.

She pulled him closer.

Was she also drunk last night? he wondered. *Is she going to be disappointed when she realizes I'm the one laying here?* He knew well that he didn't look like one of those otherworldly pictures of masculinity that he saw flirting with her at the bar. How could anyone less than one of those guys possibly attract her attention unless she had also been inebriated?

"Good morning," she whispered, gently reaching over and touching his cheek.

He opened an eye, with a cautious smile.

Okay. She's not drunk, and she knows it's me. "Hi," was all he could muster.

She kissed his cheek.

He was hesitant to ask: "What happened last night?"

She shifted under the covers towards him, and he could feel more of the warmth of her body press against his. A flush of something intoxicating rushed through him, but it wasn't wine. It was something more chemical.

"I came up to see if you had made it into your room, you looked like you might pass out in the pitcher plant in the hall." She giggled, which nearly stopped his heart cold. "And I found you laying in the hall, half in, half outside of your room. I decided you looked cold, so I thought I might... warm you."

Andrew swallowed. "Did we?"

She walked her fingers up his chest and touched his

chin. "Oh, wouldn't you like to know," she flirted. "I can tell you that last night was good for me. *Very* good."

At that, he couldn't help but feel his cheeks bloom with heat, and she laughed, but not at him.

He turned away, but she sat up on an arm and gently pulled his face back to hers.

She was smiling. "Why do you do that?"

"What?"

"Turn away when your cheeks turn red?"

He sighed and started to turn away again out of habit, but she stopped him.

"I think it's cute. And no, we did not. I kept you warm. That's all."

"That's all? That's *everything*," he mumbled shyly, which she heard, endearing him to her even more, and she laid her head back on his shoulder.

CHAPTER 26

After Feyloren fed Andrew a light breakfast and left him with a gentle kiss, Andrew tended to Brynlee and made his journey back to Lithuel.

"Hey! There he is!" Lithuel called from around the back corner of the house as Andrew approached. Jasper quickly dashed across the yard and through puddles of water to welcome him.

"Hey boy," Andrew laughed, climbing off of Brynlee and petting the scraggly dog behind his wildly flopping ears. He let Bryn walk herself the rest of the way into the fenced area.

Lithuel used his cane, with some effort, to rise to his feet from where he knelt applying some tar to the underside of his upturned fishing boat. "How was your journey? Are you well?"

Andrew embraced him, which didn't happen often since Andrew had become a young man.

Lithuel looked down at him for a moment, wondering what this was for, then returned the embrace. "You doin' alright?"

"Yeah. Just glad to be home," Andrew replied.

"Well, come on in. I'll put the kettle on and warm some of that bread. I saved part of the loaf for your return."

"That sounds good," Andrew replied.

As often as Andrew wondered about who his family might be, it was always Lithuel he missed when he was gone.

Lithuel asked about Andrew's journey after some lunch and small talk about how things had been around the "farm" while Andrew was gone, which is what they both playfully called their little shack in the swamp.

Andrew told him about the Shimar Etsell and everything that had happened. He also decided to share how he had met a wonderful herbalist woman in Jatoba who had helped him and the unusual conversation with Elrift, but that he had run out of answers. He wasn't quite ready to mention Feyloren, yet.

"I thought I could help her," Andrew said, referring to Lorna.

"Maybe you did. Just not the way you thought you could."

Andrew shook his head. "You should hear the way everyone in town talks about her. Some of the older folks don't mind her, remembering when her mind was healthy, but the kids can be mean."

Lithuel just nodded.

The sky was beginning to grey and the sun was setting, dotting the horizon with freckles of orange.

"I don't exactly know what I expected to find, or do, but it somehow *felt* like I was supposed to be there. Like everything was leading to me meeting that...Night Watchman."

Lithuel sighed, not quite wanting to share what he was

thinking, but Andrew could tell he was holding something back.

"What is it?" Andrew asked.

Lithuel did not raise his eyes from the knothole in the floor he had been staring at while Andrew was talking and petting Jasper's side. Then he slowly stood, packed two long wooden pipes with herb, lit them both and handed one to Andrew. Andrew accepted it and pulled a long draw through the stem, which helped calm his nerves. Lithuel then sat down at the hearth and Andrew joined him.

"Have you ever thought that you might be seeing what you want to see?" Lithuel finally said, looking up at Andrew with some caution, not wanting to hurt his feelings.

"What's that supposed to mean?"

Lithuel thoughtfully pulled another slow draw from his pipe and let its blue-grey tendrils of thin smoke rise from his nostrils like a dragon.

"You've always been meant for something more than..." and he waved his hand through the air to signify the cabin. "*This.* I can see it plain as day. I had to fight to find things to keep you interested by time you were nine 'cause you could do everything I could with twice the skill, and in half the time."

"Lithuel, now come on..."

Lithuel held up a hand to stop him. "It's time I speak and you hear me now. I never had any of my own children, and when I found you, I was sure someone would show up at that very door and whisk you away from here. But no one ever came. Year after year, I raised you as my own. Honored to get to see you grow into a man, grateful for the time I had already been given. And, ever since you was a boy, you've been itchin' just *itchin'* to do somethin' more. Hell, I encouraged it! Because, you have...a *gift*...for this. Some of those drawings in your book are years beyond me. And I'm not just talking a new hitch lever or leg brace, I'm talkin' *academy* stuff."

Andrew's eyes raised, listening carefully and smoking his pipe.

"Oh, don't think I don't know about your designs. They're *brilliant*. You think bigger than these here four walls. And when you look, you're lookin' out past the horizon, like a bird waitin' for the moment he can finally stretch his wings and fly. Cause' that's *exactly* what you're meant to do! But, that don't mean it's today."

Lithuel thought carefully about his next words, letting his pipe vapors slowly surround his head in a cloud of calm and comfort. Then his eyes rose and met Andrew's. "Sometimes, an old woman with a sick mind is just an old woman with a sick mind. Sometimes in life, there are no cures; sometimes there are no answers."

Quietly they sat together as the sun went to bed for the night and the fire began to dim. Jasper had fallen asleep between the two men's feet and was now snoring.

Andrew rose and laid more logs on the flame. "Maybe you're right. Maybe it was a fool's errand."

"Nothing wrong with a little adventure, just don't let it become something that pulls you down is all I'm sayin'. Embrace it for what it was."

Andrew nodded, poking at the embers and blowing on them until the faint flickering flame grew to ignite the new logs he had added.

The crackle-pop of the wood was hypnotizing as he stared into the wisping orange-red light, his mind rolling around the things he had heard and seen over the past few days and letting Lithuel's word slowly set it. Then he quietly said: "But something doesn't add up."

Lithuel raised his eyes. "Oh?"

"When I asked Lorna about the chest, that morning over breakfast, she said that someone was keeping her secrets from her."

Lithuel nodded.

"And when I asked the craftsman about it, he said that only seven had been made, as gifts to hold something of great value or importance, and that it wasn't for me to open it." He was talking to himself as much as Lithuel now. "He said that it was a particularly *moody* box."

"A moody box?" Lithuel asked, wondering at the strange comment. "How exactly is a box moody?"

Andrew turned to the only man he had ever known as a father. "The craftsman said that the box was alive, and somehow suggested that it could *decide* whether or not to open."

Lithuel leaned forward. "Alive you say?"

Andrew nodded. "Whatever that means. When I mentioned it to Daphnie, it seemed to get her attention, which is why she sent me to Elrift, but he grew too tired before I could ask him about it."

Just then Lithuel started laughing.

Andrew turned.

"Oh, no," Lithuel said, rubbing his face. "Oh goodness."

"What's wrong with you?"

Lithuel had a mischievous grin Andrew had not seen on him before, like a young man who had just got one over on the sheriff. "I remember now where I've seen something like that, only...it wasn't a box."

Andrew sat back in his chair. He couldn't remember the last time he had heard Lithuel laugh like that. "Where?"

"Oh..." he thought for a moment. "Has it been that long?" he asked himself. "I was traveling through Nevarii doing some trading, and I met another tinker," he said, raising an eyebrow. "We had drinks."

"Another tinker? Anyone I know?"

Lithuel shook his head.

"Were they any good?" The first question any tinker ever asked when talking about another, which was actually the kind way of asking: Are they as good as I am?

"Yeah...*she* was."

"She?"

Lithuel nodded.

"I've never heard of a woman tinker. Why haven't you mentioned her?"

"Well, some things a man keeps to himself."

Andrew raised an eyebrow wondering what that could possibly mean.

"Years ago, I was traveling through Nevarii, trading honey with the governor's baker when I saw a tinker's cart near the gate. Only, it wasn't any ordinary tinker's cart, it was beautiful! Unlike anything I had ever seen. It was crafted from a single piece of strange bright-red and honey colored wood, drawn by four horses."

"Four?" Andrew asked, having never heard of a tinker who could afford four horses to pull their cart, or why they would even need that many.

Lithuel nodded, staring listlessly at the firelight.

"That night I saw it again, parked by the tavern on the outer ring of the city. I figured I'd have a drink with them and wish them peace on their journey; see if they'd had any good fortune in town, perhaps trade wares, you know how it is. Well, I hadn't paid any attention to the coachman, for the brown cloak he wore, until I was close enough to see into the cart, and that's when he, *it*, turned to me." He looked up at Andrew. "The coachman was stone. Solid stone. Of course, I thought maybe it was a mask, until I realized his eyes were empty, unblinking holes with these... floating dead blue orbs where the eyes of a man should be. I needed a drink after seeing that face, I tell you."

Lithuel started smiling again. "When I found her, she was sitting at the bar eating alone. I greeted her and asked if she had found any fortune in the city, but she ignored me. I even tried buying her a drink, but she wouldn't have it, until I offered her a piece of honey candy."

Andrew smiled. The honey candy was one of Lithuel's specialties, but he could only make a few times a year when honey was in season in the swamp, and even then it was hit or miss because the hives often moved.

"After that, she started talking. We spoke all night before..." Lithuel said, with a fond smile of remembrance on his face.

"The Night Watchman's sword, the one that..." Andrew gently touched his lip. "It had a wooden handle, fiery-red and honey-colored."

Lithuel's eyebrows rose.

"Any idea who she was? Where she was from?" Andrew asked.

"No idea. I often wished I knew. It was a good evening. I even got her to laugh once or twice, but by morning she was gone."

"What do you think her coachman was?" Andrew asked.

Lithuel shook his head, still slowly petting Jasper. "I've never seen anything like him, before or since. The way he moved—turned his head—was unnatural somehow."

"Do you think she knows the Shimar Etsell?"

"No idea. But she looked well off. Her clothes weren't what you'd expect a tinker to wear, the usual leathers. It was all fine quality. I do remember glancing her boots several times thinking they must be worth a half-sovereign."

Andrew whistled. "Any guess how I might find her?"

Lithuel shrugged. "Maybe ask around Nevarii?"

The presentation of a new opportunity to find answers for Lorna, even a remote one, lifted Andrew's mood.

"But be careful," Lithuel added.

Andrew nodded. He knew why.

Then Lithuel grunted and pulled himself up and out of his chair. Jasper sat up as he did and yawned. And that's when Andrew saw the plume of red behind Lithuel's knee that looked to have dried sometime earlier.

"What happened here?" Andrew asked, pointing at Lithuel's leg.

Lithuel partially turned then waved away the question. "Don't worry about that."

Andrew stopped him, knelt and gently lifted Lithuel's trouser leg. His bad leg had crusted blood near the place where he had hurt it years earlier. "You need to have this looked at!"

Lithuel sighed. "No need. It's already healin'. Besides, I know how to take care of myself."

"Let me at least wrap it for you."

Lithuel started to shake his head, but saw the serious you-don't-have-a-choice-in-the-matter look on Andrew's face, so he scowled, looked away and sat down to let Andrew tend to his knee.

"You *need* to take it easy for a few days," Andrew told him, applying a cloudy salve and cloth bandage they had bought in Quincary the last time they had passed through.

Once Andrew was finished, Lithuel rose to the cupboard

in the kitchen and took down a small cloth sack the size of a money purse and tossed it into Andrew's lap.

"What's this?" Andrew asked, picking it up and pulling it open. Inside were the last remaining pieces of honey candy in the house.

"If you find her, give her one of these. Maybe she'll remember me."

Andrew smelled the bag. The candies smelled sweet and made his mouth water, but he didn't eat one. There were only a few and he'd rather keep them for her.

THAT NIGHT, after Lithuel and Jasper had gone to bed, even though he was exhausted, Andrew couldn't sleep. He wrapped himself in a blanket and curled up on Lithuel's large chair by the hearth. It was good to be home. The fire-light, familiar smells and familiar sounds of the swamp comforted him.

He opened his leather-bound book and wrote out some of his thoughts—looking at the canvas portrait of the woman he assumed must be his mother.

Jasper rose from his bed and laid down at Andrew's feet.

Why are they called the Shimmering? Why did he say it was not for me to open it? Could someone or something else open it? Perhaps there's an herb or intuition that might help Lorna remember. Should I look for a way to restore her memory or focus on the dumb box.

'Dumb' was underlined several times.

CHAPTER 27

Nevarii was different than Jatoba in almost every way. It was a wealthy city, hundreds of years old, with high, white stone walls and large carved statues of armored guards towering above the seven city gates that never closed. The buildings within the city grew up and packed into every nook and cranny while the city beyond the walls spilled out like a sack of grain split open at the belly.

Nevarii had been built on the ancestral homeland of Lithuel's people, the Nimic, though Longbeards now populated most of the homes and shops, along with more than a dozen other races filling in the cracks.

Dym caverns also dotted the hills along the north and could be found giving the city a second life after sunset.

The Dym were a, pale, nocturnal race who lived underground and thrived in darkness. Thanks to the Dym, Nevarii truly was an entirely different city after dark. They had their own laws, their own marshals, their own businesses, and their own way of life that existed in the same city but entirely separate from Nevarii day-folk—what the

Dym called daylight dwellers. A Longbeard or Nimic shop-keep would use a storefront by day, and a Dym shopkeep would then use the same storefront by night. They would pack up their wares, sweep up shop, and welcome their co-habitants. Rent was cheaper this way.

Nevarii's magistrate didn't mind the Dym's presence since she collected taxes from the Dym as she did any other resident of Nevarii. If anyone in Dym society caused trouble, they had their own methods of dealing with it.

Andrew preferred the city at night since the Dym didn't care if someone was Human, Longbeard, or a figment of one's imagination, as long as they paid. But Andrew needed answers, and Lithuel had said that the tinker he had met had been trading with the magistrate's baker. That was day business. It also meant Andrew had to pass through wealthier districts—replete with nosy guards—and possibly even ask around the magistrate's villa. And though the laws forbidding Humans from entering the city were old and mostly ignored, they were not gone. If anyone were to judge Andrew for the color of his skin, it would be there.

Even outside the wealthier districts, Andrew tried avoiding larger cities as much as possible—though he was starting to have to visit more often since Lithuel had hurt his leg. A tinker needed certain supplies, like teefite, that were difficult to come by in Quincary or some of the smaller towns scattered across the countryside. Life in the city was very different than what he was used to. It was harder and more cutthroat—at least, that's how he perceived it. He had to watch his purse and his cart, when and if he brought it.

Nevarii's three crown jewels stood at the city's center, facing each other: the Lincarna Academy, the temple to Ruach, and the governor's village, all built from the same white stone.

Andrew had only seen the governor's property once from a distance, with its high-carved gate, stone figures, and armed guards. Beyond the white stone gate that glistened in the sunlight lay carefully manicured gardens, pruned and flowering trees, and flourishing fountains.

"Hello, sir," Andrew said, approaching a guard in tarnished armor.

"Keep clear of the gate," the guard replied, not looking directly at him, standing at his post with a shield resting against both legs and a longsword at his side.

"I was wondering if the governor might be in need of a tinker today. Sharpen knives, fix..."

"No need today."

Andrew rubbed the back of his neck. "I'm actually looking for someone. Maybe you know her. I understand another tinker comes by sometimes with a red and honey-colored four-horse cart. Her coachman might be stone."

The guard glared at him. "Keep clear, I say."

Andrew took a few steps back. "I really need to speak to her. I might be able to make it worth your time."

"Ey, you daft! I said, clear out, Human, before I clear you out!" He cleared his nose and spat a sizeable green glob onto the ground towards Andrew, who threw his hands up and quickly left.

For the next several hours, Andrew asked around shops and stores, trying to find anyone who might recognize the tinker and her cart, but most either knew nothing or slammed their door in his face. While Humans had once been the majority culture, any sign of Human rule had been torn down and burned long ago. They were now seen as a weak, non-intuitive race best forgotten.

Having no luck, Andrew approached the narrow window of a carvery facing onto the street where pieces of roast ox leg hung in the window. As he stood there considering the food, an old Longbeard man with snow-white hair stepped up to the window and ordered a bap from a heavy Nimic woman with braided white hair and a white lace dress. Nimic script, Andrew could read from having lived with Lithuel, was tattooed in white ink up and down her arms and neck. She handed the elder Longbeard a sandwich wrapped in a thin sheet of paper and wished him a Happy Eden Vale.

"That'll be tupenny," the woman said with a warm smile.

The man handed her two copper coins, took the sandwich, and left.

Andrew had missed breakfast, and the smell was tantalizing. He approached the window. As he did, the woman's face changed.

"How can I help?" she asked.

"I'll take a bap, please," Andrew said as a young girl, maybe five or six, peeked out from behind a curtain and smiled at him. Andrew returned the smile and waggled his pinker finger at her to say hello. The girl's skin was not as dark as her mother's, but she too had the white script on her dark skin, though her's looked more painted than tattooed.

The woman scowled and pulled the curtain back. "That'll be trepenny," the woman said, setting a sliced meat and butter sandwich on the counter before him. Only two thin slices of meat hung from the edges of the bread.

"I thought I heard you say a bap was tupenny."

"Last one of the day. We're almost out," she replied.

Andrew looked at the counter beside her, where a stack of sliced sandwiches lay waiting for customers. Then he opened the sandwich. The meat was thin and grey, not fresh and glistening like the meat he saw in the window.

"Really?" he asked, leaning the bread towards her.

"That'll be trepenny, or I'll call the warden," she said.

Andrew's shoulders dropped. He didn't want a fight. So, he took three coins from his purse, laid them on the counter, and thanked her kindly. Then he scraped the nasty meat onto the street and ate the bread only.

"I heard you're looking for Rya."

Andrew turned to see an older Nimic man with snow-white beard and white clothes wiping soil from his hands.

"Rya?" Andrew asked.

"The tinker? With the cart? And that coach driver made of stone?"

"Yes! Do you know her?"

The man looked around. "Why don't you buy me a drink."

CHAPTER 28

The Nimic man led Andrew to a tavern that didn't look like the usual Eagle and Child or Hiddy Coo Andrew was used to. It was in a back alley where someone was either sleeping or dead on the ground, and the small space inside was dark, smelled of mold, and had only three taps behind the bartender. No, this was definitely a bar, not a tavern.

"He's with me," the man said to the bartender as he and Andrew sat at the long, sticky table.

The bartender was the skinniest Dym Andrew had ever seen, with pale blue skin, facial piercings, a narrow gaunt frame, and the telltale Dym ears, with their three points like the webbed barbs of a fish. Only, this bartender's third, bottom lobe, hung in a low hoop of skin pulled by a heavy metal earring.

"Bitter, sweet or spicy," the man asked Andrew.

"Uh, whatever."

"Two bitters," the Nimic man told the bartender, who nodded, turned, and began pouring the drinks.

As the Nimic man sat, he caught Andrew staring at his white tattoos.

"Don't know many Nimic?" he asked.

"Actually, my father is Nimic," Andrew replied.

"Your father?"

"Adopted."

The man grunted.

"How do you know, uh, Rya, was it?" Andrew asked.

"I didn't say I knew her."

"But..." Andrew pointed in the general direction back to where they had met.

"I *said* I heard who you was askin' about. I *didn't* say I knew her."

The bartender sat two drinks in front of them, sloshing suds onto the table with a splash.

"I see her 'round," the Nimic man said, picking up the stout mug and taking a long drink.

Andrew picked his up and took a swallow. It was dry like he was drinking liquid sand, which made him grimace. He set the mug back on the bar and coughed.

The man raised an eyebrow at him. "What are you doin' here? She owe you money or something? Maybe you got a thing for her?"

Andrew shook his head. "Nothing like that."

The man took another drink. "What is it then?"

Andrew considered how to answer this. "I have a friend who's sick, and I think she might be able to help. That's all," he replied, slowly pushing the mug further away.

"I've never seen her with any medicines or anything like that."

Andrew noticed the man's hands. He had dark soil underneath his fingernails. His shoes were also caked with the same dark soil.

"How'd you hear I was looking for her?" Andrew asked.

The man pursed his lips and took another drink.

"The only place around here I've seen soil like that is in the governor's gardens. You heard me talking to the guard, didn't you?"

The man grunted. "Governor's gardens? Those are *my* gardens."

"They're beautiful."

The man's look softened. "What do you know about gardens?"

"Not a lot, but a friend of mine knows something about them, and she's shown me hers. She keeps rare plants, like brynlee phalaenopsis."

This got his attention. "*Really?* Who is this friend of yours?"

"Her name's Daphnie. She lives in Jat..."

The man laughed. "I'll be dipped in pig fat and fried on a spit. You know Daph?"

Andrew smiled. "Yeah. I do. Just saw her a couple of days ago."

The man slapped his knee and looked around. "My days. She's toured my gardens. Good lady."

Andrew smiled. "Yeah, she is."

The man thought for a moment, then leaned over and took Andrew's mug. "You gonna drink this?"

Andrew motioned him to have it.

"I work the gardens—have for damn near twenty years now. Seen three of them governors come and go," and he looked around and dropped his voice to a whisper. "And if you ask me, this one is the laziest yet. But yeah, I've seen your lady come by now and again. And that driver of hers," and he shivered. "Those blue eyes. I never seen anything like 'em. You see, no one pays any attention to the groundskeeper, but I've seen things, I tell you," he said, tapping a finger on the side of his head. His voice was beginning to slur.

"How often does she come through town?" Andrew asked.

"Once, maybe twice a year."

"Any idea where she's from or where she goes?"

The groundskeeper shook his head.

"Any idea how I can find her?"

The man shook his head again and tipped back the last of Andrew's drink.

This isn't going anywhere, Andrew thought to himself.

Then the man sat the mug down on the bar with a bang. "But, I know who can."

Andrew's eyes widened.

"My wife. She's the governor's cook, but you can't just go back up to that gate again, or Melpas 'll skewer you *and* your horse. I'm pretty sure if it was closer to the end of his shift, he pro'ly woulda' whooped your ass just to prove a point."

"What do you suggest?"

"You have to bring somethin'."

"Like a gift? For the governor?" Andrew asked.

The man touched his nose. "Just to get passed the guard."

"Well, what does she like?"

The man rubbed his forehead, belabouredly trying to think. "Jewelry?"

Andrew shook his head. He didn't have any jewelry.

"Art?"

Andrew shook his head again. "Maybe I could make her something."

196

"This isn't a woman who needs her *knives sharpened*. You've got to think bigger, son."

"I don't have anything like what you're suggesting. I'm just a tinker, not an art dealer."

"I'm not suggesting you buy your way in, but you gotta *bring* something—something interesting. Like some kindda weird fruit or something my wife can cook. You need to look like you're there on purpose, and don't go back to that front gate again. Go 'round the side where all the deliveries happen. No guard there. You'll have to ring the bell."

"What kind of food?"

The groundskeeper shrugged. "How in the hells am I supposed to know? My wife's the cook."

They both sat, trying to think of something else.

"Where'd you say you're from?" the man asked.

"Aitecham Tioram," Andrew replied, expecting the man to grimace or give him grief, but he didn't even seem to hear him.

Then he slowly turned to Andrew. "Are there lagoons?"

Andrew thought. "Yeah. To the East, along the coast."

The man smiled and shook Andrew's shoulder. "Pulmari. The governor has a thing for seafood, especially Pulmari." Then he belched.

Andrew scrunched his brow. "What's Pulmari?"

The man smiled. "The eggs of a land octopus."

CHAPTER 29

Andrew didn't like traveling through the swamp after dark, but the days were growing shorter as winter approached, and he was close enough to home that he decided to push through. Fortunately, the raven moon cast just enough light across the shallows to let him see his path, and he made it back with no trouble.

He had never come home after dark and didn't realize Lithuel left a small lantern burning for him in the window, which made him feel both loved and missed as he turned down the wick and watched the small light flicker out for the night. He tiptoed around each and every squeaky board and gently peaked in through Lithuel's open bedroom door. Jasper, who usually slept by the front door but apparently slept with Lithuel when Andrew was gone, lifted his head and twitched his tail when Andrew approached. Andrew held up a hand to stop him from waking the older tinker. Jasper set his head back down on Lithuel's arm with a sigh.

As Andrew fell into bed that night, he thought about what the old Gardner had told him: "She has a thing for fresh seafood, especially Pulmari." Where was he supposed to find a land octopus?

Then, as the sounds of the swamp began to sing him to sleep, he thought about Feyloren. He imagined her smiling at some patron ordering another round of drinks as Brutste slipped out for the night with her *bald* husband—a thought that made Andrew smile again. He imagined himself slipping in quietly and watching her from the back of the tavern. Maybe she would look up and see him and smile. In his mind, he was always the confident hero. He'd tell her about his trip to Nevarii, how he fought a guard who spat at him, told an old racist woman where she could shove her bap, and laughed with a wise old gardener, even though none of these things had actually happened.

It was a good dream.

ANDREW AWOKE the next morning to the smell of Jasper farting and something fatty cooking on the hob.

"Good grief, boy!" he exclaimed, waving a hand over his nose. At that, Jasper jumped up on the bed and began licking Andrew's face. "You need a bath," Andrew said, laughing and trying to pull away.

Over a comforting breakfast of tea, beans, bacon, eggs, and sliced bread, Andrew gave Lithuel the rundown of how things actually went in Nevarii and how he had met the old groundskeeper who suggested he find some eggs to bring back to Nebi, the groundskeeper's wife.

"Land octopus eggs, you say?" Lithuel asked, rubbing the stubble on his chin that he only bothered to shave down about once a month.

Andrew nodded. "I've never seen one. Have you?"

Lithuel paid no attention to the question, deep in thought. Then he slowly rose from the table and hobbled over to a large cabinet built into the wall in his bedroom, lined with rows of small drawers. Andrew followed him.

"You always wondered why I'd collect these bits and bobs from around the swamp," Lithuel said, glancing at Andrew, who stood in the doorway. "It's in case we ever came across a day like today. You see, all these little pieces are like a map of this here swamp." And he began opening drawer after drawer, looking for something in particular. A feather. A small mollusk shell. An insect casing. A slender piece of reptile skin. Various flowers dried and pressed flat. Leaves. Rocks. Every item had a small, handwritten label reminding Lithuel where he was when he had found the specimen. Then his eyes narrowed into a sly look, and he grinned at Andrew. "Land octopus," he said, handing Andrew what looked like a strange bird beak, though it was unlike any beak Andrew had ever seen. It was neither smooth nor beautiful, like so many other bird beaks, but instead looked like a beak made of bone that had grown inside of something—rough, white, and barely the size of Andrew's fingertip.

"Eastern shallows," Lithuel squinted, trying to read his own handwriting on the small label in the drawer.

"Eastern shallows. Okay," Andrew replied, rolling it around in the palm of his hand. "But the shallows are thousands of cubits. How am I supposed to..." But before he could finish, Lithuel snatched the beak from his hand.

"Like this," and he held out the tiny bone to Jasper, who stood up with curiosity and approached the strange object. With excitement, he began sniffing it, then paused, his tail stiff in the air, then wildly began sniffing it again. Then turning, he started for the door.

"His nose is the key to the map," Lithuel said with a broad smile.

Andrew quickly grabbed his coat as Lithuel hobbled alongside him, pulling an empty jar with a wooden stopper off a shelf and handing it to him. Andrew fit Brynlee with her tack and harness as quickly as he could and pulled Jasper up onto the saddle where the dog was used to riding —legs hanging down on either side. Then, holding onto the old dog, Andrew, Brynlee, and Jasper made their way to the Eastern Shallows—Jasper's tail vacillating with excitement.

CHAPTER 30

The smell of salt water was thick in the air as Andrew guided Brynlee carefully across slowly deepening water where green and golden grasses grew up to her chest. It was becoming difficult for him to see where they were stepping now, the water nearly up to her knees. He didn't like this at all. *Snakes, or worse, could be lying just below the water's surface,* he thought, carefully watching for any movement and remembering his encounter with the marsh dragon the night he had collected the brynlee phalaenopsis for Daphnie. Thankfully, he knew most predators hunted in early day or early evening, but that didn't mean there were no sudden holes she might step into and break a leg.

Just as he decided he had gone as far as he was willing to go with her, the water thinned away into a sandbar that Brynlee stepped up onto. From here, he could now see where lanes of water ran between grass flats with edges dropping straight down three or four feet into nearly crystal-clear water. Most were inaccessible without somehow climbing down into the water and back up the steep bank of the next flat, but there might be just enough of them interconnected to allow Andrew to carefully walk Brynlee and Jasper out to see what might be lurking in the shallow salt-water pools. He could hear the distant sound of ocean breaking against stone shoals maybe a quarter mile away.

He helped Jasper down from the saddle, then dismounted Brynlee to lead her on by hand from here. The ocean breeze was cool in his hair, and the sound of serpent gulls sang overhead.

He had never been to this place before. As much as he thought he knew every nook and cranny of this place once known as the Dry Places, his home continued to astound him, both with its beauty and its ferocity. While a part of him wondered if he could build a home here with a window looking out over the ocean, he knew that these lanes of water, scoured deep into the land, existed because of how violently the ocean battered the shore during the season of Macpella, named after an angry ocean spirit the Algi still offered tribute to; probably a fay tale, but who could know for certain.

As he looked down into the clear water, small fish darted back and forth beneath his reflection. White spider gar and purple crabs he didn't know the names of also fled from his shadow. In one pool, he found a baby peconis trapped by the tide, so tiny, so deadly. For several minutes he knelt by the water's edge just marveling at it.

"Alright, boy," he said, rising and holding out the small bone beak for Jasper to have another good sniff and get to work. And to work he went.

Andrew kept a hold on a lead that Jasper didn't often wear, but here, Andrew wanted to make sure that the old boy didn't get too distracted and into a mess that Andrew might be unable to get him out of. It also kept Jasper from jumping from one flat to the next, leaving Andrew and Brynlee behind. At one point, something low and long pushed aside the grass and disappeared into the water without Andrew ever seeing what it was.

After some time, Jasper finally let out a sharp bark, with his butt high in the air and his tail wagging.

"What is it, boy?" Andrew asked, shortening the lead and kneeling next to Jasper to peer into the water, trying to glimpse what the old dog had found.

Down, beneath the completely calm surface of the water, underneath an overhanging bit of root-bound mud, hid a nearly impossible-to-see creature, its textured skin perfectly matching the dark brown-grey soil.

"That can't be right, can it?" Andrew asked Jasper. "Why is it called a land octopus if it's in the water?" Of course, Jasper didn't answer. He just stared hard at the hiding creature wagging his tail.

From that distance, Andrew couldn't tell if it was an octopus or if it had any eggs. He began slowly reaching for it, but it was too far.

"Let me know if anything sneaks up on us, would you, girl?" he told Brynlee as he laid on his stomach and began stretching again toward the hiding creature, but before he could get within two feet of it, it fled its hiding spot with a push of its eight legs and released a burst of an iridescent, color changing cloud behind it, obscuring its escape. Andrew thought it was actually quite cute that it was trying so hard to escape, since the decapod only had one way to swim: directly down the water lane. Fortunately for both Andrew and Brynlee, there was enough land bridge along this particular waterway for him to carefully follow the swimming creature through the once-again clear water, trying to keep a distant eye on where it might go but not wanting to scare it again in case it might successfully vanish out of sight. But before it got too far, a Shoal Shark shot out from under another mud bank and swallowed up the fruit-sized octopus in a few violent bites, three still-curling legs dropping to the sandy bottom.

Andrew winced and turned away, sorry to have scared the small creature right into the mouth of a waiting predator.

He slapped his leg in frustration.

The sun was getting high, and the day was slowly warming, so he draped his long coat over Brynlee and kept searching.

This place where the ocean met land was so full of life. If he let his eyes gently relax, the way Lithuel had taught him to do when hunting to see movement through trees, he could see how much life there really was. From clouds of elim flies, nearly invisible for their tiny size, to some large flying lizard he could see on the mirror-like horizon, bobbing on the distant chop, periodically disappearing below the water for some aquatic breakfast. He wasn't a quarter mile from the ocean any longer. They must have been slowly walking for nearly an hour.

Now, on the outer edges of giving up, Jasper let out another sharp bark, this time tilting his head this way and that, and scratching at some grass.

Andrew clicked his tongue and gave the lead a tug for Jasper to back down as he carefully peaked through a patch of particularly thick grass to find a much larger version of the octopus he had found hiding in the estuary. The creature was nearly the size of Jasper and partially covered in the sandy soil.

He pulled Jasper back, not wanting either of them to get hurt, and pushed on Jasper's backside for him to sit. Then he slowly and carefully looked again at the mound of creature.

It wasn't moving.

Was it dead? It probably should have sensed either him or the dog, but it just lay there. Did it have eggs? If it did, where were they? He wasn't after the octopus itself.

He broke off a long piece of grass and gently touched the edge of one of its tightly curled legs. It didn't move.

He stepped closer to it, unsure of how it might be able to defend itself.

He poked the leg a bit harder.

This time, it moved, but only just.

Leaning towards it, he blew on it the way he often did with bugs to see if they were still alive, and when he did, the creature's skin slightly tensed, and its color shifted, but only barely.

It was alive. It knew he was there, and it wasn't fighting back. Not yet.

He studied it for a minute or two, then leaned closer and gently touched its leg with the back of his hand.

It flexed away from him but did not pull away.

If he had to guess, Andrew thought it looked like it was dying. Could that be?

He stood and looked around. They were close to water but not in it. *Insects tend to lay their eggs somewhere near food or safety and leave. Fish often keep their eggs close by, even carrying them on their body if necessary,* he thought, considering the possibilities.

He found nothing in the shallow waters that looked like eggs nor anything on this small finger of sandy soil.

Jasper rested nearby Brynlee in some grass that Bryn had stamped flat.

Sea turtles live in the ocean but come to land to lay eggs.

Several times, Andrew had seen them bury the eggs in the sand by moonlight and leave them behind. *Perhaps...*

Andrew found a flat piece of driftwood about the size of his hand, knelt a few feet from the octopus, and began digging. Jasper just tilted his head and watched the foolish human.

Soon, Andrew found what he was looking for. The octopus had buried a clutch of semi-moist eggs, each about the size of his thumb, deep enough to draw ocean water into the nest but not completely drown them, and had then buried itself on top of the nest. Why? He wasn't sure. Perhaps it planned on protecting them for as long as it could. Perhaps something was prematurely shortening its life, and under most circumstances, it would have been ready to violently protect its clutch. Or perhaps, the large body of the parent would end up as food for the hatching young. What he did know was that the large creature did nothing more than slightly shift color once in a while at the presence of his digging.

Once he had access to the nest, he could begin to see that there must have been several hundred eggs buried there in the sand, but he had no way to carry that many; he didn't need that many; he didn't *want* that many. There was no reason for him to take every egg. Perhaps egg hunters often did, greatly decreasing the survivability of the species, which probably contributed to their scarcity and delicacy, but he wasn't here to make a few crowns. He was here to help his friend and hoped a small jar's worth would suffice.

Pulling the stopper on the vessel Lithuel had given him, he leaned down to the water's edge and slightly filled the jar with salt water. Then he, careful not to break them, plucked ten leathery, pliable eggs from the nest and nestled them into the jar. Each was oblong and matched the dark honey color of the parent.

"Pay no attention to me," he told the parent, who he was pretty sure was watching him with a single, nearly closed eye but who no longer had the strength to do anything about the theft. "I won't take many. You've done well to protect them," he said.

Then, having filled the jar, he pushed the sandy soil back into place, hoisted Jasper up onto the saddle, and mounted Brynlee. Before leaving, he turned once more to the large creature.

"Thank you for your gift."

Then he slowly led Brynlee back to solid ground.

CHAPTER 31

Back home, Andrew touched base with Lithuel, letting him know about the effectiveness of Jasper's sharp nose and showing him the eggs in the jar before returning to Nevarii, hoping to make it by evening. He was acutely aware of how fragile the eggs were and did not want them to spoil or break.

He made Nevarii in good time and approached the side gate just like the groundskeeper had told him. A small, black, cast-iron bell hung from the gate by a thin chain.

Andrew pulled the chain but heard no ringing. He tugged it again and again, but nothing.

"Alright, alright, I'm comin'," he heard holler from the house.

A short, portly, Nimic woman opened the gate, wiping her hands on her apron. "You only need ring it once!" She snapped at him. "Can I help you?"

He held up the jar. "Is Nebi available? I've brought her something."

The woman's look changed from annoyance to curiosity. "I heard you were coming and might have something for me, but the old codger wouldn't tell what. And what a handsome lad," she said with a smile. She took the jar from him, carefully removed the lid, and tipped the portly little pot towards her. Then she smiled. "Pulmari! You must be jokin'."

She plucked one of the eggs out and sucked it into her mouth with a slurp. Her eyes grew large. "Oy! And they're fresh!" she sighed—eyes closed. She stopped the jar shut and grabbed Andrew by the arm. "You've made a friend of this house, that's for sure! Have you eaten?"

"Well, no."

"Come, come. Stable your horse 'round the side there, and let me feed you. You look like you barely eat."

Andrew saw the gardener a few dozen cubits away, on his knees, planting something around the base of one of the trees. He glanced up at Andrew, then went back to work like he had no idea who Andrew was, peacefully whistling a tune to himself.

Two distant guards watched the interaction, but when Nebi waved at them, they returned to the front gate. As far as he could tell, now that he was past the outer perimeter, Andrew could go anywhere on the grounds he wanted without much trouble.

The stables where Andrew put up Brynlee smelled better than most homes he had been in, with large bales of hay and oats for her to eat. Then he hugged her neck, assuring her he'd be back to check on her and went to the side door of the main house Nebi had disappeared into.

At first, Andrew entered the bustling kitchen cautiously until he realized that no one but Nebi paid him any attention, and within minutes, she had set out a spread of food before him on the servants' dining table. Sliced bread with fruit preserves. A pile of thinly sliced roast meat. Cheeses. Boiled eggs. A full pot of hot tea. Fresh fruit!

He lifted a large purple citrus he had not seen before, smelled it—the rich, sharp, sweet smell immediately making his mouth water—and peeled back the rind to find layers of even darker, juicy flesh underneath.

Nebi sat two more dishes before him, one with golden puffed pastries and another with cooling porridge.

"You really don't have to," he said, purple juice dripping down his lip.

She smiled. "Oy, this? This was breakfast for the house. It's about to be tossed out."

Tossed out!? Who would throw all this out? he wondered, his eyes large at the thought.

He and Lithuel could eat like kings for a week on what sat right before him. He didn't know where to start, but start he did. Andrew piled an empty plate with two more pieces of the purple fruit, some scoops of a sliced fresh fruit cocktail, two cooked sausages, a large scoop of porridge, one of the puffed pastries that he took two more of as soon as he realized they were filled with meats and cheeses, and he didn't even make it on to the sliced bread and charcuterie before his stomach demanded that he stop or burst.

"I hear you're lookin' for someone. How can I help?" Nebi asked, only pouring herself half a cuppa and sitting across the tattered and worn table from him.

Andrew nodded. "A tinker. Woman tinker. Your..."

Nebi's eyebrows raised.

"*Someone*...told me that she might be by these parts couple times a year."

Nebi nodded her head. "Short. Beautiful. That coachman of hers," she said. "Ay, I know who you're

211

speaking of. Name's Hemtee. Come with me." She rose from her seat.

Not wanting to seem ungrateful but still bewildered by the thought of it all going in the rubbish bin, he slid another pastry and two pieces of fruit into his pocket, smiling at Nebi, seeking her permission, who smiled back and motioned him to go on then. He followed her to a locked pantry down the hall from the kitchen.

"If you do find her, she may not speak to you. She's an upity one, that one. Won't lift a finger to fix a cracked pot. Mostly trades in expensive spices and bobbles. But, some of her spices, I can't get anywhere else," Nebi said, removing a ring of keys from underneath her apron and unlocking the double doors. Inside were rows of narrow shelves filled with various unique items, one of which was a bell jar protecting what looked like a small tree with long, needle-thin branches and tiny leaves that slowly opened in the light. What looked like tiny blue pearls hung beneath two of the branches.

Nebi gently plucked one with a pair of tweezers that sat on the shelf next to the tree and returned the plant to the bell jar. She then cupped the tiny berry in her palm and gently blew onto it. As she did, it began to glow a blue light and opened in her hand. A tiny bug unrolled itself from the now-open husk of the berry and shook off its sleep. It then stretched forth wings so tiny Andrew could barely see them, rose from her palm, and in a moment, vanished down the hall, around the corner, and out through the keyhole in the front door, a trail of mist-blue vapor vanishing behind it.

"How long?" Andrew asked.

Nebi shrugged. "Never know. She could be 'cross town or dead in a ditch somewhere. But she's never taken more than three days," Nebi replied, closing the pantry doors and re-locking them.

Three days, Andrew thought to himself, not wanting to be in such an unfriendly town for that long.

She saw his hesitation. "Have you a room at the tavern yet?"

Andrew shook his head.

She nodded decisively. "There's a boarding room above the stables where you'll stay until she arrives."

"Oh, I couldn't," Andrew said but implied he wanted to with the tone of his voice.

"Enough. It's already decided. Besides, I need to put some meat on those handsome cheeks o' yours. Round 'em out a bit."

Andrew didn't mind the sound of that at all.

As NIGHT DREW NEAR, the lights of the main house flickered to life, and Andrew settled into the room above the stables. It was nicer than his house or any tavern he had ever stayed in, with its furniture covered in lacquer, cotton sheets, and end tables dressed in lace. *If this was for passers-by, what's the main house like?* he wondered.

He could see partially into the main house's dining room through a side window where a well-dressed butler set out plates of cooked meats, pasta, rice, bread, soup, and wine on a large table lit with candlesticks. Everything Nebi had presented looked like afternoon tea compared to this spread.

Across the city center and beyond the gates, three bells rang out from the temple's high tower as a lamplighter made his rounds around the property, lighting gas lights and blanketing the grounds in a lovely, warm glow. Soon after, there was movement in the courtyard, and Andrew peaked out his loft window to see Nebi smiling and welcoming someone he couldn't see because his view was blocked by most of the barn. Then a four-horse carriage made of glossy red and honey-colored wood pulled into the lamplight near the kitchen entrance, and a woman, barely half Nebi's height, climbed down off the wagon where she had been sitting next to some enormous mass of a coachman who caused the cart to noticeably list to his side.

It was a Bantam woman. She had dreadlocks dotted with metal trinkets. Copper wire held her hair up and back, except for the few strands that hung low across her eyes. A long leather coat with a high popped collar hid most of her tiny figure save for some metal items that reflected the lamplight from the backs of her gloves and the buckles of her boots. Her coachman did not move. He did not turn his head to watch her warmly greet Nebi and follow her into the house, nor did he even rise to tend the horses. He sat entirely unmoving, like a large bolder draped in drab, unassuming, coarse-brown fabric.

The cart glistened beautifully in the lamplight. Andrew had not seen wood like it before encountering the Night Watchmen, but it was unmistakably the same pattern of honey grain in the fire-red wood that held the Watchman's blade, and looking at it made his top lip sting.

The back of the cart was draped in a fabric so black it was difficult to see, save for the red wood that stood out along its edges like a frame of unmoving fire holding total darkness.

And if Andrew still doubted whether she had dealings with the Shimar Etsell, those doubts were dashed away when he realized that three of her four horses were green.

Most might not notice for the saddle blankets and some paint tinging their hair dappled grey, but Andrew recognized them. The shape of their legs. The spots behind their knees where the paint had faded. Their incredible size. The prehensile tail carefully pulled up and tied underneath the blankets that he could see from his angle, knowing what to look for.

But how? he wondered. Her cart. Her horses. Was she trading with the Shimar Etsell somehow? If so, she *must* know what they might want. Perhaps she even knew of the chest and how to open it. He had to talk to her.

Andrew watched carefully until the side door to the house finally opened, and the Bantam woman came out with an empty wooden crate in her hands, followed by two surprisingly muscular Nimic servant boys. She set the crate on the ground near the back of the cart, threw back a corner of the black cover, and climbed up. Then she motioned to the boys and filled their crates with something Andrew couldn't see in the dark. Once they were full, she waved them back into the house and followed them inside.

For the next hour or so, there was no sign of her, and never once, even for a moment, did the coachman move at all. He was so still Andrew forgot he was even there until the Bantam woman exited the governor's house with a half-full crate, which she quickly set in the back of her cart and motioned one of the servant boys to open the gate for her. Only after her coach slowly backed up and pulled forward to leave the grounds did Andrew see her coachman flick the reigns to guide the horses—the slightest sliver of a chin and lower lip jutting out from the hood just enough for Andrew to see its light grey stone edges.

As the cart was leaving, Nebi came out of the house to wave the Bantam woman off, then looked up at Andrew, who was peeking out from behind the dark curtains, shooting him a look like "What the hells are you waiting for?"

At that, Andrew grabbed his bag and his coat, collected Brynlee, thanked Nebi, who retrieved a small bundle of food wrapped in cloth from where it was hiding under her apron, handed it to him, and made him promise to return the next time he was in that part of the world. He warmly agreed, told her to thank *that certain someone*, and began following the Bantam tinker into the night.

CHAPTER 32

Andrew kept his distance, not wanting to startle the tinker or arouse suspicion. He planned on waiting until she stopped for the night. He would then approach and ask if he could share her fire. He wasn't sure what reason he would give for approaching her along the road instead of in a town as is common for tinkers, but he would have to work that out when necessary.

Over hill and valley, he followed her cart, which never sped up nor slowed.

Sometimes, he would lose sight of it for a few minutes around a bend or just past a clearing, but her cart moved steadily enough that he always found it again.

And the night wore on. As the faint crescent moon climbed high in the sky, the Bantam tinker's cart dipped behind a hill, but as soon as Brynlee crested the hill, Andrew could see her cart again, still slowly moving when suddenly, the cold, sharp metal of a blade pressed against his throat.

"Do not turn. Do not take your hand from the reins," a female voice whispered.

How did she get on my horse? Andrew thought for a fleeting moment and swallowed.

"If you so much as change the speed of this crusty old beast, I will end you in a moment."

Andrew tried to nod but couldn't. The blade was pressed too tightly against his throat.

"What do you want, and why have you been following me?" she asked.

"You knew my father," he was barely able to say.

"Who is your father?"

"Another tinker, and I a tinker myself."

There was silence. Then she asked:

"Where's your cart?"

"I'll tell you whatever you want to know, just..."

The blade pressed harder as a warm bead of blood crawled down his neck.

"I've traveled a great distance to find you. My mare is not as young as she used to be. I left it at home to keep her from growing weary on the road," which was only partially true. "I'm no threat. Please," he pleaded.

Silence for another moment, then a question: "Tell me, *tinker*, what is the one tool a tinker can not live without?"

"His wits."

"What is heavier, copper or iron?"

A tricky question. He had to think for a moment. "Copper?"

"Is that a question?" she spat.

"Copper! It's copper."

"And how many pure gold sovereigns can you lift with a magnet the size of your thumb?"

This was definitely a trick question. "None. Gold is not magnetic."

She lowered her blade, but as soon as she did, he felt its point press into his side just below his right elbow.

"Pull over," she said, as he realized her cart had pulled off the road and come to a stop along the edge of some trees. He did as she asked.

"You get down first," she told him, and he listened, slowly sliding off of Brynlee opposite her knife. Even if he had wanted to run, there was no use. As easily as she had mounted Brynlee without him—or possibly Brynlee—knowing, she quickly dismounted and re-approached Andrew with the knife he could now see: a narrow dirk with a black blade twice the length of his hand.

That's when the coachman rose from his seat and approached Andrew, who could now see his stone face and empty eye sockets with their floating orbs of blue light. The coachman was twice as tall as Andrew and several times his width. No, neither by force nor fleet footedness was Andrew getting out of this without a clear and honest explanation. So, he leaned into the one tool no tinker could do without.

"My father is Lithuel."

She didn't seem to recognize the name.

"He met you a few years ago in Nevarii and told me about your cart."

"My cart?"

"I know where you got that cart, and I need to ask you about them."

She slowly lowered her blade but did not yet put it away.

Then he remembered. "I have something for you!" he said, holding up a finger.

She lifted the blade again.

He held out his hands to calm her. "It's there, in my saddle bag. The small pouch."

Not taking her eyes off him, she stepped backward towards Brynlee and opened the saddle bag. Inside, she found the small pouch of honey candy and opened it. She wasn't sure what it was until she smelled it, then a smile of remembrance slowly grew across her face, and she ate one.

"He said you might remember that."

She sheathed her dagger.

Andrew sighed, rubbed the back of his neck, and touched where she had drawn blood.

She nodded to her coachman, who turned to fetch some things from her cart and began building a fire.

"Why do you want to know about my cart?" she asked, tossing the small bag back to Andrew.

For the next fifteen or twenty minutes, Andrew told her about Lorna, the chest, his encounter with the Shimar Etsell, and how he had run out of options until his father remembered her, her cart, and her coachman.

"I try to keep as low-key as I can, but he's not easy to miss," she said, looking at the towering being standing on the outer edge of the firelight, near the cart, staring like a stone statue—completely unmoving—at Andrew.

"What is he?" Andrew asked, scooping up a spoonful of beef stew that had just finished cooking over the raging campfire.

"I don't know. He's completely harmless unless someone tries to bother me. Then you would be surprised how quickly he can move," she said.

Andrew's eyes grew as he wondered what that meant.

"Do you trade with them?"

She looked up from her food. "Who?"

"The Night Watchmen?"

"I don't make a habit of discussing my business with

anyone, but no." She was quiet for a moment, then added: "I wish I did."

"Then where did you get your cart and your horses?"

She glared at him, not wanting to divulge where she sourced her unique wares.

Andrew could feel that he was pushing and looked away.

As she watched the fire flicker, she considered the strange situation and the chest, wondering what a chest like that might be worth. Then she slowly looked up at him with a sly grin. "Give me some more of that candy."

Andrew smiled, pulling the small pouch out of his pocket. "There's not a lot left," he said with a shrug, playing with her just a little.

She rolled her eyes.

"What about him? Does he want a piece?" Andrew asked, nodding to the coachman.

The stone statue moved for the first time since they had settled in for supper and slowly turned his head towards the small pouch.

Andrew smiled. What was this figure? A machine of some sort? An enchanted statue? Beyond the faintly flickering blue orbs in his eyes, one would assume he was ornamental and nothing more.

Hemtee smiled and grunted. "Go on then," she told her coachman with a wave of her hand.

The stone figure knelt towards Andrew and held out this massive paw of a hand nearly as big as Andrew's face. Now, Andrew wished he had brought more because only six pieces remained.

Andrew counted out three and put them in the stone being's palm, who rose and let them roll into his mouth, letting out a contented grunt—not unlike a purr; the first sound Andrew had heard him ever make.

"I made the mistake of giving him a piece once, like forever ago, and now he's hooked on the darn things," Hemtee said, shaking her head.

"There's three left," Andrew told her, tossing the bag across the fire to her.

She smiled at the memories the sweet smell brought back as she held the bag to her nose.

"My father smiled just like that when he spoke of you."

She held one of the pieces out to the firelight, marveling at the translucent yellow. Then she glanced up at him. "Really? And what did he tell you, exactly?"

"Not much. He said men keep some things to themself. Only, I've never known him to keep anything from me."

She smirked. "How is he?" She slowly ate one of the pieces.

"Tired. Grey. His leg hurts. He tore up his knee in an accident a few years ago, but good."

She nodded. "When I knew him, he was beautiful. Like you."

Andrew smiled. "It sounds like it was a good dinner."

She demurred. "He was being a gentleman. It was more than dinner."

Andrew didn't ask for more details. He just sat and considered what Lithuel's life must have been like before finding a small child in the back of his cart and pivoting his entire existence to help that child survive in an unrelenting world.

"I remember his hands...like oiled leather," she said, slowly savoring the last piece of honey. "And his gentleness. And..." she swallowed and touched her throat. Then she glanced at Andrew, who was watching her. "Well...it was a good night."

Andrew could see what his father had seen in her. She was beautiful, especially the way she grinned a scant, playful grin looking at the candy. It reminded him of Feyloren and made him miss her. Then he rubbed his arms for the cooling night creeping through his clothes, and he held his hands out towards the fire to warm them.

Just then, it began gently snowing.

CHAPTER 33

Even though Hemtee didn't tell anyone where she sourced her wares, she figured it probably wouldn't hurt to answer Andrew's questions since she had already returned to the places in her story several times, hoping to find what she had found before—but never with any luck. The chest, however, was interesting. Hemtee knew from her dealings with the Shimar Etsell that anything from them was worth a stack of sovereigns taller than she was, taller than this strange boy, taller than even Bip, her coachman. Maybe if she told this silly boy what he wanted to know, he might lead her to this Lorna. And that *had* to be worth something.

"Maybe ten seasons ago, I tried finding a shorter route to Kleek Ooba when I passed into the Ki Lo Kan Forest," Hemtee began. "As I stopped to water my steed, a woman approached me next to the river, which was alarming since we were hours from anything, but she didn't seem threatening, and she had nothing with her, no horse or bag."

Andrew listened closely as the firelight danced in Hemtee's eyes, and Bip stood like an unmoving sentinel on the outer edge of the camp near the horses, which he had untied to roam freely for the night, two of which had climbed a large tree nearby and were nibbling the high leaves.

"What I remember most about her were her eyes. They were an odd shape and green, with two small pupils. All of her was green. Even her nearly black hair had a green shine to it, and her clothing looked like fabric made from woven moss or something.

"She asked if she could see a stone in my cart. I didn't know what she was going on about, but she was quite adamant that there was a stone in my cart she was very interested in. So, I pulled back my covers and poked around until I found a small basket of white stones I had forgotten about that I had collected a few weeks earlier when I had traveled to the Giant's Causeway. I hadn't seen any like them and was curious if they could be carved down into ornaments or trinkets."

"Something you could sell," Andrew said.

Hemtee gestured in agreement with her hand. "She poured out the basket and began picking through the stones until she came to a large one, which she looked at closely and then held up to me. "Protect this one," she said, setting it aside, then kept digging and sorting until she found another, different in color than the others. It had this Fuchsia-colored moss on it like dust in the tiny cracks.

"She asked if she could have it. Well, I'm not in the business of charity, so I told her I'd sell it to her, but she had no money. Even the idea of money seemed strange to her. I suggested a trade, but she didn't have much with her, and what she offered me didn't seem of any value, just her cloak, so I declined. I told her I'd be back through the area in about a week, and maybe we could meet again, but she didn't look thrilled with that idea.

"She asked where I had found it, but by now, it was clearly worth something to her, so I said I didn't remember.

"I was starting to think that she might not give it back, but she did. Then she just walked off into the trees.

"That night, I camped near the top of the falls. And when I woke the following day, I found the horses and the cart there waiting for me, but the stone with the moss was gone. I had even hidden it underneath my pillow, but somehow... Well, it must have been important to her because in the cart was a pair of quality shoes, a pair of gloves, a walking cane made of the same wood as the cart, a small wooden hand-carved figurine, and a set of the most beautiful woodworking tools I've ever seen, most of which I've sold, save for the cart and the horses. As I was packing to leave, having moved everything from my old cart to the new one, I found my satchel was heavy. When I opened it, I found the large white stone she had told me to protect, wrapped in a thick blanket.

"A couple of weeks later, it hatched," she said, gesturing to Bip.

Andrew's eyes were big. "He hatched...out of a rock?"

"Or maybe an egg that looked like a rock. Who knows, but yeah. I didn't know what the hells to do with a stone baby, but he didn't really move or make any sound. He barely eats! So, I just left him in the back of the cart most of the time. Sometimes, I'd even forget he was back there, just sitting like a lump on a log, until the first time I ran into trouble.

"He was barely my height by then, but the drunken fool's knife didn't affect him. He nearly crushed the guy's skull until I told him to stop. And that's when I knew he could be useful. So, I kept him around. I just had no idea he would get that big," she said, gesturing to Bip again. "Hells, I'm not even sure he's done growing. He moves so slow. If it weren't for those damned eyes, I wouldn't know he was alive, but maybe that's part of why we get along. I'm used to the quiet and the solitude, and that's what he gives me, even though he's always here."

Andrew was impressed by the story and how much affection he could see she had for Bip, though he could also see she was guarded about it.

"I've returned to both the causeway and the forest several times, trying to find her again, trying to find more stones like him or the one she took from me, but never any luck."

Andrew's eyes were growing heavy, and he welcomed the warmth of the fire and the company. It was now at least the third watch of the evening.

"May I camp here with you tonight?" he asked. It had been a long day, having traveled from home to collect the eggs, on to Nevarii, and now here with Hemtee by the side of the highway.

She nodded, uncapped a water skin, took a drink, then offered it to Andrew. He waved it away for his own skin, then unrolled a blanket that had been tied behind Brynlee's saddle and curled up next to the fire.

The last thing he remembered before dozing off was Bip's blue eyes glowing out from the darkness on the edges of the trees.

WHEN ANDREW AWOKE the next morning, the fire was out, and Hemtee was gone, but she *had* left him a small rolled note tied to the horn of Brynlee's saddle, which read:

The Giant's Causeway is two-day's ride northeast of Eetoomba, along the coast. There's nothing there. Trust me. Of course, you won't, so be careful.

Say hello to your father for me. – H

Andrew slid the note into his saddle bag. Eetoomba was at least a day's hard ride north of the Eastern Shallows, where he had found the land octopus eggs, probably a good half-day's ride from where he was now, which meant he and Brynlee had a long way to go.

CHAPTER 34

Etoomba was once a bustling trade port turned into a mighty naval fort during the Granarleen War, with beautifully carved arches, marble columns, and tall statues of decorated soldiers, all of which now lay in ruins beneath the surface of the azure blue water in the bay.

Without his cart, Andrew had little to trade and no tools to fix any wares or make any coin, so he stocked up on some supplies and continued on.

Off the coast, he watched Algi fishing boats bob on the water. Some were barely large enough for three hands, while others were massive ocean-dwelling vessels with gold and green banners flowing in the wind to mark who owned them. The Algi were an aquatic race of jellyfish-like beings that absorbed sunlight through their translucent skin during the day and dove deep into their sunken cities at night. This made them ideal pirates, fishermen, and resort owners, if you could believe that. They often enjoyed sunning themselves in the afternoon on warm beach sands.

On the darkest nights, the faint light of their cities could be seen glowing from the ocean's depth.

Andrew set up camp and kept Brynlee close as the low thrum of crickets welcomed another evening. He was grateful for the warming rod, which never failed to provide a full and brilliant fire and always made him think of Lorna and his friends now so far away. When the clouds broke, he looked up at the stars, thinking of Feyloren, still wondering if her thoughts were ever for him. Perhaps he could bring her a gift or something from his travels for the next time he saw her. Then, as he poked at the campfire, he saw, through the firelight, a distant bush that he quickly recognized. It was a rare leaf he could smoke that gave off a sweet smell with a sharp ginger-like pinch. He couldn't smoke the wet leaves on the plant, so he carefully foraged for a handful of dry leaves that had not yet fallen to the ground where they would have been spoilt by moisture, dirt, or bugs. Having found a handful, he laid them in his leather smoking pouch and crunched them into the little smoking herb he had left.

Then he packed some wet leaves into his saddle bag for later and sat next to the fire. He tapped the bowl of his long, narrow pipe on a piece of wood, blew into it, and ran the corner of his shirt along the inside to clear the bowl of any old leaf, then filled it halfway—okay, two-thirds way—full. He carefully plucked a thin glowing twig from the fire, dipped its red tip into his bowl with one hand, and cupped the top of the bowl with the other. In a few draws, the leaf was smoldering.

The smoke was welcome, and the experience of the herb multi-faceted. Packing his bowl was like a dance that drew him closer to Lithuel, who had hand-carved the pipe for him when he was only fourteen. It was tactile: the feel of the leaf in his fingers and the texture of the wood pipe—

rough on the bowl and smooth on the stem. It was olfactory: the smell of the semi-damp smoking leaf; the first taste of smoke filling his mouth and pinching his tongue. It was audible: the crackle of the glowing ember against the leaf; the hollow sound of the draw of smoke through the stem. It was emotional: the triggered memories of home; the softening edges of his mind as its chemical components kicked in. This particular herb made his entire campsite smell like leather and spice. He was happy.

As he dozed off, he dreamt of home and hot meals and awoke the next morning sore in the saddle but ready to continue on.

Brynlee was an ever-welcome traveling companion, often listening to Andrew ramble for hours about the Shimar Etsell or Daphnie. Might he set up a shop in Jatoba one day? If he did, would Feyloren have him for longer than a meal and a night? What sort of life was there for a tinker who didn't travel? He had asked himself these questions before and still had no answer. Perhaps he was meant for something more than the tinker's life, but if so, what? And what of family? How could someone who had never really had a family know how to raise one of his own?

He had never been this far from home and was astounded by the incredible beauty of his country. In some places, along the coast where he would stop to lunch and give Brynlee a rest—the wild coastal grasses blowing in the ocean breeze—he would look out over the distant water, sure he could see for hundreds of miles.

On the night of the second day, just as Andrew was falling asleep under a large hornbeam growing on the peak of a hill, he heard a succession of short grunts followed by a long hollow bugle echo out across the valley below. He rose and looked to see a vintnew moving slowly across an open field. Standing at a height of what must have been thirty feet, the mythic elk-like creature was magnificent, with glowing fur, eight legs, six eyes, and a rack of antlers as wide as the governor's stables. It gave out a loud bugle again, then pulled nearly all the leaves off a nearby tree in a single mouthful. It cast a warm glow over the entire valley like the light of the setting sun. Its presence made Andrew feel safe. He had heard stories of how vintnew drove predators away from their lands, even using their massive and powerful antlers to fend off dragons, but he had never known anyone to have actually seen one. Until tonight, they had existed for him more in myth than reality, but having seen this extraordinary bull with his own eyes, he knew the stories must be true—all of them.

How many other creatures of myth were real? Were there really creatures that sounded like crying children in the night that would feast on unsuspecting travelers through the forest? And what about Grace Givers?

He began to sense that he was approaching a place of powerful intuition.

The morning of the third day was cold, and a low-lying fog blanketed the crest of the hill, forcing Andrew and Brynlee down into the valley where he had seen the great elk the night before. The landscape was also changing. The lush green coastal grasses and scattered trees he had been riding through the day before had given way to short, rough scrub and fiery-red bushes with no leaves scattered across rocky cliffs, leaving little for Brynlee to eat. There were also miles of knee-high fences made of thin stacked stones, many of which were now broken down and overgrown.

The ruins of an old lighthouse stood on an island off the coast, perhaps a distant outpost for naval soldiers at one time. The crow's nest that would have held the large signal fire was now crumbling into the ocean below.

Andrew could imagine why these shores were known as the Giant's Causeway, with their tall grey columns of stone growing out of the ocean's crashing waves like frozen beings from another age. Ocean birds and small pterodactyls barely the size of housecats dipped and glided on the strong, up currents and nested along the steep stone faces. As he watched them, Brynlee suddenly stopped.

A large, flat crater of loose white stone lay before them down a steep embankment. Only, they were not just stones, but pieces of hands and faces, arms and feet—faces like the stone visage of Hemtee's coachman, Bip, scattered for hundreds of cubits; however, many were easily twice his size.

Andrew climbed down off of Brynlee and approached the edge of the embankment. It was too steep for Brynlee to descend safely—nothing but loose rock all the way down—but he wasn't sure he wanted to descend anyway. To him, this looked like a grave site. Except, why were the scattered faces with their hollow eyes left unburied? He had no idea. But now he really knew why this place was known as the Giant's Causeway. Andrew looked around. Where had they come from? He had passed no village or dwelling for at least a day. Where would beings of such size have lived? Why were they here? It felt so sudden and out of place. He saw no sign of any life save for ocean birds and a rock dodger now and again. Perhaps he was getting closer to what he had come to find. But how would he find it? What did it look like? A small stone with some pink moss? This was absurd. What possibly made him think he could find some small stone scattered in this vast and barren landscape? Perhaps something was drawing him from deep within himself. Perhaps something powerful was drawing him from the outside? He had tried to leave it all alone more than once, but the further he put his mind from it by day, the closer it drew to him in his dreams until he would wake in the morning, unsure of where he was. No matter how hard he tried, he could not run from whatever was leading him on.

Andrew rubbed the back of his neck. Was he to wander the cliffs and crags until his supplies ran out? Thanks to the oatcakes, that might not be for a few days at least, assuming he could find fresh water.

He was tired of riding, so he walked on for a while, letting Brynlee follow loosely behind him.

The sun was bright, and the day was finally warming just enough. He had developed a blister at the back of his ankle that was now bleeding, and he was hungry for more than oatcakes, apples, and a dry hunk of cheese he had purchased in Eetoomba.

Then, as he crested another rise, he saw a ramshackle hut of broad, flat stones and a grass-covered roof built into the side of the hill in the shape of a squat beehive. Beyond it, a hundred cubits or so, sat a small figure in a dark, fading grey cloak, hunched forward on a rocky outcropping. Puffy white sheep grazed on scrub grasses around the hillside below him.

"Hello there!" Andrew called, but the wind must have carried away his voice because the figure did not turn.

Andrew carefully led Brylee down the hillside, past the beehive hut that looked carefully kept though spartan, and hollered again. "Hello!"

Only when Andrew was close enough to reach out and touch him did the old shepherd turn to Andrew. He was Bantam, with yellowing skin, possibly from disease. A long white beard hung out over his robe—wild and unkempt—down past his knees and piled on the ground in front of his stone perch. He was missing an eye and had an open and weeping sore on his cheek, which made Andrew step back when he saw it. Pieces of a broken shepherd's crook lay beside him in the overgrown grass.

"What do you want?" the Bantam shepherd spat.

"I don't mean to trouble you, sir..."

"Trouble me? It's too late for that. Can't you see I'm busy and can't be bothered?"

Andrew looked around. Everything was calm and quiet, the sheep grazing peacefully.

"I won't keep you. I've traveled quite a distance looking for a stone..."

"A stone, you say?" the old man interrupted. "If it's stones you're after, take your fill and leave. The hills are covered in 'em." And he turned away.

"I'm looking for particular stones covered in a pink moss or lichen. Have you seen anything like that?"

The man turned back to him. "These lands are bare. Does it look like any sort of purple moss might grow here?"

"Pink," Andrew corrected.

"Be gone! You're upsetting my sheep," the shepherd hollered, then took up a handful of rocks and threw them at Andrew and Brynlee, one hitting Brynlee in the side and startling her.

"Hey! You don't need..."

The shepherd threw another handful, pelting and stinging Andrew's arm and shoulder where they struck. The shepherd might have been old, but it was clear his strength had not left him. Before the shepherd could launch another volley, Andrew turned and led Brynlee away.

As they passed a small pile of kindling near the side of

the hut, Andrew tugged Brynlee to stop. He looked again towards the shepherd, considering the angry old man and his broken staff. Then Andrew sighed and climbed down off of Brynlee.

He carefully selected three strong, flat pieces of wood, each twice the length of his hand, removed a long strip of leather from his saddle bag he used to tie it shut, and returned to the shepherd, motioning Brynlee to stay where she was, out of stone's throw.

His movement made no sound over the wind.

Andrew carefully lifted the sections of broken crook and used the leather cord and three pieces of wood he had collected to bind and repair the old staff. Then, he carefully laid it against the rock and turned to leave.

The shepherd slowly lifted the staff and ran his thumb over the repair. "What have you done?"

Andrew turned back.

"Why have you done this?" the old shepherd asked.

"I was taught to do good whenever it is in my power."

The shepherd slowly looked up at Andrew. "But I was rude to you, even cruel," he said, his voice beginning to change.

"It's okay," Andrew replied.

The shepherd considered again the repair. "Many have come before you. Threatening. Bribing. Looking for the secrets hiding in these hills," his voice growing clear and strong as the wind surrounding them fell utterly still. "But you were willing to help an old man who was cruel to you. And you honestly expected no reward, did you?" he asked, surprise coloring his voice.

"I said it's fine. I'm sorry to have bothered you."

The shepherd stood, and as he did, his stature grew and grew, his old robes falling away and his appearance changing from an old diseased Bantam shepherd to that of a towering being of almost pure light—his shepherd's crook now a long and powerful sword of crystal fire. He had three arms, two sets of powerful wings, and armor covering his entire body. His face was featureless except for six eyes that looked unblinking at Andrew. The sheep also vanished away in a haze, leaving behind terrible warhorses stationed with armored riders across the hillside. This powerful and terrible army's brightness and sudden appearance startled Andrew, causing him to fall back and cut his hands on the rocks—blood pouring out. When this Lord of Terrible Aspect spoke again, the ground trembled.

"Do not fear Andrew, son of Lithuel. You have found favor because you have acted with grace, so a grace you will receive." Then he opened the hand not clinging tightly to his sword and the old shack vanished away, revealing the mouth of a stone cave. When this terrible being spoke again, Andrew felt the voice deep in his chest igniting like revelation in his mind and burning like poison in his bones. "You may enter, but be wise, Andrew, son of Lithuel. Do not hunger for more than you can eat. Do not reach for more than you can carry. Do not lust for more than is yours. Or you *will* be consumed."

Andrew rose and looked at his hands. The gashes were gone. Only the pain of the cuts remained.

Then he looked to the entrance that had appeared in the hillside—a faint green light spilling forth, and just before entering, he turned back to the Lord of Terrible Aspect. But he was gone. In his place sat a lowly shepherd with a mended staff, calmly watching his sheep.

CHAPTER 35

Andrew followed a gently sloping path as the green light grew brighter. He could hear the sound of dripping water. The path opened into a large cavern of pools reflecting the light of an oddly shaped tree. It had a bulbous trunk and low branches that reached out over the pools, somehow dripping water into them. White ghost-like fish, about the size of Andrew's finger, swam towards him to see the stranger approaching, then darted away.

A delicate Human girl of nine or ten stepped out from behind the thick trunk of the glowing tree—a whisper of a thing, hair wild, thin dress tattered at its edges.

"Hello?" Andrew asked. "What are you doing here?"

The girl looked at him curiously. "Please remove your shoes and jacket," her gentle voice asked.

An odd request, Andrew thought, glancing around.

"You would not think it odd if you knew what ground you stood upon," she replied as though she heard what he was thinking.

Andrew removed his boots and jacket and lay them at the cave entrance. When he did, the girl smiled.

"Why have you come?" she asked, stepping to the pool's edge.

He almost opened his mouth and told her everything he wanted, everything he was seeking, but then all the warnings he had heard poured through him, and he paused.

"Be wise," the being of light at the entrance had told him. The Night Watchman had nearly struck him down for speaking too casually of the Grace Giver. Truth and illusion, Elrift's voice reminded. So, Andrew took a breath, decided to slow down, and chose his words carefully. "I've come for my friend," he finally replied.

The girl's smile grew. "Then welcome. Step across the water and sit with me." But she turned away before he could ask her exactly *how* to step across the water.

He thought for a moment. The pools must have been deep because he could not see the bottom, though the water was crystal clear. Lithuel had taught him how to swim, but he was nervous swimming in water with an unseen bottom. Fortunately, the other side of the pool was not far, so he cautiously began to step in. When he did, the water did not give way beneath him. Instead, it held his weight and barely splashed up over his bare toes. This took him off guard, and he almost lost his balance and fell over. Once he regained his footing, he slowly crossed over. On the other side, he lifted his foot and saw that his ruptured blister was gone, and the skin on his feet that had turned to calluses from years of riding was new and supple.

The girl now sat on a large branch—legs gently swinging. She looked familiar, but he wasn't sure how. The shape of her jawline? The color of her eyes? He couldn't quite place it. She was clearly a child, but somehow, he knew she was ancient. She was older than the rivers and the trees; older than the mountains or the vintnew; perhaps even older than that being of light he had encountered at the mouth of the cave. Was she present when the world was born, when time was still an imaginary dream? Was she...the Ruach Hakodesh?

She giggled a sweet, innocent giggle that resonated in Andrew's heart. "I am not the Great Kadosh. If He were here, you could not survive in His presence. I am one of his children." The eyes of the tree blinked as she spoke. "It's been so long since I've had visitors. Tell me, what of the night?"

What of the night? Andrew didn't know what this meant or how to reply.

"It's day."

She looked confused by his answer. "You've recently been with my people."

"Who are your people?" he asked.

"The Night Watchmen. So, tell me, what of the night?"

"I'm sorry, but I don't know what you mean."

She looked away for a moment, then returned his gaze. "How are things in the world? Is there peace or war?"

Andrew shrugged. "Fine, I guess. There are no wars. None that I have news of anyways."

"And what of Mentanii?"

He thought carefully about her question. "I don't know what that is."

The girl looked away for a few moments, then asked: "What about my people? Have they sent word?"

"No. I don't really know your people. I've only met them once, and they didn't exactly stick around to chat."

Disappointed, her eyes dropped. Perhaps she hoped to

hear news of her people or something more, but Andrew had no news to give her.

"Then make your request," the young girl said with a sigh, the eyes of the tree blinking again.

This was it—what he had been waiting for—though he had not expected to find a Grace Giver ever, much less on his journey for some moss. Perhaps he should ask for the moss.

He shook his head. That didn't feel right.

Andrew considered the portrait in his pocket. Who was the woman? What if she was no one? Perhaps he should ask about his mother, but what if she was dead? If he used his request on these things, they might lead to nothing, and what would it cost him? Would he lose Lithuel? Perhaps he should ask for Lithuel's health. But Lithuel wasn't that bad off. His leg hurt, but he was otherwise healthy and happy. This was more than a bandage. Then he thought of Lorna. How could he help her in a way that would be life-changing? Could this girl give her her memory back? Would that be enough? Again, what would it cost him, his own memory? Or maybe Lorna would get her memory, and they would forget each other.

"Ask for the least possible, else nothing at all," Daphnie had told him. What was the least possible thing he could ask for that would still change Lorna's situation and keep his life intact? Maybe nothing. Maybe there was no way to make a request without it costing Andrew a great deal, and maybe that was right. Maybe it was supposed to cost him something.

If a king, or a god, agrees to grant me one request, how should I answer? he wondered then, after some consideration, decided: *with humility.*

"I am not here for myself but for my friend," he said.

"Go on," the girl replied.

"There is a woman, Human, like me, far from here who saved my life, and I would like..." he hesitated. "I don't know how to help her. I request that *you* might help her."

The girl thought for a moment. "You have asked rightly," she said with a smile.

Now in Andrew's hand was a small, glowing, green shoot with long hair-like roots. And when he looked up to where the girl had been sitting, both she and the tree were gone. Only the dark husk of a long-dead hornbeam stood in its place. The pools, the fish, and anything the pools might have held were also gone. He was now in a large, dark, empty cavern, only able to see by the light of the glowing shoot.

He collected his boots and his coat and climbed the path again to the mouth of the cave, only this time, there was no Giant's Causeway beyond the entrance, but the misty Shadow Falls where he had camped the night he met the Shimar Etsell. He also saw Brynlee casually eating grass like she had been there waiting for him all day.

When he turned back to the entrance, all he saw was forest behind him. But the tender shoot was still with him.

CHAPTER 36

A ndrew tried to process what had just happened as he set up camp for the night in the same hollowed-out tree he stayed in the night he met the Shimar Etsell. Having soaked a small strip of fabric in water from the river and wrapped the roots to keep them from drying out, he laid the tender shoot on an exposed tree root. Why had the Grace Giver brought him back here? Had the last three days not happened? Had he not met a shepherd that was something else entirely?

He opened his pack. None of the oatcakes were eaten.

He opened his smoking pouch. There were no fresh leaves waiting to dry.

Andrew shook his head. Everything inside of him told him that his trip to the Giant's Causeway *had* happened, but there was no sign of any of it.

He sat on the tree trunk inside the hollow and pulled off his boots. He had no calluses; his feet were soft and supple. It *had* been real; it just hadn't cost him anything—not even time or a trip.

He looked again at the small plant lying on the leg of the tree. What was he supposed to do with this?

"Even closed doors are still doors. You just have to find the key," Elrift had said. Perhaps this was the key.

Hours passed, but no one came. *Maybe they only come after nightfall*, he wondered.

It began to drizzle.

Andrew fed part of an oatcake to Brynlee and ate some himself. Then he thought about his friends back in Jatoba.

More time passed. Nothing.

His fire began to dim.

He went out to find more wood, but it was hard to keep dry and harder still to find dry wood for the drizzle that became heavier after sundown. The warming rod helped, but the wet logs didn't burn well, and he kept having to relight them.

This isn't what he had imagined: sitting in the damp hollow of a tree with thinning food rations, waiting for someone he wasn't sure would come.

Andrew wrapped himself in his coat and tried to stay close to the fire, but it gave off very little heat, and as he waited, his eyes grew heavy.

What was he expecting? The craftsman had said there was no way to open it without a word, song, or phrase that only the possessor of the chest knew. Perhaps the craftsman had thought of something since last they spoke. Andrew didn't know what to expect or what to do. He was out of options. He had asked the Grace Giver to help Lorna, and the Grace Giver had given him the small plant and brought him here. What else could he do but wait? If this didn't work, perhaps nothing could be done for her.

As his eyes grew heavier, he stared at the tender shoot, wondering what it was or what it might grow into. Was it a piece of the Grace Giver? Had he even *met* a Grace Giver? Would it grow into a tree like the one he had seen, glowing with those strange eyes? And who, or what, was that little girl?

He closed his eyes and felt himself beginning to doze. Then he jerked his head up and looked around. There was no one. Again, he faded, and again, he jerked his head up. The fire was now only a smoldering pile of ash, and still, he was alone.

He rubbed his hands together, trying to warm them. Andrew carefully piled the last of his semi-dry sticks in the stone circle, not wanting to go back out into the rain in the middle of the night, and used the warming rod to light them. Then he leaned back against the wood trunk again, with his legs crossed, and tried to take in some of the warmth of the low fire. And before long, he was asleep again.

When he woke next, the craftsman sat next to a brightly roaring fire, looking closely at the glowing plant.

Andrew sat up quickly and rubbed his face.

"I see you've returned," the craftsman said, glancing at Andrew. "Dangerous."

"I've brought you something."

"Where did you find this?" the craftsman asked, carefully studying the leaves and roots lying across his palm.

"In the Giant's Causeway."

"Do you know what this is?" the craftsman asked, his voice gentle. "No. I don't expect you do." Then he gently wrapped the glowing plant in an ornamented piece of blue-green fabric and carefully slid it into a shoulder bag.

"It was given to me," Andrew replied.

The craftsman looked at him with a stern and questioning look. "Given to you? By whom?"

"A little girl, in a cave, sitting on this huge glowing tree with eyes."

"By what color of light did this tree glow?"

"Green," Andrew said.

The craftsman's eyes grew large. He knelt down in front of Andrew and held out his hands. "May I? Please?"

Andrew wasn't sure what was happening, but he needed this man, so he obliged and held out his hands.

"You have touched grace," he said, gently kissing the palms of Andrew's hands and touching Andrew's hands to his forehead. Then he rose. "Please, come with me," he said, gesturing to the entrance of the tree hollow.

Andrew followed.

CHAPTER 37

"It is not lawful for outsiders to enter my home, but these are exceptional circumstances," the craftsman said, handing Andrew his cloak. "Put this on."

Andrew did as the craftsman asked. Then, the craftsman mounted his tree horse.

"Your mare will be safe here until you return. Please. And leave your things," he said, holding out his hand for Andrew to join him.

Andrew wasn't comfortable with any of this, but there was no way he was turning back now. His only real fear was for Brynlee, but the craftsman had assured him she would be safe, and somehow, Andrew believed him. Andrew sat in front of the craftsman on his mount, and he quickly knew why. He could immediately feel the muscular power and heat of the beast as the incredible creature reached and carried them into the trees, climbing vertically as quickly as a racehorse might cross an open field.

For several minutes, the horse climbed straight up the tree until it sprang onto a massive branch and began galloping across the wood, leaping and jumping, grabbing and pivoting from one tree to the next until they were far into the canopy of the Ki Lo Kan Forest—with no more sight of ground beneath them.

Andrew was initially scared, but he could feel the powerful arms of the craftsman steady him while guiding the horse with the slightest touch, which calmed Andrew, allowing him to embrace the beauty of this strange new world.

Entire ecosystems thrived around him of plants and creatures he had never seen nor heard of before. Bright flowers sang as they rode past. Birds that looked like feathered cats with wings. A purple and orange Marsupial with two babies clinging to her back, twice as large as the tree horse. Orchids and vines. Amphibians and snakes. None of which existed on the ground below. It was like the heights of the trees kept their own temperate climate.

Then, as they pushed through a particularly thick cluster of hanging bushes, signs of civilization finally appeared.

They were now on what looked like ground, but it was not soil. It appeared to be some thick, spongy moss that had connected the branches of the trees into a landscape of hills. Somehow, there was also water flowing out of hollows of trees, creating creeks and streams, pools, and even a small lake where Andrew could see colorful fish darting past as they rode along its shore.

"How is this water here?" Andrew asked.

"These trees grow hollow, drawing water up from the ground below, until they are mature and begin to break open, releasing their waters," the craftsman replied. "Very pure; very delicious."

"It's beautiful," Andrew exclaimed.

"You think this is beautiful? I wish you could see what I see. I can see the Chimcary of the plants, resonating in colors invisible to Humans."

"Chimcary?"

"You might call it a kind of intuition. It's how plants talk to each other."

Talking horses? Talking plants? What's next? Andrew was beginning to wonder how little he knew of the world.

Soon, they passed a small home. Then another.

"No one from the lands below have entered our lands for a countless age. You can not be caught here."

Andrew pulled the hood further down to hide his face.

To Andrew, the Shimar Etsell looked like a feudal society of hardworking but happy people living closely with the forest. Their clothes were beautiful, loose, natural fibers, colored in such a way that made them look like a living extension of the forest. Their homes were beautifully carved timber with adornments of the red and honey wood they had used for Hemtee's cart. Their tools were also wood. There were no fences. They kept goats and chickens, and children played openly. As they rode past, a small girl playing out in front of her house saw Andrew and dropped a small carved figurine that looked like a toy, but when she did, she just smiled and waved. Andrew waved back.

In one area of open moss near a small pond, ten or fifteen Night Watchmen stood in rows and formation wearing only a pair of thin shorts, practicing what looked like a form of kata—a cross between dance and martial arts with bow staves. Then, the craftsman stopped in front of a small home with beautifully carved pillars of animals, flowers, and trees. A small fountain sat on the front porch, trickling water over rocks.

The craftsman dismounted and opened his front door,

which was only a translucent cloth of ink-wash shapes over a wooden frame. Andrew followed him through his beautiful home, full of carved wood furniture, and out the back door into a small, private garden. The plants in the garden were beautifully shaped and carefully pruned. To one side of the garden was an open workshop with tools, a long bench, and shelves holding various colors and shapes of wood. Any other time, Andrew would have loved to explore the craftsman's workspace, handling the strange-looking tools, and "talking shop," as it were, but it could not be so— not today.

Towards the back of the garden, the craftsman pulled aside a small pot he quickly filled with handfuls of loose soil from a nearby trough and took the small green plant from his shoulder bag. The plant was noticeably lean and tired-looking from when Andrew received it, but it quickly strengthened again when the craftsman rubbed a blue ring he wore on his left hand, causing the soil to moisten. He then moved the pot into a stream of light breaking through the trees high above.

"Guard your mother well," the craftsman said as Andrew watched the surrounding trees move to give it more sunlight. Then, the craftsman slowly rose and dusted the soil from off his hands. He sighed and turned to Andrew with a look of sorrow. "It is a fateful day, this one. A day of life. And death. Very well," he said. "Come with me."

Andrew followed him back into his workshop, where rows of tools hung in neat rows on one wall and orbs of colorful glass sat on another.

"Neekoo el hoo mam," the craftsman said as a yellow, beautifully ornate chest flexed like a muscle and opened to display rows of small, colorful glass vials. He selected one and held it up to the light. Then he looked at Andrew.

"Because your mare has assured me you are here for someone else and not yourself, I will grant you what you seek." And he slowly handed the small vial to Andrew. "But it is a grave thing."

Andrew held the tiny jar up to the lamp. It looked like some sort of thick, brown oil. "If I put this on the chest, it will open it?"

"Kill it, actually," the craftsman said with a tone of hesitation and sorrow. "I hope whatever is in your chest is worth it."

Andrew swallowed. He had not realized he would have to kill the chest to open it.

Just then, a loud horn blared from somewhere in the distance, and the craftsman looked with worry in its direction. He grabbed Andrew's arm with incredible strength and ushered him outside. "You must go. Now! My steed will return you to your mare, and when you find her again, do not be afraid to push her hard. She will find the strength to take you from this forest. If you can make it across the Vondermarden, you will be safe. They will not follow you across it," the craftsman said, helping Andrew up onto the tree horse, whispering something to it that caused it to bristle and stomp the ground. "Close your eyes. Do not look back. They have been trained for war and have never found any, which means their blades are hungry and their arrow swift. If they catch you, they will kill you without question or hesitation. Do not return to this forest. Do not cross the river again. Now go! And Grace be with you!" And with the shout of a word Andrew could not discern, the powerful green horse reared and ran.

It took everything Andrew had to hold onto the mighty animal's mane—its broad, muscular body beat beneath him as more horn blasts blew behind him.

Andrew's hood blew off his head, and he was sure some of the people outside of their homes could now see him as he quickly passed by, but he did what the craftsman told him: he closed his eyes, put his head down, and held on for dear life.

Andrew felt the force of the wind pushing against him until the force of gravity pulled him from below as they descended vertically. And as they went, Andrew began to hear the crashing of branches and the hooting of powerful voices from behind and gaining on him. Suddenly, the horse pivoted left, then right. Andrew gripped until his knuckles, thighs, and knees ached as they rode faster than he could have imagined.

It took only minutes to return to Brynlee, and when they did, the craftsman's horse slid to a stop, breathing heavily and soaked in sweat.

Andrew slid off the creature, which, in a moment, dashed back to the trees in a different direction as though it were trying to mislead the oncoming soldiers. But it would not work for long; it might only buy Andrew moments. So, he quickly mounted Brynlee and did something he had never done: He tapped her hind quarter with the heel of his boot, which startled her at first, but she quickly turned out of the hollow tree and began to run. Again and again, he tapped her backside, urging her on faster and faster. "I'm so sorry girl," he yelled. "I've no choice. You have to give me all you got, or neither of us will make it out," and as he said it, it was as though the old girl found a new gear. She narrowed her head and began galloping a smooth, steady gallop—powerful and fast. The craftsman was right. She never slowed, not even for a moment.

Through the forest they ran, and as they did, Andrew heard the violent crashing of branches again, only this time it was overhead and quickly closing in. Suddenly, an arrow whistled past his left shoulder and another just past his right ear, landing in a tree beyond them. But he did not look back. He only held on tighter and pushed Brynlee on.

When Andrew saw a place in the river narrow and shallow enough for Brynlee to cross without losing her footing, he pulled her right.

She jumped and splashed through the water as it quickly rose to her chest and pushed against her, trying to pull her back downriver towards the falls. Andrew could feel this one whom Lorna had called Mother Mare fighting for her foal as she did the night of the blizzard. An arrow splashed the water, then another. Three more flew past him, but none ever found its mark. Why? How? These were well-trained soldiers, and if the blade of the first Watchman had taught Andrew anything, it was that they knew how to use their weapons. So why did they keep missing? "Grace be with you," the craftsman had said. And perhaps it was more than a wish. Perhaps it was a word of intuition. Or perhaps the young girl back in the cave knew this chase would come and had somehow made provision for it. Whatever it was, Brynlee finally found her footing on dry ground, pulled them out of the water, and began running again.

Now, across the Vondermarden, she began to tire and slow. She was breathing so heavily that Andrew began to worry she might fall from exhaustion right beneath him.

No longer hearing any horns, crashing of branches, or hollers from oncoming soldiers, Andrew slowed Brynlee to a stop and climbed off. He lay down in the grass, arms and legs splayed, exhausted.

"What just happened?" he asked Brynlee, who had also laid down.

After he finally caught his breath, he sat up. He was still wearing the craftsman's cloak, which was somehow shifting shape and color in his hands, like the skin of the land octopus he had watched dart out from underneath him in the tidal flats days earlier.

"The Shimmering," he said aloud, looking at the strange fabric. He remembered the Night Watchman almost disappearing into the darkness that night he stepped out of the tree hollow and away from Andrew's campfire. This must have been why. And perhaps, this is what caused the soldiers to miss their mark.

He turned to Brynlee.

She wasn't moving.

CHAPTER 38

Andrew awoke sometime after dark to the sounds of the forest. At some point, he laid on Brynlee's stomach and covered her in the craftsman's cloak, trying to keep her warm. She wasn't moving, but she *was* breathing, and her steady breaths comforted him. Without shelter, they were not safe in the forest. He didn't know how far he was from either the road or Jatoba, but he knew they needed to keep moving if he could rouse Brynlee to her feet.

Then he had an idea.

Andrew took out one of the oatcakes and fed her as much as she would eat, and within minutes, she was standing and moving about.

"How are you, old girl?" he asked. She leaned her forehead down, touching his, and told him in a way that he could understand that she was alright.

He did not mount her again, not for at least an hour.

As they walked, he struggled profoundly with the decision he now had to make: Kill the box and help Lorna unlock her secrets, or let it live? What if the box held no secrets? What if there was nothing more that could be done for her? The craftsman said the seven chests were given as unique gifts to keep something extraordinary, but perhaps it was *already* dead. Perhaps that is why it was in Lorna's house. Perhaps it wasn't even the right chest. Maybe Lorna had spent her life collecting other people's junk before growing old and losing her mind. And therein lied his problem: He had no way of knowing for certain if opening the box would help her. She had saved his life, and he owed it to her to help her if he could, but what if killing it did nothing? If the box was alive, and this oil would kill it, was it right to end an innocent life—such an exceptional life—just to help himself and his friend? Maybe this was the cost of such a grace. Or perhaps the Grace Giver was testing him. Perhaps he was supposed to protect the chest and, in so doing, somehow help Lorna.

The guardian's warning at the cave entrance came to mind: "Do not lust after what is not yours to take, else you will be consumed." Had he gone too far? Did he want it too much? To be Human. To have family. To help the woman who saved his life.

He and Brynlee finally made it back to the bend in the road—the full raven moon now high in the night sky as a question paralyzed him as he stood looking at his beloved mare: Would he kill Brynlee to open the chest? Of course not. If not Brynlee, then how could he kill the Igbaya?

Andrew carefully mounted Brynlee, and together, they made their way back to Jatoba.

CHAPTER 39

It was late. The homes scattered along the mountainside were all dark and quiet, and it was beginning to snow again.

Andrew was so exhausted he could lie down in the middle of the road and sleep for hours. He didn't know what he was looking for besides a friendly face. Unfortunately, but unsurprisingly, Daphnie's shop was all locked up.

Dark doors. Dark windows. Failure. He felt vulnerable. That's when he saw the only light in the street: a single flickering candle in the tavern's front window—its warm glow drawing him in. He slowly approached and pressed his hand against the cold, frosted glass to see if anyone was still awake. There, behind the bar, washing what looked like the last of the evening dishes, was Feyloren, and seeing her made him almost start to weep. Had she left a candle burning just for him? He had faced both gods and monsters and survived. Now, here he stood, safe and whole, though entirely more exhausted than he ever thought possible.

Exhausted from riding. Exhausted from traveling. Exhausted from running. Exhausted from taking his life into his own hands, more than once.

With trepidation, he tapped on the window, unsure where he and Feyloren stood in their relationship, uncertain if she could even be bothered with him in the middle of the night. Were they still strangers? Were they friends? Were they more than friends? All he knew was that he didn't have the mind to sort it all out just now. Not tonight.

She opened the tavern door, and at first, she looked confused, probably wondering who could be out of their mind enough to come banging at this late hour, but when she saw Andrew, she quickly hugged him.

"What are you doing out here?" she asked.

He sighed. "Trying to find my way home."

She pulled back to look at him. She could tell he was hurting. "You've found it," she said, ushering him into the warm bar where the fire had not yet wholly gone out from the night's revelries.

The sound of her voice was like a balm to his soul; the touch of her skin soothing like a warm bath. Where he had felt vulnerable moments earlier, he now felt safe and welcome.

She did not question him. She just sat him down in front of the hearth, pulled off his jacket and boots, massaged his hands for a moment where she thought he might have been holding onto Brynlee's reins for what must have been hours, and rose to fetch some hot tea and a plate of whatever she could find.

The soft leather chair embraced him, and the firelight brought him new life. He held his hands up to it to let them thaw. His shirt was becoming wet from melting snow, his feet ached, and his mind listed from his journey, but he had made it back.

Having Feyloren close after such a long and difficult journey made him realize that with her, he really was home. It had no longer been Lithuel that Andrew longed to see after such an ordeal. It was her.

Somewhere out on the open road of his journey, he had fallen in love with her. He didn't know what that meant for either of them. He had no idea if her family, whatever family she had left, her people, or the town would respond well to her marrying a Human or if she would even have him. But he now knew beyond all knowing that he wanted to stick around long enough to find out.

She returned with a pot of steaming tea, a small plate of apples, cheese and bread, bowl of hot water, and two towels. Then she slowly removed his shirt and carefully washed his hands, his neck, his face, and his chest. He took intentional mouthfuls of food and drink between her carefully wiping him down and drying him off. But she never asked. She never cared. Wherever he had been, whatever he had been through, it didn't matter. All that mattered to her was that he was there with her now and that he clearly needed her.

Watching her quietly in the glow of the firelight, he realized something else. Her jawline. The color of her eyes. The Grace Giver had chosen someone he loved upon which to fashion the little girl's appearance, and that person was Feyloren. Young. Female. Human. The face of someone he loved. All attributes meant to disarm him, to keep him calm, to make him feel safe. And it had worked.

What would have happened if I had asked wrongly? he wondered. The hair on the backs of his hands bristled at the thought. He had been in the presence of—and spoken with —a being that could rewrite time itself.

As the firelight glinted off Feyloren's copper skin, he leaned forward and took her by the arm. She looked at him.

"Why?" he asked.

She smiled that gentle smile that totally disarmed him. That smile that had caused him to drop his prices the first time he met her. That smile that was like a drug he couldn't get enough of. "Why what?" she asked.

"Why me? Why here? Why this?" he said, motioning to the food and the towels.

She turned away and dipped a towel in the hot water.

He wasn't shy anymore—not after all he had been through. Perhaps that was the grace that was left for him.

He gently reached for her chin and drew it back so that he could look into her eyes, and when he did, there were tears.

"Because you never wanted to *take* anything from me. You've always wanted me for who I am."

Then he kissed her. And she kissed him back.

THEY WOKE INTERTWINED and interwoven the next morning, again in room one of the tavern. And this time, Andrew could clearly remember everything that had happened the night before.

On the morning he had left for the Ki Lo Kan Forest, Feyloren had made him breakfast. Now, he wanted to return the favor. He knew the tavern would not open until lunch; he just didn't know what time it was, so he carefully slipped out of her arms, put on his trousers, and snuck downstairs.

The morning was cold but fresh with possibilities.

He blew into his hands and started lighting the fire, this time the old-fashioned way, not with his warming rod but with strikers and kindling. Half a dozen broken strikers quickly reminded him how hard it was to get logs to burn if not properly lit and made him grateful for the rod. Then he went behind the bar and into the back room, where he poked around the dry goods, wet goods, and shelves of foodstuffs for something to put a smile on Feyloren's face. And when he returned to the bar, arms full of bread and oats and berries and honey and an apple in his mouth, there stood Brutste with a surprised look like she wasn't expecting to find a "tiny tinker" tinkering around her food pantry.

"What in the hells?" she asked, eyeing his bare feet. She didn't know why, but somehow she sensed that where something of a boy had entered her tavern the first time, a man now stood in his place.

He smiled, slowly set down the food, pulled the apple out of his mouth, and tried to think of a way to explain what he was doing there, but no words came out.

Brutste looked around. The front door had been locked. Nothing looked amiss. Had he been in the tavern last night and passed out somewhere, and Feyloren hadn't noticed when she locked up? It wouldn't have been the first time.

"Where is that sexy naked ass I saw last night?" Feyloren hollered as she came down the stairs with nothing but a sheet wrapped around her. And for what seemed like the longest minute in Jatoba's history, the three of them stood there staring at each other, all equally dumbfounded, until Brutste waved a hand, slightly bowed her head, and left the tavern.

"I...will be back in an hour," she said, eyes large. Then

she paused just before closing the door behind her. "You had *better* not hurt her," she said, flexing a bicep the size of Andrew's head. Then she slammed the door to punctuate that she was serious.

Andrew and Feyloren looked at each other and burst out laughing.

CHAPTER 40

As Andrew set the kettle onto the iron hook over the hearth, he felt at home, but quickly, his heart grew heavy again, and Feyloren could see it.

"Was last night a mistake?" she carefully asked, pulling the sheet up over her shoulders, afraid of his answer.

He turned to her and answered her question with a long and passionate kiss. "Absolutely not."

"Then what is it?"

He thought about how to answer as he cracked a couple of eggs into a bowl, stirred them with a fork, pinched in some cinnamon and vanilla, and dipped slices of bread into the batter.

"What are you doing?" she asked, confused.

"I had an idea." Then he thought more about her first question. "Sometimes I cook to keep my hands busy."

She watched his strange ritual as he dropped a small knob of butter into a hot pan, which began to sizzle immediately, and laid the dripping bread on top of it. The smell of cinnamon and melting butter filled the tavern.

She didn't want to pry, but she thought that if he talked

about whatever was bothering him, it might help him heal. "Did you find what you were looking for?" she asked.

Andrew nodded. "Yes. But I've been warned it could cost me." He flipped the piece of toast and let the second side brown.

Feyloren wasn't sure what that meant. "If you're in any kind of trouble..." she began.

He shook his head. "Nothing like that. I have an awful decision to make, and I'm not sure I can make it."

"Do you have to make it?"

That was a good question. *Did* he have to make it?

He pushed two more pieces of battered bread around on the pan and flipped them once they reached what he thought might be a good color. The pop and sizzle of the cooking butter with the cinnamon and vanilla fragrances were starting to make Feyloren's mouth water.

Just then, bells began ringing outside in the street.

Andrew and Feyloren looked out the window. He was confused, but she was smiling. Then she turned to him. "Happy Eden Vale!"

"It's today?"

"Tonight," she said, reaching across the counter for him. He piled the bread onto two plates, pausing long enough to take her hand. "I want you to come with me," she told him. "Tonight, all things are made new."

He grunted, remembering that he had actually missed Eden Vale. It was the night he saw the vintnew in the valley, but that was before his time was returned to him by the Grace Giver. The thought of it tingled the back of his neck. Three whole days had been erased from history. Just like that. *Tonight, all things are made new.*

He nodded, then cut a corner of the golden-battered toast and took a bite. His eyes widened. It was good, but it was missing something. He added a drizzle of honey. Better, but not quite there.

The changing looks on Andrew's face amused Feyloren as he tasted his experiment and explored ways to improve it. "Well? How is it? It smells good," she asked.

He held a finger up to his mouth, thinking. "Does your sister have any cream?"

"She should. Back in the larder. Check beneath the door in the back corner."

He slipped into the backroom and opened a small wooden door in the ground. Beneath it were jars of various cheeses and other dairy products. He lifted one, looking thick enough to be cream, and returned to Feyloren, her incredible beauty catching him off guard as she sat there waiting for him, wrapped in nothing but white cloth like some sort of wonderful gift.

He smiled at her, and she smiled back, a flirty, fantastic, "hey you," kind of smile.

Andrew tossed a handful of fresh berries onto his toast and drizzled it with cream. Then, he took a bite.

His eyes lit up. This was it. The warm, eggy toast, melted butter crust, sweet honey, sharp berries, and rich cream all sang in his mouth like a beautiful chorus of wonderful flavors. Then he cut a bite for Feyloren and offered it to her.

She took the bite and smiled, catching a drip of cream running down her chin and laughing.

"Hmmm?" he asked, cutting another large piece for himself.

"Mmmm. Oh god," she replied—her face looking a bit like it had last night. "What is this?"

He shrugged. "I don't know. I just had an idea."

She took another bite. The second was better than the first.

He watched her eyes close, and her head sway with pleasure. Yeah, he was addicted to her, alright.

"We have to put this on the menu," she told him.

His eyebrows rose. *That's not a bad idea,* he thought, then walked around the bar and sat next to her. She scooped her arm up underneath his without asking.

She was right. He had found his home. Then, together, they enjoyed breakfast.

CHAPTER 41

Andrew approached the leaning cottage he had first seen just a week earlier through the haze of a late-night blizzard that nearly ended his life. A snow-white squirrel with black stripes watched him from the roof as he approached. He wondered if all the little critters crawling around Lorna's house were an extension of her eyes and ears. Probably.

Over breakfast, he had explained to Feyloren some of what had happened on his journey, not quite ready to share everything. He wasn't trying to keep anything from her, he just hadn't had time to process everything since he came into possession of the oil.

"Do you want me to come with you?" she had asked.

"No. I need to do this myself," he had told her.

"You should take her some of this!" she replied, forking the last bite of her toast.

Not a bad idea. Food seemed to help Lorna's memory. However, he decided to bring the supplies with him and make her some fresh rather than trying to carry the battered toast in his bag, along with everything he needed to brew her some fresh tea.

In his pocket was the oil.

Tufts of leaves blew past her window. The house looked as quiet as it always did. He didn't see the sparrow. Perhaps she was out.

He looked around. The forest was quiet—patches of snow hid from sunlight beneath trees and bush.

"What do you want!" came a sharp, cracked voice from the side of the cottage.

Andrew turned to see Lorna kneeling over a slender garden running along the side of her house. It was tidy and tenderly kept—looking out of place in her forgotten ramshackle of a yard. Her staff leaned against the wall next to her. She pulled a bulb from the soil with long orange leaves and dusted the debris off its roots on her robe.

Andrew was glad to see her. "Happy Eden Vale!" he hollered, lifting the bag of food up for her to see.

She was confused. Who was this strange boy? His mare looked familiar, but he didn't. Then her sparrow flittered about and whispered to her: "Do not fear him, mother. He is a friend."

Lorna rose and dusted the dirt from her hands.

"I've brought you some tea and supplies," Andrew said.

Lorna studied him for a moment. He looked like no threat. Then she turned to the mare and whispered something to her. After some listening, Lorna turned again to the boy. Her right eye twitched, trying to remember who he was even though everyone else seemed to know him.

"Come in," she told him, and Andrew followed her into the house.

The jars of tea he had left for her were scattered around the counter—one leaning on its side and empty. The markings he had written on their surface were now smudged from use.

Andrew set down the food, refilled the jars, put the kettle on, and re-marked the proper portions on the jar's surfaces. He then dug around in the pantry for a pan as the small lizard with feathers he had seen days earlier darted out from a top shelf, up the wall, and out through a crack in the ceiling. This didn't surprise him anymore. In fact, he wondered if the lizard had a name—just another of Lorna's tiny friends.

"Today is Eden Vale, and I wanted to check in on you. Maybe brew you some tea. I thought we could have a meal together," he told her as the butter began melting in the pan. "I came up with this just this morning. I hope you like it," he said, turning to her.

Lorna watched him without argument, rocking back and forth and twisting a long strand of hair. She still had no idea who he was or how he knew his way around her home. As much as he felt like a stranger, he also somehow felt like a friend, so she let him get on with his cooking.

"I saw your gate fell again," he told her, scooping battered toast onto a plate, dropping on a handful of berries and a drizzle of cream, then handing the plate to her. "I still need to bring some proper hinges for it, but I'll tighten it up again while I'm here." He turned to her front window, feeling a sharp breeze crawling along his feet. The bottom corner pane, which had been cracked the last time he was there, was now missing, so he rose and found some paper to put over the hole, making a mental note to bring back a few pieces of window glass as well.

For the next few hours, Lorna quietly watched him flutter around her home, fixing what he could and telling her about his journey to Nevarii to find the tinker who might know something about the Shimar Etsell, on to the Giant's Causeway and meeting the Grace Giver. He had not shared any details about the Grace Giver with Feyloren, but he shared every detail with Lorna. He thought she deserved to know and hoped that some small detail, any detail, might trigger a memory—anything that might help open the box without needing to use the oil.

Then he took the small jar out of his pocket and set it on the table in front of her.

"This is it," he said, looking at the poison. "He said this would open the box, but to do so will kill it." Then he looked up at her.

Her face was worried and confused. He wasn't quite sure whether she understood what he was saying. Then he leaned forward. "Do you remember the chest in the other room?"

Lorna didn't respond. She just sat, slightly rocking back and forth, looking down at the floor and picking at the edge of her robe. Her sparrow had long since fallen asleep.

He spoke to her now in clear terms. He had decided along his journey that he would take care of her, whatever that involved, and that she deserved to know what was happening, even if she didn't understand or remember everything he told her.

"You told me that someone was keeping secrets from you. I think you mean the chest."

She squeezed her eyes and rubbed her face, rocking faster now. "He won't help me," she finally said, having not said a word for most of his visit.

"He won't help you?" Andrew asked, surprised at her response. "Who? The Watchman? Did you go to him for help?"

She didn't respond.

"Well, he helped me. I think," Andrew told her, picking up the vial and holding it up to the firelight. "But it will kill it unless you can remember. Do you understand what I'm telling you? This is poison. It will open your chest but kill it in the process."

She glanced at his eyes for a quick moment, then looked away.

Andrew sighed. He was learning that looking him straight in the eye was hard for her. He wasn't sure why. Perhaps it had something to do with the malady with which she suffered.

He swallowed and looked again at the dreadful potion.

"Can you remember anything like a word, song, or poem? Does anything like that sound familiar?" he asked. "Anything that might be close to you...a name, perhaps?"

There was no reply.

He set the oil back on the table. It was no use. She didn't understand. The faster pace of her rocking showed him that this was starting to disturb her. Perhaps the thought of killing something or something dying was causing it, which didn't surprise him. It was a thought that troubled him as well.

Lights began flickering outside the cottage windows, drawing Lorna's and Andrew's attention.

Andrew rose and went to the front door. Feyloren, draped in a beautiful fur-trimmed robe with blue and gold satin, walked up the path and smiled when she saw him. It was nearly sunset now and a long processional of Long-beard and Minotaur people, all dressed in gold and blue, slowly walked the path just a few cubits past Lorna's front door on their way down into the valley for Eden Vale, all carrying candles and torches. Even the children all carried candles—their hands shielding their flickering flames from the mountain breeze. A tall Minotaur at the front of the processional rode the back of a stately black steed wrapped in its own blue and gold robes; he carried a long circular brass horn underneath one arm. Gold ribbons tied bundles of the yellow flower to his horns.

Feyloren stopped at Lorna's gate on the edge of her yard, looking at Andrew, who smiled and turned to Lorna.

"It's beginning. Come with us."

Lorna looked past him but did not rise. She simply shook her head and turned away.

Andrew's eyes dropped. He turned back to Feyloren, who was waiting for him. The processional was now mostly past the cottage and on down into the valley.

He didn't want to leave Lorna, but he had promised Feyloren to go with her.

"I'll be back," he told Lorna, whose rocking had slowed. Then he donned his coat, took Feyloren's hand, and followed her—with the last of the processional—down into the valley. As he did, a small Minotaur child handed Andrew her candle, and the mother hugged the child for thinking of someone other than herself on this most special night.

CHAPTER 42

Eden Vale was a celebration of grace. A night of joy, to give thanks for the year past and to pray over the year ahead.

As the processional came to the mouth of the valley, Jatoba's citizens stood scattered all along the hillside, holding out their firelights and quietly waiting.

Feyloren pulled Andrew close and laid her head on his shoulder. It was beautiful on so many levels.

Then, as they stood there in the quietude of the evening, waiting for the last light of the sun to disappear behind the horizon, the voice of a small child echoed across the valley:

"Thank you for your gifts and grace,
    May they find us in this place,
    Let our light shine true and bright,
    On this most important night."

Feyloren squeezed Andrew's arm, and he squeezed hers back. Brutste and her husband stood nearby, first smiling at

Andrew and Feyloren, then turning their attention to the lights. Daphnie was also there, not far off, holding her flickering candle.

And just as the last of the evening sun vanished, the yellow flowers scattered all throughout the valley opened a tiny pearl of a petal in their centers and released a glowing bloom that floated into the air.

Andrew watched a stream of the golden flowers gently drift down the mountainsides, becoming a river of flowing light as the Minotaur who led the processional lifted his brass horn and blew three short, sharp blasts and one long note that he held for several seconds. Then, other trumpet sounds rang out from other villages across the mountains.

Once all the blooms had gone, the villagers used their firelights to make their way home, posting their candles and torches along doorposts and on window sills throughout Jatoba, giving the rustic village the feeling of a multilayered candelabra climbing the snowy mountainside.

"How did it go?" Feyloren asked.

Andrew shook his head. "I'm not sure she understood a word I said. I asked if she could remember anything, where the chest came from, perhaps how to open it, but she didn't reply. All she said was: He won't help me. Whatever that means."

Feyloren thought about what Andrew was saying, then asked: "Are you staying in Jatoba tonight?"

He remembered how lovely last night had been. Then he sighed. "I need to return to her. Brynlee is still there. She has a spare bed I might use."

Feyloren nodded. "Come back to me before you leave for home?"

He nodded and kissed her.

CHAPTER 43

Andrew returned to Lorna.

Brynlee was standing quietly at the corner of the house in the darkness.

He gently tried the front door, which opened without trouble.

Inside, Lorna lay on her cot, the small vial of poison lying next to her on the floor. When he saw it, his heart stopped.

He quickly picked up the small bottle, but the lid was on, and there was no sign any was missing.

As he turned to her, she gently moved, and when she did, he sighed a heavy sigh of relief and leaned against the large tree in the middle of her living room. Then he looked at the bottle again. How awful of a solution this was. The momentary fear of Lorna's death was still high in the back of his throat, making him literally taste death, and in so doing, he knew he did not have the stomach for it. Not just yet, anyway.

He set the small bottle on the mantle of the hearth and

went back into the backroom of the cottage, where he knew the chest was waiting.

It was just as he had left it, once again draped in raven light piercing through the crack in the ceiling, a gentle few flakes of newly falling snow alighting on its lid. The raven moon carved in the lid was glowing such a bright blue-grey light that Andrew no longer thought it was a reflection of anything rather than a source of light itself.

"You sure are a lot of trouble, aren't you," he told the chest, blowing snow off the lid and gently touching one of the corners.

Vines had somehow grown up through the floorboards and wound themselves around the bottom edges and corners of the box, which he had not previously noticed. He removed a knife from the kitchen and carefully cut away the vines. He then assessed the condition of the wood. As beautiful as it was, he could see it had been neglected for years and possibly decades. Hairline cracks ran along its corners, and tiny brass filagree feet had come loose at its base.

Stepping out to his saddle bag, Andrew fetched a small tool and piece of refined leather that he used for polishing metal. He then dug around in the kitchen until he found a small tub of oil he had seen sometime earlier and returned to the chest. The raven light had moved on, and it was now hard to see the features and wood grain of the chest, so he gave it a nudge to feel its weight, which felt far lighter than he thought it should be, so he carried it through the house towards the fire where he would be able to see it more clearly.

Once it was close enough to the hearth, he knelt next to it and used his tool to tighten the loose brass fittings.

"I'm in a difficult spot," he told it, feeling a bit foolish talking to a box, but he was beyond caring. "I'm trying to help my friend, and I think you might be able to help," Andrew said, dabbing some oil on his rag and beginning to wipe the surface of the wood. "But I don't know how to open you. I met the man who made you, and he said you're alive and gave me that oil up there." He pointed to the oil still sitting on the fireplace mantel. "But, he said it would kill you."

As he wiped, the wood drank up the oil from his rag, and he couldn't be certain, but it looked like the long, hairline cracks were actually healing.

"Was he right? Are you alive? Or are you just some tattered and forgotten junk chest?"

As he continued to rub the oil into the surface of the wood, the chest released what sounded like a long sigh of relief and moved.

Andrew leaned back on his knees and watched as a seam appeared along the top edge of the chest and rose open. Andrew's heart beat fast. He had chosen well.

Inside were rows of books that looked much like the ones in Daphnie's shop, a small bone figurine shaped like a dragon, a stack of letters in old envelopes, and a hand-painted image of a young woman with long blonde hair on canvas...wearing a green necklace. As Andrew picked up the image, he immediately recognized it. Then Lorna spoke from behind him.

"What are you doing?" she asked, rubbing her face.

Andrew turned, both excited and ready to calm her again, worried she wouldn't remember him, not wanting a repeat of his first morning with her. "I know you don't remember me but..."

"Of course, I remember you," Lorna said.

"Wait. You remember me?"

As he watched, the cracked folds of her wrinkled skin tightened and healed into the skin of a healthy woman. She was beautiful—eyes sharp and bright.

Lorna looked at him. She wasn't afraid of him, but she couldn't quite place him yet, either. He felt familiar, but she didn't know how. Faint figments of him talking to her the night before came to mind. Fixing her food. Mending her fence. She glanced at the dirty plate with small scraps of the battered toast and touched her lips. Tea. Something about tea. It felt like a light in a dark room that kept flickering on and off. Then she looked down at the chest. This, too, looked familiar, like an old friend or lost pet returned home.

When she did not answer, the immediate thought that this had all been for nothing stung Andrew's mind and bloomed into frustration. Then, the image.

"Why do you have this?" he asked, holding the miniature portrait out to her.

Lorna glanced at it, trying to find the piece of memory that might offer an answer, but as soon as she thought she had one, it was gone.

She gently touched the rows of books. These felt like old friends, too. Were these the memories she was looking for?

She lifted one and let its clear pages gently open in her hands, and as she did, it all came back.

CHAPTER 44
16 YEARS EARLIER

Lithuel polished the copper buttons and set them in place. It had taken him all morning, but they fit perfectly. A sense of work well done washed over him and he smiled. He had been trying to ignore the crying baby and sharp words tossed back and forth in the house since he had arrived.

None of my business.

The coach he was working on had once been beautiful and expensive but was now fraying at its edges. The silk curtains were threadbare; the copper fittings were tarnished. He had been asked to repair the broken buttons along the edges of the interior seats, causing them to lose their padding, and he was glad to be finishing up before evening because it was his last job before heading home.

He wiped his hands with a rag that permanently lived in his pocket and approached the back door of a two-story townhouse nestled at the end of the lane in one of Nevarii's more affluent neighborhoods. Upon first knock, no one answered, so he knocked louder.

"Do I have to have Jinto see you to your coach?" came the voice of an older woman from behind the door.

"I'm not a child, mother!" a younger woman yelled back. Then the bolt clicked on the door, and it opened.

The lady of the house stepped forward, brushed a stray, greying curl away from her face, and tucked it behind an ear. "Yes?"

"Oh, ma-lady, I'm sorry to bother. I wasn't expecting..."

"Yes. You will have to excuse me. My manservant is... otherwise occupied at the moment. What can I do for you?"

"He's hired me to fix your coach seats," Lithuel replied, stepping back from the front door out into the street. A woman with curly blonde hair looked out of the second-floor window from behind sheer curtains.

"Oh, of course," the elder woman replied, clearly flustered. "What do we owe you?"

"Do you care to see my work first?"

"Yes, yes. Of course." She glanced back into the house before closing the door and following him to the open coach door. She was twisting a white handkerchief.

"I had a stamp in my kit that resembled the flower on the old buttons. It's not the exact same, but I thought it added a nice touch," he told her, showing her the careful work he had put into each button, pushing back the stuffing where he could and repairing a corner of the seat where the ruffles had torn. He wasn't a clothier, but he was good with his hands and thought it didn't hurt to do what little he could with the fabric.

"Yes, yes. Fine, fine. It looks fine. What do we owe you," she asked, still distracted.

"Oh, I figure four pennies should do it."

"Let me find the purse. Please do come inside," she said, returning to the house.

Lithuel stopped at the door, uncomfortable going inside the once wealthy home where the furniture was draped in fabric and there were discolored spots on the walls in the shape of picture frames. Wood crates lined the hall with labels such as 'kitchen' and 'parlor.'

"Are the words of binding in place?" the woman asked, coming down from upstairs with a small leather pouch as she dug for coins. "Yes, my lady," a male voice replied from the other room. There was no more baby crying.

"You will have to excuse us. We are just packing up for the summer. So many things going on."

"Oh, no problem at all. I'll be out of your way."

"I didn't catch your name."

"Lithuel, ma'am."

She handed him five coins and smiled, actually looking at him for the first time instead of being distracted by everything else. "Well. Lovely work. Thanks so much."

"Oh, ma'am. This is too much," he replied, seeing the fifth coin.

"No, no. I won't hear of it."

It was rare to receive more than the agreed-upon price for work completed, so Lithuel wasn't sure how to respond. He tipped his hat and said, "Very kind of you, ma'am." Then he turned and left.

Lithuel had been in Nevarii for nearly two days and needed to stock up on a few supplies before leaving town.

He pulled his cart up to the tanner to collect a harness he had dropped off for repairs the day before and stepped into the blacksmith next door for a new hammer, his ball peen having split its handle after ten good years of work. The coach station across the street was buzzing with activity as people came and went. One overweight Bantam man, who was barely as tall as Lithuel's waist, hollered at a tall and slender Dym servant with long grey hair hanging down over a well-tailored ash-grey suit.

Lithuel ran his hand along Brynlee's neck, assuring her he was ready to leave as a cool wind blew, causing him to prop up his collar and blow into his hands.

He was glad to be leaving town. He didn't care much for all the noise and problems a large city created. There was too much danger in the world. Too many wandering eyes and too many roaming hands.

He clicked twice, and they were on their way.

He wouldn't make it home before evening, but that was fine. There was a quaint little hideaway hole of a tavern about an hour's ride due south known as The Plough he liked to stay in instead of Nevarii whenever it made sense, and staying tonight meant an easy ride home just after a hearty breakfast in the morning always put forward for travelers by the tavern owner, and the barmaid wasn't bad on the eyes either.

Nearly thirty minutes into his journey, he heard something as his mind was drawn to what might be on for supper. He didn't pay any attention to it at first due to the chatterly sounds of the wagon on stones and soil, but then it grew louder. He pulled over. As he did, the sound turned into crying.

Lithuel climbed down from his driver's seat and pulled back the tarp on his cart to find a small bundle wrapped in a blanket. Inside the bundle was a Human baby.

Lithuel looked around. He hadn't seen anyone since he left Nevarii other than a distant farm hand finishing work in a field more than ten minutes ago. How did a baby get in the back of his cart?

The baby started crying properly now that it could feel the cold evening air on its face.

Lithuel pulled off his cap and rung it in his hands. Then, the baby started crying louder.

"Shhh, shhh," he said, picking it up and starting to bounce it. Perhaps the movement of the cart had been what was placating the child until the cart stopped. He didn't know why he was bouncing it; he had just seen some woman somewhere doing something like bouncing at some point and had no idea what else to do, but it seemed to work until the little pisser decided he had had enough and really let out a proper scream.

This startled Lithuel, who had no idea what to do.

He went to the front of his cart and opened his bag. He couldn't feed it apples or bread. The child had no teeth. He opened his water skin and tried to give the child a drink, but the child coughed and cried harder. That didn't work.

Lithuel looked around again, trying to quiet the now-wailing child, but there was no sign of anyone other than Brynlee, who looked back at him like they had just run over a small animal.

"Come on, come on. What do I do here? Please. Shhh. Shhhh."

The baby cried so hard its little face started turning red, spittle running down its cheek.

Lithuel's mind began to race. The crying child was making it hard to think clearly. There was so much urgency in the cry now that Lithuel felt himself starting to panic. Then he had one more idea.

He opened his bag and pulled out a small jar of honey that was nearly empty. It was the last of what he had collected that summer, often saving himself a bit of the comb for long trips as a kind of treat. He quickly popped off the lid, dipped his finger down into the bottom corner, and put his honey-covered finger into the child's mouth. At that, the baby quieted. When he removed his finger, the child started crying again, so he re-dipped his finger and let the baby pacify itself.

With one hand, he carefully pulled himself back up into the driver's seat, turned Brylee around, and made his way back as quickly as he could to the only Human he had seen in probably five years: the woman in Nevarii.

The bumping rhythm of the cart must have helped because the infant was asleep by the time he made it back into Nevarii, up the dirt streets that became cobblestone near the finer homes and around a corner when he pulled Brynlee to a stop.

He carefully set the child aside in the driver's seat next to him and climbed out. He could not believe what he was seeing.

The townhouse was gone. Completely gone. There was a gap in the mortar along the building next to where it had stood and an empty space in the cobblestone street exposing the compact soil.

Lithuel threw his hat down in frustration. Then he turned to the Human baby asleep in his cart. What was he supposed to do now?

CHAPTER 45

Andrew woke in the bed in the small room at the back of Lorna's house, but the bed was no longer dusty and leaning. There were no more cobwebs in the rafters or snow falling in through cracks in the ceiling. The cottage was no longer leaning either, nor was there a large tree tearing the house in twain.

The smell of salty bacon drew him out of his room and towards the kitchen, where Lorna stood whistling a tune to herself that Andrew somehow recognized—a child's lullaby.

"What is that?" he asked.

She turned and smiled. "Breakfast!" she replied. She was standing upright. Her clothes were beautiful, clean, and the richest, darkest green. Her hair was long and the most beautiful grey he had ever seen, pulled up in curls on her head. She was still the same Lorna but vibrant and full of life.

"No, that tune you were whistling," he asked.

"A bedtime song I used to sing to your mother."

He trembled, and he had to steady himself against the corner of the table. *My mother. She knew my mother.*

Everything about the house was healthy and new. There were no longer small creatures taking over her pantries, no grey knickknacks on the shelves being swallowed by dust. It was like everything had been cleaned and rebuilt.

"What happened to your house?"

"You saved my life," she told him, setting a plate of eggs, bacon, beans, fruit, and sliced toast before him. "I locked old Melphas there and forgot how to open him. He had all my books. Without them, I began to fade, and as I began to fade, so did the cottage. It was foolish of me. I should have kept one or two out, just in case."

She set a cup of tea in front of him.

He first smelled it, then took a drink. It was his special blend.

"Remember that?" she asked him with a smile, sitting beside him at the table.

"Remember it? I mixed it!"

"You did. And you did so much more. You refused to give up on me, even after I almost killed you."

He looked at her. "You remember *that* now, too, do you?"

She nodded. "Thanks to you, I remember all of it. As soon as I opened one of my books, it all came back."

Andrew took another long drink of tea. "Can I ask what it was? The keyword?"

She smiled, leaned forward, and touched his arm. "The name of my grandson: Andrew."

CHAPTER 46

A ndrew and Lorna rode together into town. She had answered some of his most burning questions, and he was processing.

They dismounted their horses next to the posts outside the tavern and went in, which always opened early on the weekend for anyone who wanted roast carvery.

Feyloren saw Andrew, ran to him, and embraced him.

Brutste was slicing everyone thick pieces of ham and roast fowl. She was starting to enjoy seeing her little sister happy again.

Then Feyloren turned to Lorna, who was draped in a hooded robe so deeply purple it was nearly black. Feyloren's eyes were wide. She knew who she was but had never seen the old woman so...healthy.

Lorna pulled back her hood and smiled. "Is this who you wanted me to meet?" she asked Andrew.

He nodded. "Feyloren, this is my grandmother."

Feyloren looked at him with confusion and surprise—a hundred questions flooding her mind. But this wasn't the time.

Andrew's eyes told her that he was having difficulty believing it himself, and he nodded.

"Okay," Feyloren said with a laugh and hugged Lorna.

"I get the feeling you two are close," Lorna told her.

"We are," Feyloren replied.

"I knew your parents," Lorna said.

"My parents?"

Lorna nodded.

"Yes. You have your mother's eyes."

Feyloren's eyes welled up, and she wiped a tear away. "Well, come in. Both of you. Let me get you some food!"

Andrew took her hand. "Actually, we can't stay."

Feyloren's countenance dropped. "Oh?"

"I'm returning home. I need to speak with my father. It's time he knows what's happened," he glanced at Lorna. "All of it."

Lorna nodded.

"When will you be back?" Feyloren asked, clearly shaken.

"I want you to come with me."

Feyloren's eyes widened. "What? Why?"

Andrew smiled. "I've found family—some new, some old. And I want to introduce both of you to my father."

A smile slowly grew on the edges of Feyloren's mouth. Then she nodded.

Turning back to the bar, she took off her apron and whispered something to Brutste, who looked confused and disapproving at first, then sighed, nodded, and waved her off. Just before they left, Brutste walked over to Andrew and squeezed his shoulders. "Remember what I told you yesterday?"

"How can I forget."

"You better not," she said in her most threatening voice,

then she picked him up and hugged him. "She deserves the best. That had better be you," she whispered. Then she set him back down on the floor.

As they mounted their horses in the city center, Lorna asked Andrew: "How has the branch of my staff been treating you?"

"Oh, this?" he asked, taking it out of his inside coat pocket and handing it to her. "Fine, I guess. I almost blew myself up once, but I've gotten the hang of lighting fires with it."

She looked at him like she had given him a prize race-horse, and he was using it to plow fields. "You know it can do more than that, right?"

Andrew shook his head. "Like what?"

She smiled. "I guess I have a lot to teach you."

"Where are we going?" Feyloren asked.

Andrew hesitated like he was about to tell her he lived in a trash heap. He was suddenly second-guessing the trip. His meager shack on the swamp. His scruffy, scraggly dog. Sure, they were his family, his home, but what would Lorna and Feyloren think of them?

"Aitecham Tioram," he told her sheepishly.

Lorna laughed. "Really?" she asked, drawing her question out slowly. "The Dry Places?"

He knew it. This was a mistake. But he nodded anyway.

"How delightful. My grandson just so happens to live in one of the *most* powerful places of intuition on the continent. That can't be a coincidence."

Andrew's eyes grew. He looked at Feyloren, who simply shrugged.

Lorna held Andrew's warming rod up to her lips and whispered: Elmana peltum Ke-orsay, Aitecham Tioram. Then she pointed the branch out before them and moved it in a circular motion. As she did, a mirror-like fog appeared. Through the fog, Andrew could see his house.

"How?" Andrew asked.

Lorna smiled. "Oh, you have no idea," she replied with a smile. "Follow me." And follow her, Andrew did.

CHAPTER 47

T hrough the mist they came: an elder woman in long robes, a young tinker whose life was about to change, and a copper-skinned beauty. When Lithuel saw them, he rose to meet them.

"Well, what is this?" he asked, trying not to get so excited that his leg would start acting up.

As Andrew dismounted and approached the front door, Jasper sprang up and jumped into his arms. "Hey, boy," he said, laughing. "Lithuel, I have some people I'd like you to meet."

Feyloren and Lorna dismounted their horses and approached him.

"This is Feyloren. She and I..." he shot her a glance, and she just smiled at Andrew, curious what he would say next. "We'll be spending some time together. Perhaps a lot of time."

Lithuel wiped his hands on his trousers and reached to shake Feyloren's hand. Then he laughed. "Mighty strong handshake you have there."

She smiled.

"And this..." Andrew said with some hesitation, stepping aside so they could see each other. "This is Lorna, my grandmother."

Lithuel paused and looked at Andrew, trying to determine if what he had just heard was what he had just heard. Then he looked at Lorna. She smiled a gentle smile and reached for his hand.

Lithuel slowly shook it. "I remember you."

"Hello, Lithuel," Lorna said with a smile.

"Wait, you two know each other?" Andrew asked with a look of confusion.

"Maybe you should all come on inside," Lithuel replied.

"You remember how I told you I found you in Nevarii?" Lithuel asked as he put the kettle on to heat some water for tea.

"Yes," Andrew replied, slowly sitting at the kitchen table.

"I had met a Human woman earlier that day."

"Your father repaired my coach seats," Lorna added.

"After you started cryin', I went back to where I'd seen her, but she was gone. Her entire house was gone."

Lorna nodded. "Nevarii was our holiday home, and I was going home that day."

"What happened to the house?" Lithuel asked.

Lorna smiled. "I spoke a word of intuition and shrunk it down into my book and took it with me."

Lithuel shook his head. He had never heard of such a thing.

"I loved that home. I was forced to sell it some years ago to make ends meet."

"Why didn't you tell me any of this?" Andrew asked.

"I didn't know it was her, not for sure. And I didn't have her name, so what was I supposed to tell you: some Human woman left you in my cart, and that I went back trying to find her? Cause I'm pretty sure that's what I did tell you."

"You could have told me you met her!"

"Don't blame your father, Andrew. Jilian was on her way to university, but after three weeks of no work, I wrote the headmaster and was told she never arrived."

"My mother's name is Jilian?"

Lorna smiled and nodded. "I'd love to tell you about her."

Andrew wiped away a tear. This was all so much.

"So, you have no idea why your daughter, his mother..." he glanced at Andrew, unsure if calling her that was fair, "left him behind or what happened to her?"

Lorna shook her head.

"We used to be a family of means, but that had slipped away. All I had from her was a note, and she was gone."

"What did it say?" Andrew asked.

The question was heavy, the memories heavier. "She told me not to try to find her and that it wasn't my fault— even though I'm not sure that's entirely true," Lorna sighed. "And that your name was Andrew." Lorna smiled, scratching a piece of fabric on her sleeve. "That was my father's name."

Andrew looked at Lithuel, seeing clearly that this was all hard for him to hear as well.

"When I found you, you was so little. All you had on you was three silver crowns, and that there image," Lithuel said, pointing to the portrait Andrew had removed from his pocket. Then he rose and stood by the fire.

"I tried finding your mother but never could and figured a Human child didn't stand a chance."

Feyloren squeezed Andrew's hand.

Andrew rose and put his hand on Lithuel's shoulder. "I wouldn't have survived without you."

"I can't thank you enough for taking care of him," Lorna added.

"You're still my father, and this will always be my home," Andrew said.

"But," Lithuel said.

"But, she's asked me to come live with her. And I think I need to," Andrew looked at Feyloren. "I *want* to," he added, and Feyloren gently smiled.

Lithuel turned to Andrew; his eyes were wet. "I always knew you was better than this place." Then he pulled Andrew close and hugged him. "I always knew this day might come," Lithuel told him. "You deserve to be with your family."

"*You* are my family."

Lithuel nodded and wiped his face. "Now they are too, and there's room for all of us. Just not here."

Andrew didn't argue.

As evening began to set on another day, Andrew packed a few bags, hugged Jasper, and promised to be back to see Lithuel soon and often.

Lithuel nodded, though he knew how life had its way.

"I want you to take Brynlee," Lithuel told him.

Andrew shook his head, but Lithuel held up a hand. "You're hers as much as you was mine. She won't survive long if I took her foal from her." Somehow, Andrew knew he was right.

"What will you do? You need a horse."

"Oh, I've got on just fine while you was travelin'. I'll make do until I find another."

Lorna rose. "I think I can answer this." She took a small, wood-carved figurine from off a shelf Lithuel had crafted for Andrew as a toy when he was a boy. Then she left the cabin, walked to the edge of the small island the shack was built upon, and stepped out onto the water.

Everyone followed her as far as they could, but she continued on, distancing herself from them.

She held her hand over the top of her staff and spoke words Andrew could not hear as blue light drew into it. Then she stretched her staff out over the dark water and said, "Em-noo, ley-fee loo, Aitecham Tioram! Hear me now. Bring me a child of your dark waters. A spirit of strength, steady and true."

The water beneath her began to move.

"Not by might, nor by power!"

The water swirled and pushed away—her hair blowing back and her robes flourishing behind her—but Andrew felt no wind. "But by the name of the Ruach Hakodesh, do I call thee! Come and serve me now!"

From the dark waters came a horse of shadow and mist standing nineteen hands.

She lowered her staff, and the wind quieted, her robes and hair came to rest, and the dark water beneath her returned to its calm, murky state. But the horse remained.

She turned and approached Lithuel, and the horse followed. Upon the water, the horse was like fog, but upon the land, it became corporeal, with powerful sinuous legs, shining black coat, and a flowing mane more beautiful than any woman's hair.

Lorna handed the small figurine to Lithuel, who had

seen a lot in his day but never anything like this. "Keep this close, and it will serve you well."

Lithuel took the figurine. It was warm.

"Oh, and one more thing," Lorna said, touching Lithuel's knee with her staff. As she did, Lithuel's face brightened, and he slowly shifted his weight onto his bad leg. Then he laughed and started jumping around. The pain was gone.

Andrew laughed and hugged Lithuel's neck. Then he turned to Lorna. "Thank you!"

She smiled and nodded.

After another goodbye and a squeeze for Jasper, Andrew looked into his bedroom. He had grown up in this place. Now, it was time to go.

Good memories, he thought to himself, turning to Feyloren, who took his arm.

"I plan on being up through Jatoba with this new horse o' mine," Lithuel said, following the three to the door.

"You had better," Andrew replied. Then he took Feyloren by one hand and Brynlee's reins by the other as Lorna called forth the mirror mist.

Lithuel watched until they were gone and the mist faded. Then he turned to Jasper, who looked at him with a wagging tail.

"How's about some supper?" Lithuel asked as Jasper rose and followed him into the house.

About the Author

We hope you have enjoyed *THE TINKER & THE WITCH* by author G. J. Daily.

Please leave a review.

Reviews can mean the difference between the success and failure of a book.

Also from G. J. Daily:
ELOREE & ARDIMUS - a cozy character tale
STRANGE CHILD - a supernatural mystery

You can also follow G. J. Daily on Instagram @authorgjdaily.

instagram.com/authorgjdaily

Printed in Great Britain
by Amazon